PICTURE PERFECT

LAURIE WETZEL

Edited by Angela Wiechmann
Design by Aurora Whittet Best

ISBN: 9798359156301

To my sons, Luke and Mason.

May you always follow your dreams,
as you inspired me to follow mine.

WARNING

I understand that we all have our own unique life experiences. Please know this story contains the following subjects that may be upsetting to some readers:

Violence

Emotional, mental, and physical abuse

Neglect

Torture

Depression

Suicidal thoughts/acts

Please do not feel guilty if you decide to put this book down now and walk away.

Always,

Laurie

ONE

THE ALL-TOO-FAMILIAR WEIGHT OF BEING watched settles on my skin like the marking of a Sharpie. No amount of scrubbing will erase it.

It's not as though I've never felt eyes upon me before. Years of pageants, cheerleading competitions, and Dad's political career should have numbed me to that feeling. And they mostly have. However, this isn't about being judged, getting checked out, or even the hostile glares from envious competitors.

It's something else entirely.

I try to ignore it. Try to focus on what the teacher is saying and not the way the hairs on the back of my neck are standing on end. Even though I know I shouldn't, I glance over my shoulder. Our eyes meet.

Nick isn't like other boys who try to get my attention. He doesn't smile. He doesn't blink. During the three classes we share and every time we pass in the hallway, he doesn't do anything other than stare. Stare with that mix of loathing and longing.

It seeps under my skin and chips away at my heart. The loathing is for me. The longing is for the girl he wishes I were.

The final bell rings, and he finally breaks away, racing out the door with the rest of our peers. That bell marked the official beginning of winter break.

I release my breath. My body sags with relief now that he—and the heaviness—is gone.

"Hey, Jessica."

Blake saunters to my desk as if he owns the place. He pretty much does. As do I. It's not some quarterback-and-cheerleader cliché. We're Northland royalty. Our families own a majority of the town.

He's especially handsome today, decked out in a charcoal sweater over a dress shirt with cream-colored pants. No doubt the doing of his mother, Georgina, though I'm not complaining.

Gray-blue eyes—the color of the sky after a thunderstorm—stare down at me. "We're one minute into winter break, and you're still sitting here like a statue. Come on, beautiful—we have a plane to catch."

Christmas in Aspen.

The plane leaves in a few hours, then it's two full weeks of skiing, hot-tubbing, and enjoying holiday traditions. Blake's driving me home now, which will be the only alone time we'll get for the foreseeable future, unless we find ways to ditch our families in Aspen.

I realize I'm staring off into space with all these thoughts. Blake gives me an amused yet concerned look.

"You OK? You seem a little out of it."

"Yeah. I guess I am kind of spaced," I say.

His face twists in mock horror. "Well, it's easy to space out in AP Macaroni."

"AP *Macroeconomics*." I smack his stomach as I stand. "You're such a jock."

Not wanting to waste any more time, he wraps his arm around my shoulder, and we move through the halls, to my locker.

Various people call out to us. It's impossible to go

anywhere without someone wanting to bend our ears. But with the time crunch, we don't slow down. We simultaneously acknowledge and dismiss them with the ease that's been bred into both of us.

"Wait up!" someone calls.

If it were anyone other than my best friend, Cassie, I'd be miffed. Each minute spent here is one less minute Blake and I get to spend alone.

Tall brown boots and light-blue jeans cling to her muscular lower body. A sweater the color of pink lemonade hangs off her shoulders. Her long brown hair is pulled up in a messy bun with a pencil tucked through.

When she catches up to us, she turns her attention right to Blake. "So, what time are you picking me up?" she asks, twirling a manicured finger through a loose strand of hair. "I have a little packing to do. I ordered a new bikini for the hot tub."

"Give me an hour to drop Jessy off," Blake says. His attention returns to me. "That cool with you?"

I nod, trying to hold my smile while suddenly regretting inviting Cassie to come along to Aspen. Is this what my vacation will be like, with Cassie all over Blake? He hates when she does this. I know she doesn't mean anything by it. Half the time, she isn't even aware that she's doing it. She's just naturally flirty.

But Cassie needs this more than we do. Her universe blew up a few days ago. Who cheats on their girlfriend right before Christmas? What a dirtbag.

Blake took the news really hard too. He and Ryan are— at least were—best friends. Ryan's sporting a shiner now, though neither guy will say why.

My eyes meet Cassie's, and she stops bouncing. Her berry lips shift into an indebted smile.

"Thanks again for inviting me," she says. "I really appreciate this."

Pushing aside my selfish thoughts, I give her one of my

patented, award-winning smiles. "You're my best friend, Cass. I couldn't let you be miserable over the holidays. Plus, this will give us an opportunity to come up with some awesome new routines!"

"Ooh!" Cassie squeals. "Heck yes! Practice Monday, when we get back?"

"Of course," I reply. "Make sure to tell the others."

"On it." She pulls out her phone. Her fingers fly over the screen as she sends out what I assume is a mass text to the squad.

On our way out to the parking lot, Cassie gushes about all the things she wants to see and do on the trip. She's already bouncing on her toes, excited to get going.

Over her head, Blake rolls his eyes and smirks at me. I hope she won't annoy him too much. He and I can pretty much kiss our already-limited alone time goodbye for the whole trip.

As we stop next to Blake's Escalade, I spot Nick again. He's standing beside his beat-up truck, trying to hide that he's watching me.

For two years, we'd successfully avoided each other, sticking to our respective sides of Northland and attending different high schools.

But this summer, tragedy struck our quiet town in the form of a tornado. Among the buildings destroyed in its wake was South River High. The school is being rebuilt, but it won't be ready until next year. So all the South River kids are now attending Northland High.

Including Nick.

As if going to the same school isn't bad enough, Nick's in my classes. In the halls. And thanks to us having the same last name—Smith—he's my locker neighbor. Making it impossible to escape him. The past. And my guilt.

I'm not the only one who notices him eyeing me across the lot.

"That freak is getting on my nerves," Blake says.

4

"I saw this movie on TV the other night," Cassie says, "where this loser was obsessed with a girl at his school, and he ended up kidnapping and killing her. I almost called you. The guy reminded me of Nick."

I snort, then I see she's serious. "It was just a movie. That kind of stuff doesn't really happen."

"If he doesn't knock it off," Blake begins, "he'll be getting a visit from me and the guys."

"Don't waste your time," Cassie says. "It's only a matter of time before he ends up in jail—just like his dad."

It's a shitty thing to say, even if there is some truth to it. Nick's dad is currently serving two years for aggravated assault. It wasn't his first offense, which was why they gave him such a long sentence.

But Nick is not his dad. As much as I want to—as much as I know I should—I can't bring myself to hate Nick. I feel like defending him, but that would only upset Blake. And who's to say he and Cassie are wrong? Statistically, Nick does have a much higher chance of getting in trouble with the law than we do.

"All right," I say with a sigh. "We should get going. Cass, I'll see you at the airport."

As Cassie and I say our temporary goodbyes, Nick finally gets in his truck and drives off. I say a silent prayer of thanks, grateful that winter break in Aspen means two weeks free of him and his overbearing presence.

As we make our way out of town, the twenty-minute drive to my house goes by too quickly. Blake and I don't need to spend it with constant chatter; we're perfectly fine with the silence between us.

Blake pulls into the drive and parks beside my Mustang—black with pink racing stripes. He then shifts in his seat to grab something out of the back seat.

"I got you something."

He holds out a small, wrapped box.

I chuckle. "You couldn't wait a few days?"

He smirks. "You know I hate waiting."

It's true. Giving me my Christmas present a couple of days early is actually really good for him. He once gave Georgina her Mother's Day present in January.

Shaking my head and smiling at that memory, I grab the present. Tearing into the paper, I reveal a black felt box. My heart races as I open it. A heart-shaped diamond necklace glitters back at me.

"Blake . . ."

Without a word, he takes the necklace from the box and motions for me to turn. I do, gathering my golden locks. Tears pool as the diamond heart finds its home on my chest. His breath hits my neck, jumpstarting my emotions in a different—and much better—way.

"I love you, Jessy."

His lips touch the base of my neck, and I shiver.

"I was planning on finding a special moment to give this to you in Aspen, but since we won't have as much alone time together—"

"I'm sorry I invited Cassie," I say quickly, interrupting him.

"Don't be."

I turn around and pull back, searching his face. He's smiling. He isn't upset about Cassie tagging along.

"Inviting her was the right thing to do," he says. "Having her there means we'll just have to be even more *creative*." The lips I crave fold into a lopsided grin, and something wicked shines in his eyes.

Excitement blossoms inside me. "I can't wait."

"Me neither, babe."

He leans over, pressing his lips to mine. Knowing our alone time will be severely limited on the trip, we make the most of it now, pouring all our emotions into the kiss.

Only when his phone rings—with Cassie's ringtone—do we break apart.

He gives me a weak smile. "See you at the airport, babe."

As I grab my stuff and slide out of the passenger seat, I hear him answer his phone.

"Hey there—I'm on my way."

He waves, then he's gone.

A light dusting of snow covers the ground. It's beautiful. But as picturesque as this snowy farm scene is, it's nothing compared to our Aspen home decorated for Christmas with the snowcapped mountains in the background. I race up the steps of the wraparound porch, eager to grab my bags and start our vacation.

"Jessica, is that you?" Mom calls from the back of the house as I step through the door.

"Yep," I reply.

She steps into the hallway, flanked by Dad. Mom's dressed in a cashmere sweater paired with black high-waisted pants, and Dad's in a polo sweater and dress pants.

"How was school, darling?" Mom asks.

I shrug, having already put the day behind me. "Fine."

As I move to the stairwell, Dad steps in front of me. With a gentle sigh, he crosses his arms against his lean chest.

"You sure it was just 'fine'?" he asks, giving me a slightly raised brow.

He perfected that look back in his glory days. That look won over voters, constituents, and even critics across the aisle. It's a welcoming, curious look. It got them trusting him and opening up to him. But much to his disappointment, it's never worked on me.

I can't help but smirk. "Your politician is showing."

He tosses his head back and laughs, just as he always does whenever Mom and I call him out on acting like a politician at home.

"Always my ego booster," he teases. Then he switches gears. "So, which teacher gave the most homework?"

I groan, thinking of the massive amount of studying I'll have to do on break—especially for my AP classes.

"It's a tie between econ and government. But I should be

able to knock a decent chunk of it out on the plane."

Mom frowns a little. I know what's coming.

"Two AP courses is a bit much on top of cheerleading . . ." she chides.

We've done this song and dance before. Mom was reluctant when I chose my classes, fearing I'd taken on too much. It all comes from a place of love, but she still voices her concern whenever I feel the pressure of my schedule.

I'll admit it *is* hectic at times. But it was important to me to get into college based on my academics and not just cheerleading alone.

Dad, thankfully, seems to understand my decision. He's concerned about me, too, but he also thrives on not just meeting but conquering challenges.

As if on cue, his arm slides around my shoulder, pulling me in tight. "Two AP classes and cheerleading is a lot, yes. But nothing our girl can't handle. She's brilliant and ambitious—just like us."

Mom gives a dazzling smile as she moves to my other side. "Of course she is. But if you need quiet time or help, let us know," she adds, leaning in close. "I'm sure your father would love nothing more than to help with whatever you have for AP Comparative Government and Politics."

"Please say one of your assignments is to interview your favorite political figure!" he begs.

A laugh bursts out of me, and Mom quickly joins.

"What?" Dad asks, feigning ignorance. "What's so funny?"

Now Mom slides up beside him. "Let's let the poor girl go so she can get ready for the flight, dear."

Hearing those words, I race up the steps.

"We'd like to leave in thirty minutes, Jessica!" Mom calls after me.

With limited time, I take a quick shower, washing away the day. I'm surprised by how good it feels. I guess I didn't even realize that my muscles were tense. I don't know why, but I feel a little wound up.

Is it because of Nick . . . ?

I quickly shake that thought away.

More likely, it's just those nerves I felt earlier about Cassie joining us. As Blake said, we'll have to get creative with our alone time. The hard part, though, will be slipping away without leaving poor Cassie stranded with the 'rents.

An idea starts forming of having her meet someone there in Aspen. I'm already picturing some of the handsome young men we could introduce her to. Maybe someone could sweep her off her feet, make her forget about Ryan—and leave Blake and me Cassie-free.

By the time I'm out of the shower, I'm already feeling better. I dress in my comfortable yet chic travel clothes, then do my hair and makeup.

Staring at myself in the mirror, I smile.

Perfect.

Suddenly, a loud bang downstairs shakes the house—and me.

I freeze in confusion. Was that the front door slamming open?

I wait to hear something to explain away the sound.

Seconds later, the reply of glass breaking, shouting, and my mom screaming my name sends my heart racing.

Then just as quickly as the noise started, it ends. Dread creeps along my skin. The sudden silence has me more worried than the noise.

My brain races, trying to fit a scenario that could possibly match those horrible, violent sounds. My parents have never been physical with each other. Not in the least. They joke around and maybe bicker a little, but that's it.

Whatever happened downstairs, I know it's not good. I race to my nightstand to grab my phone. I have to call the police.

But my phone's not there.

It's in my bag. I look all over for it, but don't see it. I

must have left it downstairs.

I hold my breath, straining to hear even the faintest sound. It's just more nothingness.

Cautiously, I tiptoe out into the hallway.

The stairs creak and groan. Someone is climbing them. For a split second, I imagine it's Nick. I curse Cassie's name for mentioning that stupid stalker movie.

The noise on the stairs continues, sounding closer. Mom walks too lightly for the stairs to groan like that, so it must be Dad. I take a step out toward the landing.

But instead of stylish salt-and-pepper hair, I see shaggy brown-and-gray hair come into view. Then the muddy eyes of a strange man lock on to me.

TWO

EVEN THOUGH I'VE LIVED IN THIS HOUSE all my life, I glance behind me, suddenly hoping to find an escape route leading me outside. Aside from jumping out a second-story bedroom window, I'm trapped.

Where are Mom and Dad?

I take a half step, but the man stops and plants himself on the landing, blocking the stairs.

Dirt clings to the creases in his face and neck. He's tall and muscular, though his clothes are ratty and torn in various places.

And then something happens that shocks me even more. His muddy eyes fill with tears. He lifts a dirt-covered, shaking hand to his lips as he stares at me.

"I've spent countless nights dreaming of this moment," he says. His voice is tender. Soft. As if he's talking to a child. "And in all my dreams, you never looked as beautiful as you do right now. Even your pictures and videos didn't do you justice."

What pictures and videos?

"You don't recognize me, do you?" he asks.

My gaze zooms over his features, scrambling to recall him. He's definitely not one of my parents' friends or coworkers. He's not from our church. Based on his rough appearance, I wonder if he's someone I've served during my years volunteering at local soup kitchens and homeless shelters. But I don't recognize him from there either. Nothing clicks.

I shake my head.

"Well, I do look worse for wear than when you saw me last." He laughs a bit. "It's been a long time, hasn't it? You've grown so much since then. And changed your hair!"

My skin crawls. What is he talking about?

"We have plenty of time to catch up now," he says.

"Mom! Dad!"

The instant I call for my parents, rage flashes in the man's eyes. He lunges for me.

Right before he can grab me, I dash into my room, slamming the door. My trembling hands fumble with the tiny lock on the door handle. I'm not quick enough.

He crashes through the door, knocking me down.

"Mom!" I scream again, sliding back on the hardwood floor. "Dad!"

Where are they?

He dives at me again, kneeling before me. He clamps a hand over my mouth.

"Don't you dare call for them!" he snarls.

I scream and cry out against his palm as I try to fight him off.

Something clatters on the floor beside me. A gun.

Oh God.

He's going to kill me. I'm going to die in my bedroom.

I stare into his muddy-brown eyes, silently pleading for him to let me go. I can't die. Not today. Not like this.

I have plans.

I'm waiting to hear back on my applications to the Division I schools recruiting Blake. I'm going to follow him. I'll be a cheerleader, right there on the sidelines, while he's throwing touchdowns. He's going to get drafted into the

NFL after that. Then we'll get married. Have kids. Spend every Christmas in Aspen with them.

Those final thoughts spur me into action. I bite the man's hand and kick him between the legs.

He reels back, crying out in pain.

It gives me just enough room to roll over onto my stomach and scramble for the gun. I've never fired a gun before. Never even held one. But in this moment, none of that matters. It's him or me. I have to win.

His hand slams down on the gun, beating me to it. He picks up the gun and leans back, holding it at his side and out of my reach. He stares down at me.

My throat dries, and my heart plummets. I should move. I should get up and fight him. *Do something.* But I can't get my body to cooperate. I just lie there on the floor, on my stomach.

He presses his knee in between my shoulder blades, pinning me down. I whimper, jaw trembling. Frozen, I watch over my shoulder, waiting for him to shoot me. Blow my brains out all over my floor.

Instead, he shoves the gun into the back of his waistband. It does little to calm my fears. Then his hand disappears in the front pocket of his sweatshirt. I shiver, wondering what else he has. I swallow, hard, as he pulls out a roll of duct tape.

"Please don't do this," I beg. "Please! I'll do anything!"

I wiggle underneath the man, trying to buck him off, trying to get away.

"Just stop it!" he grunts.

Rough hands clamp onto my wrists and pull them back behind me. I use all my strength to try and stop him, fearing what he'll do. I'm strong. For cheerleading, I have to be.

But he still overpowers me. As my wrists touch, he shifts, clasping them in one hand. Then he wraps the tape around them.

I scream, crying out in frustration. *Where are Mom and*

Dad? What has he done to them?

The man grabs my face, forcing my jaw shut. He slaps tape over my lips, silencing me.

"Hush now," he coos. His voice is tender again, like comforting a baby. "Calm down."

Violent sobs shake my body as he binds my feet next. I'm pinned. Vulnerable. It sends new waves of fear rippling through me.

The man stands, admiring his work. He's proud. Happy, even. He's got me right where he wants me.

He's going to kidnap me.

Hold me for ransom.

I think about every movie, TV show, and book where a pretty girl like me is taken. The majority of those stories never end well.

This can't be happening. I'm dreaming. A horrible nightmare of a dream. Any moment, I'll wake up . . .

I clamp my eyes shut and then open them, expecting things to be different. I do it again and again and again. A dozen times. But it doesn't work.

I know Dad will pay any ransom—whatever the man wants. Will the man release me, then? Or will he take the money, then kill me anyway?

Will he just kill me now?

Regret and anger fill me as I think of the pain my parents will go through. Again. They almost lost me once. They spent hours thinking I was dead. Even went to the morgue to identify a body they thought was mine.

Will this man make them relive the horror of not knowing my fate again?

One way or another, I don't think my parents will survive this experience. Not this time.

Then something snaps inside me. I won't let him take me.

I flip onto my back, ignoring the pain and pressure of lying on my bound hands. I kick wildly at him.

He dodges me but loses his balance. He uses my bed to stop his fall.

"Jessica, enough!" he shouts, turning back around to face me.

I freeze as if a bucket of ice water had been thrown on me.

He knows my name. He said it in such a terrifyingly familiar way.

He *knows* me.

This isn't random.

He said there were pictures and videos. How long has he been watching me? How long has he been planning this?

He grimaces as he stares at me. But then his muddy eyes brighten. He runs both his hands through his scraggly hair and lets out his ragged breath.

"Well, this isn't the joyous reunion I expected, but we're finally together, and that's what matters."

Before I can make sense of his comment, he grabs my waist. I scream, the sound lost in the duct tape. I buck as he lifts me off the ground. He grunts, adjusting his hold as I fight him.

I can't let him take me. If I do, I'm dead for sure.

His dirty fingernails dig into my skin as I flail. Finally, I succeed in breaking free from his arms.

But as I hit the ground, my shoulder erupts in blinding agony. My body curls into itself, fighting the pain. The tape muffles my cries.

"Look what you did!" he scolds. "You went and hurt yourself. Shoulder's probably dislocated. Dammit, Jessy— what were you thinking?"

Suddenly he's there, hands on my body again, moving me to sit with my back to him. His knee jabs into the middle of my back.

My pain disappears to the back of my mind; in its place, fear settles in like a thick fog.

"This is going to hurt . . ." he says.

15

His fingers curl around my dislocated shoulder, then yank it backwards.

Fire ravages my muscles. My shoulder and arm throb. After a few seconds, though, the pain lessens to a more tolerable level. Gingerly I test my shoulder, moving it slowly forward.

He fixed it.

Why would he do that? Why fix me when he's just going to kill me?

"It wasn't supposed to be this way, Jessy. I don't want to be the bad guy. Not with you." He looks deep into my eyes. "And if you think this hurt, it will hurt a hell of a lot more next time you disobey me."

My parents don't believe in violence. They've never once hit me. Not even a light spanking when I was a child. But this man . . . this stranger . . . this kidnapper . . . he won't hesitate to hurt me. I understand that with every fiber in my being. So as much as I hate it, I'll have to do whatever he says until Dad pays him.

"There're a few things I have to take care of downstairs," he says. "Can you behave if you come with me?"

No. Hell no.

But what choice do I have? Besides, I need to see what he's done to my parents. I need to know they're OK.

My jaw quivers, and a tear falls as I nod my head.

"Good girl. Now let's try this again."

His hands slide under my arms, lifting me to my feet. When he lets go, I sway, suddenly unsteady. But he's right there again, lifting me fully into his arms. Cradling me like a child.

He's deceptively strong. Not from a gym, in the way Blake is strong. This man is strong from hard work. And a hard life.

The odds of defeating him are diminishing by the second.

He stares down at me. His eyes lighten, and his overgrown beard and mustache move as he timidly smiles.

"Come on." He pauses to readjust my weight in his arms. "I have something to show you."

He carries me out of my room, through the hallway, and down the stairs.

I see the family pictures on the wall, the garland on the banister, and the furniture in the foyer. It all seems fake. Like props in a play or movie. Some Hallmark Christmas movie, where everything turns out picture perfect.

But as he takes me into the sitting room, I realize this is a horror movie.

The coffee table is knocked over. Decorative vases and picture frames lay broken and scattered on the floor. Somehow, the tree is the only thing unscathed.

And my parents are tied up in front of it.

Mom and Dad don't see us approaching. Their mouths, hands, and feet are taped like mine. They're leaning on each other, supporting each other. I want so badly to join them.

Mom's sobbing quietly on Dad's shoulder. He's trying his best to console her. Blood covers half his face. This man—this awful, horrible man—hurt my father.

My mind tries to comprehend the grave situation we're all in. Tries but fails. I cannot grasp this. It's fake. It *has* to be.

The man clears his throat to get my parents' attention. They flinch at the sound and look over at us. Their eyes bulge, seeing me tied up in his arms. Then Mom and Dad start squirming, begging through the tape for me.

I want to go to them. I want to run to them and never leave their side. But the man's grip on me tightens. For a moment, I fear he'll never let me go. I fear he'll take me away forever and leave my parents to cry out after me.

But instead, the man sets me down on the love seat.

I straighten, taking several deep breaths to try to pull it together. This man wants *me*, not them. That's obvious. I'm the key. So somehow, I have to get us out of this. I have to be strong for all of us.

The man sits on the arm of the love seat, beside me. He lifts his hand to pet my head in the way one would a dog or cat.

My skin revolts, but I hold still, not wanting to do anything to upset him. I couldn't stand it if he hurt me in front of Mom and Dad. Each stroke of his hand on my head is already causing more and more tears to fall down Mom's cheeks.

For what seems like ages, the man doesn't say anything. Just stares at my parents as he smooths my hair. He's eerily calm.

"I contemplated doing this in Aspen," he finally says.

My whole body stiffens. He knows about Aspen? How? How long has he been watching us? What else does he know?

"I went over dozens of scenarios—every possible outcome," the man says. "I figured this was the best option. Before you left for the airport. Less people around to get hurt."

Less people? Does he mean Blake and his family? Cassie? Oh God.

Dad mumbles something—a string of words lost behind the tape.

The man leans forward, taking his hand off me as he glares at Dad. His hands ball into fists, and his veins pop out along his forearms as he barely contains his rage. The sudden shift in his emotions has my stomach twisting.

"No!" the man shouts. "I'm the one doing the talking here, *Bob*."

He knows Dad's name. And he said it with that same familiarity as he said mine.

When I look at Dad for his reaction, what I see in his eyes shocks me.

Recognition.

Dad *knows* this man.

A million questions race through my mind, yet I can't

18

ask a single one. I can't even focus on a single one. This man has a gun. Our survival is all that matters. Whatever fragile grasp I had on reality is completely gone now.

I scan back to Mom, looking at her more closely. Does she, too, recognize him? But her eyes are wide, confused, terrified. No doubt what my own eyes look like.

"In order for this to go smoothly, I need you to do exactly as I say, Bob," the man says, practically spitting with contempt. "Do you think you can do that?"

His vehemence toward my father has a new fear growing in me. *Please don't let him hurt my dad. Please just let Dad do whatever it is he wants . . .*

My father is a good man. He's well known and well liked. He ran for governor and won twice. He's on many boards. He donates his time and money to various organizations. His charities are operating all over the globe. People don't always agree with his decisions, but that's politics. It's impossible to please everyone.

So why is the man beside me harboring such hatred for him?

Mom too. Why is he doing this to her? For years, Mom's been right there by Dad's side. She proudly served as our state's First Lady, leading many special initiatives to improve lives. And now she devotes herself to organizing events for the various charities and foundations.

I'm sure she's had people disagree with her ideas from time to time. But again, those things are professional matters and not a reflection of her.

There's *nothing* she—nor Dad—could have done to deserve this.

The man rises to his feet. He lazily strolls over, stopping in front of Dad. He crouches down to Dad's level. He shakes his head.

"Pay attention. I'm only going to say this once." He makes a big show of pausing, as if Dad needs time to focus.

"First, I'm going to remove the tape from your mouth. And then you're going to call Donovan Anderson."

Hearing him say Blake's dad's name makes me imagine, again, what could have happened had this monster showed up in Aspen.

"You're going to tell him there's an emergency situation involving your charity in Cameroon—some supply chain issues. You need to personally oversee it, so you and your family won't make the flight to Aspen. In fact, tell him you might be over there for a while."

Dad's forehead is wet with perspiration. Even with the tape over his mouth, I can see him grimace and falter.

"Fail to sell this story," the man says, his voice cold, "and I'll shoot Sandy."

For emphasis, he points his gun at Mom.

She whimpers as silent tears fall. Dad leans over in a feeble attempt to shield her.

The man tuts. "If you want to save her, then you'll do exactly as you're told. Are you ready?"

This time, Dad nods without hesitation.

The man roughly pulls the tape from Dad's lips, though Dad doesn't make a sound. The man then reaches into his own pocket and pulls out Dad's phone. He must have taken Dad's phone—and Mom's, no doubt—when he attacked and bound them. Does he have mine too?

He dials, putting it on speaker. In his other hand is the gun, still pointed at Mom.

The ringtone echoes so loudly through the space that I feel it vibrating in my very bones.

Pick up. Please pick up, I pray.

Dad's eyes flicker to me, holding so many emotions in their depths.

Maybe Dad can somehow subtly telegraph to him that something horrible has happened to us. They're both powerful men—they've no doubt contemplated that they might be the target of this type of attack. Perhaps they've

20

worked out some code word or something.

But as the call goes to voicemail, my whole body deflates like an empty balloon. Then that balloon plummets to the floor as I listen to Dad repeat the story about needing to tend to some emergency problem in Cameroon. Without any deviations. Without any words or expressions that could possibly be coded. He somehow even managed to keep his voice fairly steady. When Blake's dad hears this message, he'll assume Dad was merely concerned about the charity and upset about missing the Aspen trip.

We may never get another shot to call for help.

The moment Dad finishes, the man snaps the phone back, ending the call. He stares at Dad, long and hard. Tense seconds tick by. All I can do—all any of us can do—is watch and wait. The gun never moves.

Then the man straightens, seeming to collect himself. Some of the hardness loosens from his face and posture. His arm lowers the gun.

The whole room breathes a collective sigh of relief.

But I should have known the relief would be short lived.

"Why are you doing this?"

The words come from my father's mouth.

Instantly, the man hardens with hate. "Why? *Why?*" he repeats. "You damn well know why."

He takes a menacing step forward.

"You and I both know that we've had our differences in the past, but I always liked you—respected you," the man says, his voice rising. "But in my moment of need, what did you do? You stabbed me in the back!"

Dad shakes his head, denying whatever the man's accusing him of. "I tried to help—"

"Don't lie to me!" the man shouts.

I whimper and cower. I don't know what's stronger—my fear or my confusion.

"I sent you letters!" the man bellows. "I filled your answering machine a dozen times with my calls! And you ignored me! So what did you think would happen, Bob? Did you really think I'd let you get away with this?"

Dad's eyes widen in fear and disbelief, then they flash to me.

The intruder follows Dad's gaze to me. He lets out a long exhale before focusing back on Dad.

"You should have given her back to me, Bob."

Then he takes his gun, aims it at my father's head, and fires.

THREE

RED CLASHES AGAINST THE SILVER AND blue decorations on the Christmas tree. A crimson bead drips onto the white bow of a present as Dad's body slumps to the floor.

Mom's muffled scream fills the air. She doubles over, sobbing and wailing.

He shot him.

He shot my dad.

In shock, I sit there and wait for Dad to get up. To move. To breathe. I refuse to acknowledge that hole in his forehead and what it means.

Then my attention turns to his killer. He's quiet. Relaxed. Unaffected by the life he just stole. He moves, pointing the gun at my mom.

No.

Without thinking, I leap up and slam into him. We tumble to the ground, and the gun goes off.

Oh God, no.

I roll off the man and search out Mom, afraid of what I might see. But there she is, her fear-filled brown eyes scanning me as I scan her. She's OK. The bullet didn't hit her.

She screams something at me and nods toward the windows. She wants me to run.

But I can't leave her. He'll kill her. I can't lose her too.

"Dammit, Jessica!" the man snarls.

His voice shocks my system, awakening a new terror. He just got done telling me in my room that he'd hurt me if I disobeyed him. But now I just *attacked* him. There's no way he won't kill me for this.

I look back at Mom. Her wide eyes are flickering between me and him. She must realize it too—that he'll kill me. Before he can sit up, she leaps on top of him, screeching out what sounds like *Go!*

I still don't want to leave her. But now I realize that if I stay, we're both dead.

I bolt up, lurching toward the door, praying I don't lose my balance with my feet tied. If I can just get outside, maybe I can get help.

"No, Jessy!" he calls out after me.

A moment later, I hear a thud behind me. I glance back. Mom's on the ground, scrambling to stop him. But he gets up. He's coming after me.

We collide in the hallway, his heavy body dropping me onto the wooden floor like a sack of flour. Something strikes the back of my head. Everything goes dark.

‡

My head pounds as if someone took a jackhammer to my brain. Why do I hurt so much? This is worse than any headache or hangover I've ever had.

Confused, I blink and look around, trying to remember where I am and what's happened.

Aspen.

We're supposed to leave soon.

I remember coming upstairs . . . but I don't remember drinking anything or doing anything that would cause this awful throbbing in my head.

I reach up to rub my forehead, but my arm won't move. Neither of them will. They're numb. Heavy. It feels like they're stuck together by something. But that can't be right. I feel it around my ankles too. And mouth. What happened to me?

Craning my neck, I can see a familiar mirrored dresser, walk-in closet, and vanity. I'm on my bed in my bedroom.

I'm home.

I rest my aching head back on the pillow. For a moment, I feel the sense of relief and comfort that only home can bring.

But it's short lived. Images stream forward of a horror movie starring my family.

It's real.

It really happened.

My father is dead.

Tears well up. Before I can even close my eyes, the tears run out the sides.

Behind my closed eyes, I see him, my father, being shot. I see it over and over again. His blood splattering onto the tree, dripping onto the presents. Dad was there—right in front of me. And now he's gone.

Forever.

He'll miss my graduation. College. Wedding. Everything big and small left in my life. He won't be there for any of it.

I roll onto my side, giving into my grief. But then I see a shadow standing in my doorway, watching me.

Just by the slight hunch in his stance, I know it's him.

I hold my breath, not taking my eyes off him for a single moment.

Finally, he breaks away, moving down the hall and out of view.

I collapse back against the pillow. Tears continue to flow like tiny rivers down the sides of my face. I can't make them stop. I don't want them to stop. I just want this to end. I want my mom and dad.

Mom.

Where is she? What has he done to her?

Right as I'm about to scream out for her, my words get lodged in my throat because he returns. Instead of staying in the hall, he enters my room this time. My heart pounds harder with each step that brings him closer to me.

Is he going to kill me? Hurt me?

Oh God. Has he already hurt me? How long was I out? What did he do to me?

Why hasn't anyone come to rescue me? Didn't anyone hear the gunshot?

Reality quickly sinks in, though. We're out in the country. Even if someone happened to hear the shot, they would have thought nothing of it. Our neighbor down the road even has a shooting range in his backyard.

No one is coming to save us.

He's next to my bed now. He sets something down on my nightstand. It clinks, and my gaze flickers to it on impulse. It's a glass of water. My throat aches for it.

He sits on the edge of my bed, inches from me. I whimper, fearing what's next.

"I have some aspirin for your head," he says. He opens his hand to show two small white pills in his palm. "Promise not to scream, and I'll take the tape off."

I stare at the pills, unsure of what to do. Are they really aspirin, or will they knock me out again?

After several moments of silence, he lets out a long exhale and sets the pills down on my nightstand. I stare at the pills but then notice something is wrong. Something off with the nightstand. Then it hits me: my phone is missing. Normally I leave it there to charge, but I never got it out of my bag. Has he found it yet? Did he take it, like he took Dad's?

I glance over at my desk next, hoping to find my laptop.

I could use it to message my friends for help. But it's not there. He took it. Why?

The answer is obvious. I can't call for help.

What other stuff did he touch while I was out cold? What else did he do in my room, my private, personal space? It sends shivers down my spine. This place no longer feels like my own. He's tainted it all.

Why is he doing this?

He reaches for me. I flinch, but he ignores it. He grabs a corner of the tape.

"Remember, don't scream."

As he rips off the tape, my lips and cheeks burn. It's worse than having my entire body waxed. I bite my tender lips, holding in my pain.

"Good girl."

He smiles down at me, and the hardness I had seen in his eyes is gone. He genuinely looks proud of me.

I flinch again as he reaches for my shoulder, helping me sit up. He holds out the pills.

I consider refusing them again. After all, it's his fault I'm hurting. But then I remember what he said about disobeying him. Plus, when I take a closer look at the pills, they do look like real aspirins. I can even see the word *ASPIRIN* etched into them, just like the ones in our medicine cabinet.

And honestly, if they are pain meds, I could really use them. The sooner this pain goes away, the better.

I open my mouth, and he places them on my tongue. Next, he brings the water to my lips. He tips it just enough for the pills to go down without spilling, then returns the glass to the nightstand.

The tender way he's caring for me now is at odds with his earlier actions. This man *murdered* my father. How can someone be so callous and cruel one moment, then compassionate the next? I don't understand.

Why us? Why me?

Silently, he sits on my bed, staring at me. He opens his

mouth to say something but then slowly closes it again. He lets out a long exhale and then says, "You probably have to go to the bathroom, don't you?"

I doubt it was what he really wanted to say the first time. But as if on cue, my stomach tightens. I suddenly do have to pee, really bad.

"Yes," I croak.

He nods, then pulls me to my feet and helps me hop to my bathroom.

"You have two minutes," he says before he leaves the room.

I quickly get to it. It isn't easy with my hands and feet still bound, but thank goodness I'm wearing leggings, and thank goodness I'm flexible. After some impressive wiggling and bending, I manage.

Next, I have to somehow wash my hands, which are behind my back. I sit backward on my vanity, with my back pressed against the mirror so my hands can reach the faucet.

A knock sounds on the door. It's light, but it still startles me. I expect he'll just come barging in.

Instead, he waits. After a few seconds, he calls out, "All good in there?"

I can't begin to think how to answer that. After a few more seconds, he slowly opens the door and steps into the bathroom. He laughs, amused by my contortions at the vanity.

He reaches behind me, turning off the water. Then he grabs a towel. Rough hands grip my arms as he pulls me off the countertop. Before I can ask him what he's doing, he turns me around and starts drying my hands.

He's gentle. Meticulous.

He's done this before. I don't mean kidnapping—though maybe he has done that too. I mean he's taken care of someone before. Definitely. Maybe his parents? A sibling? Wife? Kids?

I don't know what he wants with me. I've been at his

mercy for I don't know how long, yet other than the initial scuffle in my room and when I tried to escape, he's been overly gentle with me. The way he's acting toward me now is almost nurturing, like a parent. It doesn't make sense.

I lift my gaze to his face. A relaxed, content smile greets me.

"I bet you feel better now. You've been asleep for almost fourteen hours, Jessy."

I don't want to believe him. But I've lived in this room long enough to know the pattern of the sunlight. With how high up the sun currently is, it's close to lunchtime. And it was late afternoon when he arrived. So it's true—I've been here in this bed, unconscious, for well over half a day.

Maybe it's a good thing. Life, as I knew it, is shattered anyway.

"Why are you doing this?" I ask. It's barely a whisper.

He stops, frowns, then sets the towel on the counter.

His mud-brown eyes meet mine, and they're back to that same scary calmness.

"Why did you try to leave?" he asks in return.

I balk.

He shakes his head, clucking his tongue. "I told you that I didn't want to hurt you. But then what did you do? Huh? You made me hurt you."

I flinch. Then in a moment of bravery, I say, "What was I supposed to do? *You killed my dad.* You were about to kill—"

"Don't bring that *bastard* up again!" He reaches behind his back and pulls out the duct tape, setting it on the counter beside me. "I've missed your voice, so I don't want to put that back on. But mention him again, and you'll leave me with no choice."

I swallow, hard. What could Dad have possibly done to him to warrant this? The way he talked to Dad and the way Dad looked at him—it was obvious that they knew each other. But no matter how much I try, I can't figure out how or why.

I take another deep breath, giving myself time to find the courage to ask him a question that terrifies me: "Where's my mom?"

His jaw tightens. "Sandy's gone."

"What?"

No. Please, God. No.

My chest constricts. I can't breathe. No matter how much air I suck in, it does nothing.

Gone. My parents are gone. He took them from me. Made me an orphan. Now I'm all alone. Alone with *him*.

"P-please," I say as tears fall. "Let me go."

His calloused fingers scratch my cheek as he wipes away my heartache. Unlike the other times he's touched me, my body doesn't recoil. I barely feel his touch now. I barely feel anything other than the crushing emptiness.

"I let you go once, Jessy. Those were the worst years of my life. I won't make that mistake again."

I don't know what he means, and right now, I don't care. I don't care about anything.

"I will never let anything or anyone take you from me again," he continues. "Do you understand?"

My mind reels as he lifts me into his arms once more and carries me back into my room. He looks around at my things, slowly shaking his head. He doesn't like my room.

That shouldn't bother me, but it does. He's judging me. The things I have, the things my parents bought.

My room is big. Bigger than any of my friends' rooms. A huge walk-in closet and a bathroom with a Jacuzzi tub. The furniture is white with gold trim, and my bed has a white lace canopy.

I had to have this set the moment I saw it. It was fit for a princess, which is how my parents always made me feel. My parents didn't even bat an eye when I asked for it. They just got me whatever I wanted. They've always done that.

I'm surrounded by everything I ever wanted, but now it's

all just *stuff.*

All I want now is them.

My lips tremble. I stare at the small chandelier, not wanting to cry anymore.

"Why don't you get some more rest," he says, looking down at me, in his arms. "Hopefully you'll be more like yourself by dinner. Don't try to escape again—I don't want to punish you."

He sets me down on my bed, tucks me in, and leaves my room, shutting the door.

Paralyzed by fear and grief, I lie in bed, watching time pass by the sunlight moving across the walls. Every time I consider getting up and escaping, I stop myself, too terrified to move. I'm afraid he'll come back if I make any noise at all. He may say he doesn't want to hurt me, but it doesn't mean he won't.

He's a killer. A cold-blooded murderer.

He killed the two people who mattered most to me. He shattered my life. And it didn't even phase him.

So I'll just lie here. I'll focus on what I need to do next.

Survive.

‡

Throughout the day, I hear him coming and going. When he's gone, the house is so quiet and still. I can't tell if he's in the yard or if he left the farm entirely. I never hear a vehicle. I don't dare try to escape if I don't know where he is.

When he's back inside the house, it's noisy. Somewhere below me, he's running a saw of some kind. At least it sounds like a saw. It goes on for what seems like forever. Then he's hammering and drilling. All I can guess is that he's building something.

What, though?

The possibilities are endless. My mind runs wild, trying to guess.

Coffins, maybe. Two of them for sure. One for Dad. One for Mom. He's going to bury them in the backyard, near the pool. At least they'll be together.

Is there a coffin for me too?

I don't know. If this were about killing me, wouldn't I be dead now? Or is this just some sort of delayed gratification, where he waits and then kills me later?

Whatever this is, it's not about money. This isn't a hostage-and-ransom situation, as I first thought. He's murdered all the people who could have paid him.

Instead, it's about . . . me.

What did the man say earlier? *You should have given her back to me.* It makes no sense.

It just hurts too much.

Please, I silently cry. *Please let someone save me.* Blake and his family. The police. Anyone. My parents are important people—doesn't anyone realize something has happened?

But then I remember how that murderer forced Dad to call Donovan and lie about canceling the Aspen trip due to a problem in Cameroon. It was the perfect cover-up, actually.

Every year, Dad takes at least one unexpected trip overseas when a charity organization has a problem. It's happened many times—supplies get caught up in customs, supplies get delivered to the wrong places, and so on. Especially in the third-world countries. Especially in Cameroon.

Each time this happens, Dad always takes it upon himself to personally sort it out. And when he does, he essentially goes offline. He even puts an out-of-office-type setting on his email and voicemail. It's common for us to not even hear from him until he's in an area with a more secured network.

The best lies are based on truths, right?

But how did this man—who certainly doesn't look well versed in international nonprofit organizations—know all this? How did he know the perfect lie? Once again, I can't help but wonder just how much he knows about us.

And why . . . ?

After several hours of listening to the construction noise downstairs, I find the courage and strength to get out of bed. My feet are still tied, so all I can do is hop around. I'm not really sure what I'm even doing.

With my hands still taped behind my back, I fumble as I check the drawers for my laptop. Even though I know it's a long shot, I check for my phone, too, hoping maybe he'd brought it up. I don't find either of them. I didn't think I would, but I still had to try.

I check the windows next. It's a long drop from the second story, but a fall might be better than whatever he has planned for me. But the windows are nailed shut. He must have done that while I was unconscious.

He's thought of everything.

I can't run. I can't get help. I'm trapped with my parents' murderer.

Knowing I *can't* leave fills me with an irrational urge to try escaping anyway—to just make a run for it, straight out the front door. But in my current state, I wouldn't even make it down the stairs before he caught me again.

At sunset, the banging downstairs stops. A minute later, I hear him climbing the stairs.

Whimpering, I hop back to bed, sitting on the edge. I hold my breath as he opens my door.

His jeans and boots are muddy. Sawdust wafts through the air. I want to know what he's been doing, but at the same time, I don't.

Before I can tug my mind away from visions of coffins, he reaches into his back pocket and pulls out a silver object. Blood drains from my face. My throat dries. My breathing quickens. In his hand is a four-inch hunting knife.

He moves toward me.

I clamp my eyes shut as every muscle inside me tightens, waiting for the moment the blade grates my skin. Will he stab me? Slit my throat?

Instead, there's only a brief tug on my ankles. Confused, I open my eyes. He's kneeling at my feet, having just cut the tape around my ankles. I can feel my circulation resume.

Without saying another word, he grabs my arm and pulls me off the bed. I think he's going to cut the tape off my hands too. But no.

"Dinner's ready."

He leads me downstairs, possibly for my last meal. Every step hurts, but I keep quiet, not wanting to appear weak.

As we pass the living room, my heart clenches. My father's body is gone. Where did it go? And where's my mom's body? Did he kill her in the same room, or somewhere else? Are they together?

The man brings me to a stop in the dining room. The table is set with crystal glasses and the china we reserve for special occasions. There's even a poinsettia resting in the center. It's like we're celebrating instead of mourning.

I choke back tears as he leads me to the table, pulling out a chair for me. I can't sit. I can't get my legs to cooperate. He finally just tugs me down.

He takes out the knife and a set of handcuffs. I hold my breath, eyeing the knife. Just because he used it to unbind my feet last time doesn't mean he won't use it to stab me now. I don't want to be stabbed. I don't want to die. But if I have to die, I hope it'll be quick.

He bends me forward in my chair until my head rests against the table. I close my eyes. Waiting for it. For the pain.

This is it. I'm going to die. My blood will forever stain the white lace tablecloth. Mom would have hated that.

I feel another brief tug. He's cutting the tape around my wrists. He rips the rest of it off me.

I'm alive. I'm free.

I sit up, rubbing my arms as blood rushes to my hands. Wide, angry red lines from the tape encircle my wrists like bracelets. In some spots, the skin is chafed. It's going to

LAURIE WETZEL ‡ PICTURE PERFECT

bruise. In a day or so, it'll be ugly.

Will I live to see it?

As I stare at my wrists, I hear a click. He's attaching one end of the handcuffs to my armrest. He then holds out his hand, waiting for me to give him mine. He's going to restrain me to the chair. I have no choice but to give him my arm. He snaps the cuff shut.

I'm not free. I never will be. Not until either he or I am dead.

And then the unthinkable happens. Mom walks in.

She's *alive*.

My heart stutters, and my vision blurs. How can this be? When I asked him where Mom was, he said she was dead.

But then my mind races back to that talk in the bathroom. I remember now—he said, "Sandy's gone." *Gone*. Not *dead*. Why would he say it like that? He had to have known what conclusion I'd jump to, especially considering that I had just witnessed him murder my father.

Mom's carrying a roast on a platter. Her hair is different—shorter and dyed strawberry blond. She's wearing a sundress with a cardigan instead of the designer outfits she normally wears. But I don't care how she looks. All that matters is she's really here.

Our eyes meet. I want to tell her I miss her. I want to tell her I'm scared. But most of all, I want to tell her I love her. But I can't. Not with him here. So I settle for staring at her, hoping my eyes say everything.

She gives me a weak smile, glances at him, and slightly shakes her head. Somehow I know she feels the exact same way. She wants to comfort me too. But not in front of him. Then her smile is gone, and she serves up dinner.

He sits at the head of the table—in Dad's chair. Mom sits beside him. I'm on his other side, across the table from Mom. I see the same markings on her wrists and around her mouth. She was bound up too.

She keeps her head down and doesn't say a word through

dinner. He gobbles up dinner, smiling and making little comments about how delicious it is.

I can't touch my food. Everything about this is wrong. *Sick. Twisted.* Less than twenty-four hours ago, my father was shot to death in the next room. And now this murderer is sitting in Dad's chair at the dining room table, eating the roast Dad bought.

"Why are you doing this?" I ask again. "Who are you? What are you going to do to us?"

Mom whimpers as the man's fork stops in midair. He lowers his fork to his plate and stares at me.

I want to appear strong. I want to be brave. But this man terrifies me.

"Eat," he finally says.

"If it's money, take it. My parents have lots."

His lips pull thin. After a moment, he repeats, "Eat."

"No. Not until you answer my questions."

"Jessy, baby," Mom pleads, her lips quivering as tears line her fear-filled eyes. "Please just eat. Please just do whatever he wants."

The man whips around to face Mom. She cowers instantly. He glares at her for several long seconds.

My mother is a proud, confident woman. Why isn't she standing up to him? Why isn't she fighting him? Couldn't the two of us take him if we worked together? Yeah, my one hand is cuffed to the chair, but I still have one hand free and both my legs. And Mom isn't restrained at all!

Then his gaze slides off of Mom and onto me. "Your mother made us a delicious dinner, Jessy. She knows it's your favorite, and she worked very hard on it. Eat."

Roast is *not* my favorite. Mom knows that. I have no clue why he would even say something like that.

The harshness in his tone makes me pick up my fork. I know he wants me to eat. But even if I tried, I know I'd just throw up. I set the fork back down.

Seeing this, he leans back and wipes his mouth with the

linen napkin from his lap. Then he stands.

Alarm bells ring inside me. I shouldn't have done that. I should have eaten. Why didn't I just eat?

I glance at Mom. She's staring down at the table.

"Mom, please . . ." I beg.

She winces.

"Your mother is doing what I ask," the man says, clamping his hand down on her shoulder. "She's being good. Don't ruin her dinner as you've ruined mine."

I swallow back tears as he walks over to me. Each step is slow, measured, precise. It's somehow worse than when he rushed me the other day.

My eyes flicker to Mom. She hasn't moved a muscle. She's not even looking up from her plate. She can't just sit there and let him hurt me—can she?

He opens the cuffs and grabs me by the arm, pulling me to my feet. He glares down at me.

My hands and feet are free for the first time. I should fight him off. I should run away again. But my brain can't seem to send out the right signals. Instead, I let him take me all the way to the basement, still watching and waiting for Mom to get up and help me.

She doesn't . . .

What did he *do* to her?

The smell of sawdust is stronger down here. Plastic covers the bar, the pool table, the home theater seats, and the projector screen. Sawhorses, a table saw, and a bag of tools are in the center of the room. In the far corner is a new plywood wall and door.

He built a room.

Is that where he put my father's body? Is that where he's going to put me? Is he going to kill me and throw my body in there too? Is that what this room is for? His own kill room?

"No," I say, struggling as I feel him lead me toward the room. "Let go!"

He whips me around like a towel and shakes me.

"Enough!" he barks.

Then he whirls me again and shoves me closer to the door. My head spins and I stumble.

When the dizziness clears, I notice three locks on the outside of the door. Why? Bodies can't escape.

He opens the door. The room is small. Barely wide enough to be a coat closet. The carpeting is gone, stripped down to the cement. A lone blanket is balled up at one end of the space, and a plastic bucket sits at the other.

"When I was away from you," he begins, "I spent some time in a room like this. No technology. No distractions. No extra comforts. Nothing to do but think about my mistakes—what I did to land me in there in the first place and the many ways I failed as a father. That's what you need now—time to reflect on your poor choices."

He shoves me inside and slams the door, locking it.

The room goes black.

I spin around, pounding on the door. "Please don't do this!" I scream. "Please let me out!"

"You're a spoiled, disobedient, selfish little girl, Jessy. You take everything and everyone for granted." He pauses. "You weren't this way before. They've ruined you. But it's OK now. I'm here. And I'm going to fix you."

"*Fix me?*" My God, what does that mean?

He doesn't answer.

I bang on the door again. "What do you mean *fix me*? Answer me!"

He doesn't. He's gone.

I keep screaming. I keep slamming my fists on the door. But he never comes. Neither does Mom—and I know she can hear me too. By the time I finally accept that no one is coming for me, my hands are numb and bloody.

I slide down the wall, bring my knees to my chest, and hug myself. Every emotion I've been too afraid to feel over the last twenty-four hours crashes into me.

This room is a cage. A prison. If he doesn't come back,

it *will* be my coffin.
I finally cry myself to sleep.

FOUR

SLEEP FADES AWAY; AWARENESS TRICKLES in. But when I feel the aches and pains in my body and the harsh coldness of the concrete floor, I go from groggy to instantly awake.

Darkness swallows me, yet I know where I am. I'll never forget it. I'm locked up in the basement—a prisoner in my own home.

How many hours have I been in here? Is it the middle of the night? Or morning?

Worry fills me. While I've been trapped down here, he's been upstairs, alone with Mom.

Is she OK? I know she heard me crying out for her. Did she fight him? Did he hurt her? Is she still alive?

Tears pool. I look up, trying to keep them from falling. And that's when I see a tiny blinking red light.

As I watch it, I notice the round object it's attached to. A camera.

He watched me panic. He watched me fall apart. And he watched me cry myself to sleep. Is he watching me now? Has he been sitting in front of the monitor the whole time, getting some sort of kick out of seeing me caged like an animal? Or is he recording it on some device so he can watch it any time he wants? Like I'm some sort of on-demand show?

I grimace and look away, catching sight of the only other object in here—the bucket. It's for pee. I suspected as much the moment he threw me in here, but I didn't want to be right. Let alone use it.

At least the bucket is positioned directly below the camera, in what's mostly a blind spot. It's like he did his best to give me some privacy. It's almost like he cares. Yet he's hurt me and locked me in here. To go from that extreme to this—I can't begin to comprehend it.

My stomach growls, and I place my hand over it, trying to appease it. The last thing I ate was a salad at school. But how long ago was that? Two days? Three? Longer? I can't tell. The darkness is disorienting. The only sounds are from the furnace and sump pump.

What about my friends? My mind tortures me, thinking of all the fun Cassie and Blake are having in Aspen. Have they noticed that I haven't liked or commented on any of their posts? Have they tried to call? Are they worried that I haven't answered?

I wish I were there with them. I wish none of this had happened.

Then Dad would still be alive.

As the pipes rattle above me again for what feels like the thousandth time, a desperate need to escape this plywood prison suddenly awakens. Once again, I punch and kick the walls and door, crying out for him. For Mom—if she's even still alive. For anyone and everyone who can hear me. My hands and feet begin to throb. I rip open the still-fresh scrapes on my knuckles and fingertips, making them bleed again. It only makes me fight harder.

When my voice and my body give out, I collapse to the floor. I lay there, in the dark, cold, pee-smelling room, rubbing my dirty and torn sweatshirt.

I glance back at the camera. I stare into it. He has to know

41

he's made his point. He's "fixed" me. He's won. Why won't he open the door?

He's not coming back.

He's never coming back.

He's going to kill me. I'm certain. The only variables are when and how. For all I know, maybe this is how I die—alone and starving in this makeshift tomb . . .

At least I can take some comfort in the fact that I've died before.

‡

We were coming home from the state football game. Ryan, Cassy's then-boyfriend, was driving his SUV. Cassy was in front, and Blake and I were in the backseat. I was leaning forward, holding out my phone to show everyone some videos of the game. We were all watching and laughing—even Ryan.

If I hadn't been playing those videos, we would have seen it in time. We would have avoided it completely. We would have seen the drunk driver veer into our lane.

But instead, we didn't see that truck until it was too late. All Ryan could do was swerve. The drunk hit us right in the side, where I was sitting. The drunk's truck bounced off our SUV like a pinball, smashing into five more vehicles as we rolled.

I remember the pain—so much pain. Then I remember faces hovering over me. Lights in a tiled ceiling.

Then suddenly it was all gone. I felt free. At peace. I wanted to stay there.

But then the pain came rushing back.

The doctor said I died on the operating table. Flatlined. I was gone for about ten minutes, but then they brought me back. I was very lucky, they said.

I didn't feel very lucky. I felt guilty. In those moments when I was gone—dead—I didn't think about anyone. I didn't think about Mom or Dad or Blake or any my friends. I didn't fight to stay for them.

But my biggest source of guilt was that while I miraculously survived, someone else didn't. Someone else died right there at the scene.

I can never forget her. I can never free myself of the guilt I carry about her. Maybe if the drunk hadn't hit us, he wouldn't have hit her. And if he hadn't hit her, both of our families would have been spared something worse than grief: hope.

Paramedics rushed us from the crash site to a small-town hospital. The staff was overwhelmed when the ambulances pulled in with so many victims.

Mistakes were made.

When my parents arrived at the hospital, the staff told them that fifteen-year-old Jessica Smith of Northland had died at the scene. My parents went to the morgue to identify my body—only it wasn't my body.

It was the body of the *other* Jessica Smith.

I'd always known about her. I'd never met her, but I knew that she was my age and that she lived on the south side of Northland.

And in some bizarre coincidence, we were both involved in that crash. What were the odds that we'd be in the same place at the same horrible time?

Our fates weren't the same, though. The other Jessica Smith died at the scene. So while I was in surgery, fighting for my life, the other Jessica Smith lay in the morgue. No one realized the mix-up until my parents looked down to see her body, not mine, on that cold table.

Ironically, Jessica and I finally would have met this year. She would have attended Northland High with all the other South River High students. In fact, she would have had a locker next to me. Right beside her twin brother—Nick.

Who decides which lives are worth saving and which ones aren't? Is there someone up there, making these decisions? And if so, did whoever is up there believe *my* life was worth saving—but *hers* wasn't?

Why? Based on what happened in my past? What would happen in my future?

If they based it on my future, well, then they picked wrong. Dying on that operating table after the accident two years ago would have been a blessing compared to the death I see in my very near future.

A jingle of keys sounds outside my door.

My panicked heart races as I scoot back on the cement floor. It's *him*. He's here to unlock my plywood prison.

The door opens and light bursts in. It's as if the darkness is abandoning me in its own race for cover. Even the darkness is afraid of the man now standing in my doorway.

What happened to him that he can ruin my life, end my father's, and be so unaffected? I don't really care. I don't give a damn about him. But it would be nice to know why he's destroying my life piece by piece.

I suppose I can ask Dad. I think I'll be joining him in a minute . . .

"Time's up," the man says. "You may come out now, Jessy. Hopefully you utilized your time wisely."

I close my eyes, savoring those words: *You may come out now.* He isn't going to kill me. Not yet.

Then I try to stand. My legs are shaky. Weak. I fall back to the floor.

How long have I been in here?

Suddenly, he's grabbing my arm, pulling me to my feet. His other arm slides around me, supporting me, as he helps me out of the box.

The brightness of the room is overwhelming. It feels like a million floodlights are blazing down on me. When my eyes adjust, I'm surprised to see that only the accent lights around the room are on. It just seems blindingly bright because I've been in near darkness for so long.

Now in the light, I suddenly can see my hands.

My fingertips are stained red. My nails have all broken off. My knuckles are bruised and bloody. My wrists are scabbed and have ugly bluish-purple bruises from the tape.

I turn away, disgusted.

We move slowly. My muscles are stiff, achingly protesting with every step.

He doesn't complain or rush me. He doesn't say anything the entire way up to my bathroom. He leans me against the vanity counter and grabs a towel from the rack.

"You may shower or take a bath now," he says. "I'll come back for you in a bit. Then we'll open presents."

Presents?

At my blank stare, he adds, "Merry Christmas, Jessy."

It's Christmas.

My dad's been dead for four days.

I crumble to the floor. Whatever strength I used to make it out of that prison and up here to my bedroom has evaporated. I remain there, in a heap.

But after a moment, I begin to fear what he'd do if he came back and found me on the floor. I get up and take a shower, as he told me to do.

Standing is too hard, so I sit down on the tiled floor of the walk-in shower. I hug my knees to my chest as I let the water rain down on me.

When I get out, I stare at the person in the mirror. Gone is the girl with the flawless complexion, perfectly styled hair, and dazzling blue eyes. The girl I see now has shallow, pale skin. Lifeless hair. Vacant eyes. Who is this other girl? And where is the girl who once looked back at me?

I continue staring, trying to come to terms with the fact that this imposter in the mirror is *me*. Maybe if I accept that truth, I can find my way back. I can become the girl I used to be. Sort of like how owning your demons helps you overcome them.

In the end, it doesn't work. Accepting my horror story of a reality doesn't suddenly make it OK. Nor does it give me any control over the situation. Even if it did, Dad is still dead. How can I possibly be who I once was without him? How can life ever be OK again?

I braid my hair, not having the strength nor desire to do anything else with it, then I walk into my room. A dress is laid out on the bed. It's a red sweaterdress Mom bought me a few weeks ago.

My heartbeat races. Does this mean Mom picked it out while I was in the shower? Is this dress her way of silently showing me she's still here with me?

Even though I know it's foolish to hope, I do it anyway. I need to. I can't face this without her.

I pull the dress on; it's loose but warm. I also toss on a pair of black leggings. As I turn to leave, someone knocks on my door. It's him. It will always be him.

He waits for me to answer, but the words won't come.

After another moment of silence, he slowly opens the door.

He's showered too. His hair has been cut and his beard trimmed, giving him a more rugged, blue-collar look. His worn-out, dirty clothes have been replaced by jeans and a sweater. I recognize the sweater. I gave it to Dad for Christmas last year.

Now that he's all cleaned up, he does look vaguely familiar. Maybe we've passed on the streets? Maybe I've seen him at a restaurant or store? Sometime when I was with Dad, because he and this man seemed to know each other? Did they work together?

I don't know if I crossed paths with this man once or many times. Either way, our encounter impacted him much more than me.

"You look very nice, Jessy," he says. "Are you feeling better after your shower?"

Do I feel better? I don't know. How am I supposed to feel?

He tilts his head, waiting for my answer.

I don't want to upset him, so even though I'm unsure, I say, "Yes."

He continues to stare. His eyebrows are raised, and his head is still tilted. It's what people do when they're waiting for something.

It's unnerving. The silence has my skin crawling. This anxious need to make it stop, to make him not look at me like that, has me desperately racking my brain. What does he want? What is he waiting for?

Somewhere, somehow, a simple phrase is pulled out of the darkness. "Thank you . . . ?" I say, testing the words as if they're foreign.

He smiles.

I was right. He wanted me to thank him. For what, though? For letting me out of the prison or for letting me shower? I'm grateful for both, of course. But having to show my gratitude to *him* for it makes bile rise in my throat.

He steps aside. "Come with me. Your mother is waiting to open presents."

Mom.

He needs to help me again. Not so much because my legs are unsteady but because my head is hazy. I have no idea what to expect as we head downstairs to the living room— where this nightmare began. Whatever hope I had gathered before is gone. With every step, I panic. Will it be Mom's blood splattered on the Christmas tree this time?

But the moment we enter the living room, my mind clears. It no longer looks like it did in my nightmare. It looks pristine. Normal.

The broken things have been removed. The tables have been righted. All the gifts that were splattered with blood have been rewrapped.

The Christmas tree, too, has been replaced. The old one was a tall spruce we had picked out together from our own land. Dad chopped it down himself. This new tree is a small artificial one. Unfamiliar, older ornaments hang from it.

I'm so confused by the scene in front of me that it takes me a moment to see her.

Mom. Alive.

She's sitting beside the tree in almost the same spot she had sat the first night. I'm relieved to see that her hands rest freely in her lap; her mouth isn't taped either.

I'm concerned, though, about how different she looks. Mom is one of the most stylish women I know. She totally rocks a glam-yet-professional look. Her makeup, hair, and clothes defy her age.

But right now, I barely recognize her. Her makeup is so . . . basic. She's wearing colors I've never seen her wear— browns and beige on her lids and dusty rose on her lips. And she's transformed her edgy shag into loose, spiral curls.

Under any other circumstance, I'd say she looks beautiful—like a homespun angel.

But in this moment, I'm filled with dread.

Our eyes meet. Her once-gorgeous hazel eyes are now lifeless. Again I wonder, What has he done to her?

"Doesn't our girl look pretty, darling?" he says to Mom, gesturing at me.

"Yes," Mom says. Her voice is just as dead as her eyes.

He turns to me, arching a brow.

There's that look again. In the weighted silence, I realize he's waiting for me to say something.

Since it worked the first time, I say, "Thank you."

Once again, he smiles.

Then he claps his hands together. "No time like the present to open presents!" He grins at his corny joke and looks expectantly at Mom.

She laughs. But it's too high. Totally fake.

As her eyes slide to me, they're no longer vacant. They're pleading, begging me. To do what? Help her? How?

Mom deliberately darts her eyes between me and the man, then she laughs even harder.

I get it now. She's begging me to help *myself*. So I join

in, laughing at a joke told by my father's murderer.

I can read it on her face: *Play along.* Mom wants me to survive by keeping him happy and doing whatever he wants us to do.

Maybe she's right. Fighting and disobeying him has only gotten me hurt. As much as my instincts tell me to stand up to him, perhaps obeying him is the right thing to do, the best thing to do. After all, who ended up in the plywood prison, me or Mom?

He motions for me to sit beside the tree, across from Mom. I do it without hesitating. Relief flashes in her eyes.

So I was right. This *is* what she wants me to do. Just play along. OK. I can do this. I can follow her lead.

He gives Mom the first gift. It's a three-carat diamond necklace—I helped Dad pick it out.

"It's perfect," she says. "Thank you."

She thanked him for my father's gift.

"Try it on," he presses.

She nods and moves her hair off to the side. I feel as if I'm having an out-of-body experience as I watch him place the necklace on her. His hands linger on her shoulders.

I study her face, expecting her to frown, grimace—do something, anything, that would mirror just how screwed up this is. But she does nothing. She doesn't react.

How can she just sit there and let him touch her?

She smiles up at him. "Thank you," she says once again. She places a hand over her new necklace.

Before I realize it, my own hand reaches up and touches my neckline. It takes me a moment to realize I'm searching for Blake's necklace. But I find only bare skin.

I look down as my hand frantically searches for the necklace. Did it fall off when I fought the man in my room that first night? Or when I was screaming and flailing in the prison downstairs? Or did he take it sometime when I was unconscious? I don't know. All I know is that the necklace is gone.

"You look worried, Jessy," he says. "Is everything all right?"

"I had a necklace. Where is it?"

He cocks his head to the side. His eyes narrow, but he doesn't answer.

"It's from my boyfriend," I continue. "He gave it to me as an early Christmas—"

"You're too young to be receiving gifts like that from admirers," he growls.

"Blake's not an *admirer*!" I blurt before I can stop myself. "We've been together for years! We're—"

"What?" he sneers. "Going off to college together? So you can cheer for him on the sidelines there and wherever he goes pro?"

Shock ripples through me. Blake and I made those plans in private. We made a pact to not tell anyone, not even our parents. We didn't want to jinx it.

"How do you know about that?" My voice is a whisper.

His mouth snaps shut, and he glares at me. I cringe, hoping I didn't upset him. If I press it more, it will only end one way: me being hurt.

He grabs a present and tosses it in Mom's lap. The discussion's over.

I let out the breath I was holding. But then a sinking suspicion settles in. This man knew us. He knew my name. Where we lived. Our habits. Our friends. He even knows my private plans with Blake. As much as I wish I could deny it, this isn't some random home invasion.

This man has been watching me. Somehow even listening in on my conversations. But how? For how long? And how did I not notice?

Did he have cameras on me this whole time? Did he hack into my phone and laptop? How much of my life has he violated?

It's too much to grasp. I turn my attention back to the gift opening. We continue for what seems like forever, opening gifts and thanking him after each one. It's the hardest thing I've ever done, but having Mom by my side gives me the strength to endure.

Everything I got—clothes, purses, makeup, jewelry—I wanted at one point. Now I'd trade them all just to have my father back. My life back.

I have to bite my lips as the man grabs the gift I bought Dad and opens it. It's concert tickets to see Chicago—Dad's favorite band. Anger courses through my veins to see this murderer holding the gift I bought for the man he killed right here in this very spot.

But then my anger is replaced by something else: shame. Next to me is a huge pile of gifts my parents bought for me, yet all I got Dad was concert tickets, and I got Mom a spa package—and both were put on a credit card Dad pays. I didn't spend a penny of my own money.

With a broad smile, the man thanks me for the tickets. "Cool! I love Chicago! Hey, we should make a weekend out of it—all three of us. Get a hotel, go out for dinner, really enjoy ourselves." He turns to Mom with an excited look. "Maybe you can go to the spa while Jessy and I go to the show!"

"No!" The word escapes before I can even stop myself.

The man and Mom both stare at me in shock.

"No," I repeat, my voice rising. "Those tickets were meant for *my dad* and me. Not you! None of these things were for you!"

The man's jaw ticks.

I know I've screwed up again, but I can't stand it anymore. The lies. The pretending. It's all so sick and twisted.

Wordlessly, he stands and leaves the room.

"Jessy . . ." Mom whispers.

I look up, meeting her fear-filled gaze.

"Jessy, baby, don't say things like that. Please, sweetie, don't make him angry anymore. I can't listen to him hurting you again."

"But Mom, I—"

He stomps back into the room, carrying garbage bags. He keeps one for himself, then tosses one at Mom and a third to me.

"Throw it out. Everything."

He kneels down, furiously reaching for wrapping paper and shoving it into his bag. But then he grabs the box still holding the bottle of perfume Dad bought Mom. His face curled in disgust, the man throws the box and the perfume into the bag, then grabs Mom's Coach purse and throws it in too.

"What are you—" I begin, holding out my hand to stop him.

"I said throw it out!" he shouts. "*Everything*. The paper. The boxes. The gifts. All of it." He points at the diamonds stretched across Mom's neckline. "That too. Throw it. Now!"

For several seconds, Mom and I stare at each other, then she closes her eyes. With trembling hands, she removes the three-carat necklace and drops it into the bag.

I focus on my mountain of gifts. Mom and Dad shop together every year, but he always buys one special gift for each of us on his own. He'll spend weeks researching and snooping to get something that makes us incredibly happy. This year it was a copy of Gabrielle Douglas's book with a personal autograph and inscription to me.

Knowing these gifts are the last thing I'll ever receive from him . . . I can't do it. I can't bring myself to toss them away.

Seeing me frozen, the man rips the bag from my hands. A tear rolls down my face as he scoops my gifts into the bag like they're yesterday's trash. By the time he's done, I'm numb, empty, and hollow.

Just when I think it can't get any worse, he pulls out two unopened presents from behind the tree. I expect him to throw them away, too, but surprisingly he passes them out to me and Mom.

With my heart sinking, I unwrap the gift I assume I'll have to promptly throw away. Once I uncover the gift, even more confusion floods me. It's a wooden jewelry box. Intricate roses are carved into the sides, and under the lid, my name is burnt into the wood. I know this isn't something Mom or Dad bought me.

Bright light flashes, momentarily blinding me. I blink away the spots to see him holding a camera. He took a picture of me? Now? Why? Why would anyone want to remember this?

He sets the camera down on the end table, then points to the jewelry box. "Do you like it?" he asks. His face is sincere. "The roses took a little over a month to carve, but I know how much you love them."

He made this?

For me?

And it took him over a month . . . ?

This wasn't some random, spur-of-the-moment act.

He planned this.

All of it.

Even down to it happening over Christmas.

How long has he been planning to break into our home, murder my father, and take Mom and me hostage?

Reaching a new level of numbness, I glance over at Mom's gift. It's a box of some sort with more carvings, but I can't make them out from here.

"For your recipe cards," he tells her. "That way, you won't lose any more—like how you lost the one for my grandmother's banana bread."

Mom had a recipe from his family? And she lost it? I don't remember her ever baking banana bread before.

"Thank you," Mom says. "That's so thoughtful."

Pleased once again, the man gets up and moves to the couch, sitting in the center with his arms resting on top.

"Come sit with me, Jessy, while your mother checks on dinner."

I don't want to. I turn to Mom, desperate for guidance. "Do you need any help, Mom?"

But she just nods at both of us. "No, sweetie. Just relax. Dinner is almost done."

I can't hide my dismay and bewilderment. Doesn't she realize "helping in the kitchen" is my chance to have a moment alone with her? Doesn't she at least see it's my chance to get away from *him*? Why did she tell me no?

He pats the cushion beside him.

My heart hammers in my chest as my legs somehow carry me over there. I sit and resist the urge to shiver as he drapes his arm around me, pulling me into his side.

"Can I get you two anything while I'm checking on dinner?" Mom asks.

The man glances at me. I think he's waiting for me to answer her first.

I shake my head.

"I'll take a drink," he says.

Mom nods. "Sure. We have whiskey, cognac—"

"Water," he snaps. "Or a Coke or something. Get rid of that other stuff." He frowns. "Teenage drinking is on the rise. I don't want Jessy getting caught up in that."

Mom subtly arches a brow, then quickly retreats to the kitchen.

I can only stare at him with my mouth open. This man has destroyed my life and *murdered* my father in front of me, yet he's worried about me *drinking*? I don't understand him.

He picks up the remote and flips through the channels on the dish, stopping on a black-and-white Christmas movie. I can't tell which one. I can see the pictures and hear the words, but they won't register.

I feel nothing.

I am nothing.

What would Dad think if he could see this? Would he be

54

outraged? Would he understand? If things were different—
if this man had killed Mom instead—would Dad have me
placate this murderer to stay alive? Or would he want me to
fight? I don't know anymore.

Sometime later, Mom announces that dinner is ready.
Just like last time, the table is done up with all the trimmings
we save for special occasions. I sit, expecting him to
handcuff me to the chair again. But he doesn't.

I suddenly realize he hasn't tied me up all day.

I could have run at any time. I could have escaped. But I
didn't. I didn't even think about it until just now.

Now my legs buzz, prepping to run.

But if I do, he'll catch me. My body is still too weak and
sluggish—I'd never get away. He'll put me back in that
room. Or worse.

So I just eat my dinner, telling myself it's to replenish
my strength.

Afterward, I help Mom with the dishes. I hope it'll give
us a moment alone, but he's there, always there. Hovering.

When we finish, he wants to watch another movie. So we
sit on the couch again. I'm under one arm; Mom's under the
other. We stay that way until he declares it's time for bed.

He gives me privacy to change into my pajamas. When I
get into bed, he doesn't tie me up. He doesn't even shut or
lock my bedroom door.

Instead, he just says, "Sweet dreams. See you in the
morning."

It's such a normal thing to say, yet the thought of seeing
him in the morning—of doing this all over again
tomorrow—makes me want to escape.

But again, I don't run. I lay in the middle of my bed,
unable to sleep.

Inexplicably, I yearn to be back in the plywood prison.
After days spent on the concrete floor, my once-comfortable
mattress is now too big and too soft. And at least I was safe
down there. I was locked in, yes. But that meant he had to

unlock the door to get inside. I could prepare myself. Here, he can silently slip in any time. I'm taunted by visions of him killing me while I sleep.

In the dark, I notice something I hadn't seen earlier. A familiar blinking red light. He's put a camera in my room.

How long has it been here? He must have installed it while I was locked downstairs. Or maybe he installed it when I was knocked out after trying to escape. I remember how *tainted* my room seemed. Perhaps I sensed the camera without even seeing it. It's impossible to say.

All that matters now is that the blinking light is taunting me. Reminding me that even though he isn't here, standing over me, he'd still know if I tried to escape.

I get up out of bed, dragging one of my blankets with me. I go into my walk-in closet and shut the door. There's no lock, but it's the closest thing to secure and private that I can manage.

I lay down underneath a rack of clothes, then grab as many shoes as I can reach. I pile them in front of me like some sort of warning system.

As I close my eyes, I say a prayer to my father, telling him I miss him and that I'm sorry for all the things I've done.

FIVE

FOR EVERY MEAL, WE DINE TOGETHER. AND after, we sit on the sofa and watch TV. It's so cruelly normal. How can the man who laughs at *The Simpsons* and guesses the *Wheel of Fortune* puzzles be the same one who murdered my father? It almost makes me doubt my own grasp on reality.

Almost . . .

When I'm with Mom, I watch her and follow her lead, doing everything this vicious man asks without hesitation. For that matter, I do everything he says even when I'm alone. There are cameras nearly everywhere now. I never know when he's watching, I treat it like he always is. The only place where I know I have privacy is the bathroom—thankfully.

He's pleased that I'm obeying him. And because he's pleased, things are better.

He doesn't hurt us.

He doesn't lock me away.

It won't last forever, though. Something will tip him over the edge. Will he kill Mom? Me? Both of us?

I keep hoping the cops will come—that Blake, Cassie, or one of my other friends called them, worried because they haven't heard from me. But it's been a week now, and no one has come. I can't continue to play house while I wait for this man to kill us. I had a family; he destroyed it. I couldn't save Dad, but I'm going to save Mom.

Somehow.

The next morning, I wake up earlier than usual. I shower, do my hair and makeup, and put on jeans and a nice sweater. When I'm finished getting ready, the house is still quiet.

Unsure of what to do, I sneak down the hall, trying to find him. I'm surprised he's not sleeping right there on the floor in the hall, close to the bedrooms so he can monitor us. He's not in any of the spare bedrooms either.

Maybe he left to run errands again? He'd put off errands while he was busy building the room downstairs. I imagine he has a few things to get caught up on.

Or perhaps he simply doesn't feel the need to watch us like hawks anymore, since we've been "getting along" so well.

Whatever the case may be, is this our shot to escape?

I head toward my parents' room. Mom is still asleep.

As I step into the room, something moves beside her in the bed. A moment later, an arm wraps around her, pulling her snug.

I stagger out into the hallway and lean against the wall.

He's in their bed—my parents' bed.

He's sleeping with her.

Is he just sharing the bed, or—

I shake my head, not wanting to give thoughts to whatever else he could be up to.

Tears well up. I press my palms to my eyes, not wanting to let them fall.

I don't know what to do. How do I save her *and* myself?

I shouldn't have to. I shouldn't have to deal with any of this. *She* should be the one trying to get us out of here. *She* should save *me*.

But if life worked how it was meant to, I'd be out in

Aspen, trying to figure out how to get Blake and myself away from Cassie and our parents so we could have time alone. Dad would still be alive. None of this would have happened.

This isn't my life.

Maybe if I keep thinking that, I can get through this.

Maybe if I pretend as if this isn't real, I can survive.

Quietly, I move downstairs. I stand in the living room, not knowing what to do next. I hadn't thought this far ahead.

My stomach growls, and I know my next move: feed him. I'll keep up this charade of being a happy little family. Then once his guard is down, I can finally escape this nightmare.

The past couple of mornings, he's ate big breakfasts. Just to be safe, I make the same: eggs, hash browns, sausage, bacon, pancakes, and toast. It's too much food. But I don't want to make him angry.

As I'm taking the bacon out of the pan, the hairs on the back of my neck stand up. *He's awake.* I just know it. I sense it in a way an animal senses a predator.

A moment later, I hear him shouting my name. There's anger in his voice. But also something else. Fear? Worry?

I hear him almost tumbling down the stairs, followed closely by Mom. They don't come into the kitchen, though. Instead, I hear the front door slam against the wall as the man throws it open in panic. Again, he shouts my name as they both run outside.

What is going on?

I rush to the hall just as they come racing back in. Seeing me, Mom places her hand over her heart and braces herself on the credenza.

The man freezes, staring at me with wild eyes. Then he races toward me. Like a deer in headlights, I'm too stunned to move.

Heavy, calloused hands grab my shoulders, shaking me, holding so tight they'll no doubt leave bruises.

"How *dare* you try to leave me again—after everything I've done? We're finally together! Finally a family! Everything is perfect! But you keep ruining it! What were you thinking? How could you do this? Did you even think about how I would feel? Or what this would do to your mother?"

He thought I had left. He's furious, but he's also scared. Taking another human's life doesn't scare him, but the thought of losing me does. What *am* I to him?

"I—I—I was just making breakfast," I stutter.

His eyes widen, looking beyond me to the mess I've made in the kitchen. His nose moves as if finally catching the scent of bacon in the air.

A moment later, he's hugging me.

"Thank God," he whispers. "I thought I'd lost you again."

Again . . . ?

That's the second time he's said that. That he's lost me before and doesn't want to lose me again. I have no clue what it means, but I commit it to memory. In the meantime, I have to do my best to save my plan.

"I just wanted to surprise you with breakfast. You know, maybe help out more around the house. Make you happy."

He holds me closer. "You do, Jessy. You make me happy every day. Oh, my sweet girl."

I don't know what to say or do, so I stand there, in the arms of my father's killer, as he embraces me.

By the time he finally lets go, most of breakfast is burnt. Mom helps dish it up and set the table. The man eats it without complaining. He smiles the whole time and keeps saying how great it is. Even Mom pretends it's good.

I can't help but think that this twisted display—this scene of a family bonding over a meal—is something an artist would create. He'd paint us and hang us in a gallery. Other families would look upon it with envy, wishing they, too, could have what we do. But that's because they would only see what's on the surface. They couldn't tell that we're puppets and he's the puppet master.

When he finishes eating, he tilts his chair back and rests his hands behind his head. "That was a delicious surprise, Jessy. Thank you."

Right on cue, I say, "You're welcome."

He stares, studying me. I try to ignore it. I try not to react. The longer he does it, the more anxious I become.

Is he questioning my motives? Does he think I'm trying to trick him into lowering his guard? Or maybe it's something else. Something worse. Maybe he does believe me, and he's trying to decide what to do next.

He's been more affectionate with Mom. I didn't want to acknowledge it, but seeing them in the same bed this morning made it impossible to ignore. She cooks for him. Cleans for him. Obeys every little command with a smile like a Stepford wife. Because that's how he's treating her—as his wife.

In this sick game that he's playing, does he view me as his daughter?

Before I can stop myself, words come flowing out of my mouth: "Why are you doing this?"

Mom gasps, shaking her head.

But I keep going. "What do you want? Who are you? What are you going to do to us? How do you know us? How long have you been watching us? What did we do to you? Why won't you just let us go?"

The questions end, and I pant, trying to catch my breath.

I wait and watch for him to come unglued. To yell or slam his fist. To break something.

"Good children obey their parents, without question," he says. "They trust that their parents know what is best for them."

The way he says "parents" has my brain misfiring.

The chair scrapes along the tiled floor as he stands.

"Do you think you know better than me, Jessy?"

He moves around the table. Each slow, measured step sends my body into a frenzy, fearing what he'll do.

"Mom?" I turn to her, begging for help.

She stares at her plate. I'm on my own against him. Again.

I stand and turn to run. As I do, I knock my glass off the table, sending it shattering into dozens of tiny pieces.

My heart stops. That glass is from the set Mom and Dad got for their wedding. I broke it.

I scramble to the floor, trying to put the pieces back together.

"Jessy," he says.

He's standing right behind me.

My fingers work faster, trying to place the jagged pieces back together, even though there is no glue. Even though the glass is slicing my fingers and blood is seeping onto the floor.

"Stop, Jessy!" he commands.

But I can't. I have to fix this. I have to make this right. I have to fix it all.

"Enough!" he booms, grabbing my arm.

Still crouched on the floor and still clutching broken pieces of glass, I stare up at him. He won't put me in the box. Not this time. He'll kill me.

I bolt up, shake him off, and race for the door. My bloody hands fumble with the locks.

Right as I rip open the door, his palm hits it, slamming it back shut.

He grabs me and whips me around. My back collides against the door, nearly knocking the wind out of me. Before I can catch my breath, he smacks me across the face with such force that I crumble to the floor.

I roll onto my side, clutching my cheek. I've never been struck before. Never even spanked. It hurts. My ears ring. I open my mouth. The bones in my jaw ache.

"Why would you do that!" he screams. "Everything was

perfect, Jessy. Our family was perfect! *And you destroyed it!*"

In his diluted brain, he really does think we're a family. He killed my father and put himself in the void. I realize that playing along and appeasing him, as Mom's done, might be the safer plan. But isn't that just feeding into his delusions? This is messed up on so many levels. I don't know if I can do this. I don't know if I'm strong enough.

"What am I going to do with you, huh?" he says. "For years, all I wanted was to come home to my baby girl. I deserve a warm welcome. Instead, you fight me. You try to leave. You're ruining everything."

He pauses. In the silence, I hear my mother crying.

"Do you hear that?" he asks, pointing back toward the kitchen. "You're breaking her heart. I thought you were better. I thought after the days spent in solitary confinement you had learned your lesson. I thought you were done misbehaving." He shakes his head. "I was wrong. I can't trust you, Jessy. You've shown that. But I'm not going to give up on you. I will *never* do that."

"I'm s-sorry." My voice cracks.

"I don't ask for much, Jessy. All I ask is that you do as I say, don't complain, and don't leave. That's it. I didn't want to soil our reunion with rules and punishments, but you seem hell-bent on doing things the hard way."

"I—I don't mean to," I say. "I don't mean to upset you. It's just . . . I can't keep doing this. I can't keep watching and waiting for you to kill us." My voice drops to barely a whisper.

He frowns, placing his hands on his hips as he stares down at me. "There are many things about our relationship that I regret, Jessy. More recently, killing Bob in front of you. But a man does what he must to protect his family. I make no apologies for that. You're not a little girl anymore, Jessy. I can't—and won't—shield you from the truth. I've never lied to you, and I expect the same courtesy." He straightens up. "Are we done with this? Are you going to be better from now on?"

If agreeing keeps me from dying or getting hurt, then so be it. "Y-yes."

"Yes *what*?"

"Yes, sir . . . ?"

He smiles. "Dad. Call me Dad."

I resist the urge to vomit. I can't do that. I can't call him that. I won't. It would be like Dad dying all over again.

"Never," I say through clenched teeth.

His smile falls. "I am your father, Jessy."

I glare at him. He's lying. He's sick. Mentally.

"It's true," he says. "I am your father."

He bends, crouching in front of me.

"As much as I wanted to be with you and watch you grow into the beautiful woman you've become, I couldn't. The actions I took—while I don't regret them—sparked unforeseen consequences that resulted in our temporary separation. And I'm sorry that the man who stepped in while I was gone failed. He failed me, and he failed you. Not only did he raise you to be a selfish, spoiled, ungrateful, little brat, but he then tried to keep you from me. He tried to keep *my daughter* from me. And for that, I killed him."

When were we separated? What actions did he take? And why in the hell is he talking like *I'm* his daughter? Like, his for-real daughter, not just some psychotic fantasy.

"I will fix Bob's wrongs," the man continued. "It will be hard on you at first. You may hate me for a little while. But eventually, you'll understand that I'm only doing what's best for you."

He stares down at me, rage burning in his eyes from his perceived injustices. His lips purse, and his expression hardens to one of grim determination. He's made a decision.

What decision . . . I don't know. And that scares me more than his rage does.

"Now, I'm afraid a time-out won't suffice for your

transgressions," he says. "You've forced me to do something I promised myself I wouldn't, but I don't see another way. Know that I'm only doing this because I love you, Jessy."

Before I can ask what he means, he pulls his leg back and then he kicks me. Hard. In the stomach.

The force knocks me on my back. Then he's there again. Kicking me. Over and over.

I can't breathe. I can't move. The pain is unbearable. Then he's punching me. In my stomach. Arms. Face. Anywhere he can. He's relentless. Not slowing down for a second.

In the half-second breaks between the blows, I pray for death. For the pain to go away just as it did that night on the operating table.

Eventually, it does.

‡

In the darkness, I feel nothing. No pain. No grief. I'm not even afraid. I want to stay here forever. It's blissful—not having to constantly walk on eggshells. Plus, if this is real— if I'm actually dead—I'll get to be with Dad, where I'm safe and free.

But then I remember my mother. I can't leave her alone with that psychopath. Dad wouldn't want me to.

I try to open my eyes, but only one cooperates. The other hurts. My eye, my eyebrow, even the cheekbone. I'm sure it's swollen and black. I try to bring my hands up to touch it—but I can't.

At first I think it's only because my body is so sore and exhausted. When really, it's because my hands are tied up again. It isn't tape this time. It's something coarse. Digging into my skin. I think it's rope, but I'm not sure.

Just then, a fire erupts in my chest.

I try to figure out why.

It does it again, and I find the answer.

I breathed.

I take a deep breath to test it. Now my lungs, ribs, and chest are screaming out in agony. I remember this pain. I know what it is because the same thing happened during my accident.

My ribs are broken.

I've been waiting for my open eye to adjust and focus, but now I realize I'm covered in darkness. Darkness I recognize—along with the cold and hard floor. I'm in that box of a room.

How long have I been here? How much longer will he make me stay?

Tears well up. As they fall, new pains ring out. My cheeks and lips are sore. My mouth isn't taped this time, so I run my tongue across it. It's swollen and split.

When he kills me, the casket will have to be closed. The people at the morgue won't be able to cover this up.

Will I even have a funeral, that is? Will he just dump my body wherever he dumped Dad's? Will anyone ever find us?

The things the man said before he attacked me come back. He thinks we're his family. He believes he's my father.

He is *not* my father. He's delusional. Psychotic. I know it.

The locks on the door click. It's him. A part of me wants to move away, distance myself from him. But it's pointless. My body is too sore to move a single inch. And even if it could, there is nowhere to go. This room is just big enough for me to lay down without touching the walls.

The door opens. He bends down beside me. "You're awake. Good."

Through my one eye, I see him inspecting me from head to toe, frowning and shaking his head at my mangled body. It's more disappointment then actual sympathy.

"I didn't want to do that, Jessy." He points at my face and bruises. "But you made me. It's your fault. You understand that, right? "

I nod—then cringe, because even that small movement creates pain.

He sighs. "I don't like to see you suffer. I take no joy in this. It hurt me a great deal to do that to you. But punishing you is the only way you'll listen. That's why I disciplined you so severely. And that's why I will not be giving you any pain medication. I need you to feel this right now. I need you to hurt so you'll remember this always and never make me do that again."

"I won't," I whisper.

"You won't *what?*" he prompts.

I swallow, cringing from the fresh onslaught of pain it brings. He wants me to say it. He wants me to call him that. Again.

Bastard.

My facial muscles tighten and harden. I clench my jaw. It's excruciating, but I do it anyway.

"Hmm," he says. "Still fighting it, huh? I don't know whether to be proud or ashamed of you." He stands. "When you're ready to rejoin your family, let me know."

He shuts the door, sealing me into the darkness once more.

For a while, I lie there, comforted by my decision to not give in to that psychopath. I'm not only standing up for myself but also for the memory of my father.

He was a great man. A wonderful father—so loving and attentive. He meant the world to me. He taught me to be kind. He taught me to be patient and understanding. He also taught me to help those who are less fortunate. He was so selfless.

He did so much for me after the accident . . .

There in the dark, my mind transports me to that night two years ago and the days and weeks that followed.

Dad immediately resigned as governor. In an emotional press conference, he explained to our entire state how he needed to put his full energy into his family, into helping me recover. Mom resigned from her duties with the foundation as well.

Recovery took a while. My leg had pretty much shattered as it got pinned in the door. A rod and some screws now keep it together. I also lost my spleen, which means I'm more susceptible to getting sick.

Mom and Dad were at every doctor appointment. Every physical therapy session. They were two extremely busy, successful people who never even hesitated to give up their careers to be with me.

They did it because they thought they had lost me. Like Nick's family had lost Jessica.

Silent tears fall.

My heart, along with everything else, hurts. I miss Dad. I miss Mom.

I miss Blake and Cassy and all my friends. Cheerleading. My phone and apps. Hanging out at the mall. Normal life.

I miss talking and laughing and not being afraid.

God, I even miss school. Had I known what was about to happen, I would have cherished my final moments in school more. I wouldn't have brushed off all those people who said bye to me. I would have actually stopped and had a conversation with them. Even my teachers. I would have thanked them for all their help over the years and let them know they were doing a great job.

And Nick. Maybe I would have said something to Nick. Now that I know what it's like to lose someone, I get what he's going through.

There are so many things I wish I could do over—but I don't think I'll have the chance.

I don't know how much more of this I can take. Even if he doesn't kill me, I feel like I'm slowly suffocating to death.

Time is meaningless in the dark. I don't know whether two hours or two days pass, but eventually, there's a knock on the door.

A knock. It's a damn *jail cell*, and he's knocking.

"Yes," I say.

"Yes *what?*"

This is it. If I don't give in, he'll never let me out. I don't want to die in here. I don't want to die at all.

What he wants me to say—it doesn't have to mean anything. It's just a word. A label. A title. A name—especially since I don't know his actual one and may never know it.

Maybe I can get through this.

I gather all the images and feelings I associate with my father—the man who exemplified the meaning of that word. Then I bury them deep inside me. It's the closest thing to a funeral I will ever be able to have for him.

I take a deep breath, "Yes, Dad."

The door unlocks, and he opens it. "You may come out now."

Somehow, I find the strength to stand through the pain. I struggle, especially with my hands still bound.

He doesn't help.

With every step out of the cell, blinding agony ripples through me. My jaw is clenched, holding back my cries, knowing they won't do me any good.

I trip on the stairs and fall. I can't hold in my scream or my tears any longer.

Still, he just stands there, watching. His face is expressionless. I finally understand. He wants this. Wants me to fall and get hurt. Wants me to suffer. All to remind me never to challenge him again.

Finally, I push myself up again and climb the rest of the way.

Keep going, I tell myself. *Just keep going.*

That mantra helps me push through the pain all the way to my room. I collapse on my bed and fall into darkness once again.

SIX

THROUGHOUT THE NEXT DAY I HEAR HIM
come and go, but I don't move. I just lay in my bed,
waiting for the pain to fade. At one point, he comes
in and unties me, but I pretend I'm sleeping.

Later, I wake to the best surprise: Mom comes into my
room, alone, carrying a cup of soup and a glass of water.

"How are you feeling, dear?" she asks.

Even though her voice is lifeless, it's still the most
beautiful sound in the world. It's a lifesaver thrown to me in
the ocean, and I desperately cling to it. I haven't had a second
alone with her since this nightmare began. He's always been
there, always hovering, watching what we say and do.

She sets the soup and water down on my nightstand, then
gently sits beside me on the bed. She brushes a strand of hair
behind my ear. I lean into her touch, wanting her comfort
more than I've wanted anything in my life.

I move just enough to glance behind her, expecting to see
him. But the hallway is empty.

"Where is he?" I ask.

"Your father?"

Her words are like a punch to the gut. She's not talking
about my real father; she meant his killer. That man is not

even here, yet she's playing his sick, twisted game.

"He left a while ago," she continues. "I don't know when he'll be back. It would make him happy to see you up and about. He's been so worried about you, dear."

His absence is overshadowed by her last statement. I'm sure that monster isn't "worried" about me. He's the one who did this to me, after all. But I bet he is waiting for me to act like the good little daughter he's molding me to be. Just hop out of bed and act as if the abuse never happened.

I cast a wary eye at the camera in the corner of the room. Wherever he may be, is he watching us right now? Is he able to access the live camera feed on his phone or some other mobile device? Is that why she's acting this way and saying this stuff?

But even if he can see us, she said he left. We may not get another opportunity like this.

"He's gone, Mom," I whisper. "Now's our chance to get away."

She drops her hand and bites her lip. For a split second, the fire—her real fire—is back in her eyes. But then she turns away from me.

"You should take a bath," she says, but any concern is missing from her voice. "It will help."

I reach out, touching her hand, needing to feel connected to her again. Once wasn't enough. Since this nightmare began, I've felt so isolated and alone when I shouldn't have. She's been here, right here, the whole time. But he's kept such tight control over us that we may as well have been in separate states.

"What did he do to you?" I implore. "Why won't you help me?"

"*Help you?*" she whispers, shaking her head. She glances back at the bedroom door, checking to make sure he's not there, even though she knows he left. "I thought I lost you that first night when he locked you in the basement. When he let you out, I swore to do *whatever* it took to keep you safe. But you just keep pushing him. Do you have any idea how hard it was to sit at the table and listen to him beat you? I can't go through that again, Jessy. I can't take seeing you in pain."

My heart aches for her. I want to hug her.

No.

I want *her* to hug *me*. Hold me like she used to and tell me it will all be OK.

But she just sits there, staring at the wall. Just like she sat there the other night.

I squeeze her hand. She flinches. Our eyes lock. Hers are cautious.

"Momma, please. I'm scared. I don't want to die."

She clamps her eyes shut, cringing as if I've hurt her. She takes several deep breaths. As her eyes reopen, I see a fire in them once more. It's small, but it's there.

"You're not going to die, Jessica. I promise. You're not expendable."

For a moment, I'm transported back to when things were normal. I picture Mom in an elegant gown at one of the charity events, giving a heartfelt speech in hopes of convincing the elite to open their pocketbooks. It works. It always does. Because when my mom sets her mind on something, nothing gets in her way.

She leaves without waiting for my response.

It takes me a moment to realize that's the most she's said to me in over a week. It was great to feel mothered for even just a moment. That spark I saw in her eyes gives me a little hope too.

Yet I can't ignore that she's acting strangely, even though the man isn't here. It's just us right now—she doesn't need the submissive charades.

I don't understand. The whole experience has left me feeling even lonelier and more unsettled.

And what did she mean by I'm *not expendable*? If I'm not expendable, does that mean she *is*? Is that what he told her?

He's different with me than he is with her.

I've fought him. Disobeyed him. Made a mockery of his rules. And for all that, he's punished me. Hurt me. It's been awful and terrifying—but not once have I ever felt my life was truly threatened. He's pushed me and tried to break me. But only in some sick way to get me to obey him. Never to harm or kill me.

But Mom . . .

He was going to kill her the first night, but he didn't. Only because I stopped him. She's alive only because of me. But even though he didn't kill her, he certainly has traumatized her. Emotionally. Mentally. Psychologically. Maybe even physically. How, though, I'm not sure. Maybe that's why he kept us separated in the beginning? Keeping us apart made it easier to break us.

I'm not broken.

Not yet, anyways.

But she is.

She can't take the risks that I have. She can't fight him. Because if she does and she loses, she will leave me all alone with him.

Oh, Mom—I'm so sorry.

Carefully, I sit up and eat her soup. It isn't much, but somehow I know it's her way of showing me she still cares—still loves me. Maybe she's not as far gone as I thought? Maybe I can help her stay strong?

As long as I have her, I can do this. I'm not alone.

Once I finish the soup, I follow her advice and take a bath. I try to keep my hands out of the water as much as possible because it makes my fingers hurt. Fresh scabs cover where my fingernails once sat, and there are many cuts from the glass. My face is healing, at least. Most of the bruises on my cheek and under my eyes are lightening.

Same can't be said for the rest of my body, though. My arms, stomach, and back are black and blue. It hurts to breathe deep, so I'm right about the ribs. I don't think they're broken, maybe just cracked. But I don't know for sure. And it's not like he'll take me to the doctor to find out.

As I soak in the bathtub, I think back to what he said before and after he put me in the box. He said he didn't want to hurt me, but that he *had* to because I didn't follow his rules. He said the same thing the first night, when I dislocated my shoulder fighting him.

I don't believe him when he says it's my fault—that I deserved to be hurt. My parents raised me to know that violence, whether physical or emotional, is never OK. That you are responsible for your own choices and actions.

Yes, I fought him. Yes, I disobeyed him. I fought and disobeyed the man who killed my father and is holding me and my mother prisoner as some twisted version of a family. Those were my choices, and I own them.

But I will not take responsibility for what he chose to do to me. Locking me up, hitting me—that's all on him.

He's the one who needs to own his own actions and choices. If he doesn't want to hurt me, then why does he? Why does he feel this way about me, yet he murdered Dad in cold blood?

None of this makes any sense.

The only thing I do know is that breaking his rules equals pain. My body can't take any more right now. So until I heal, I have no choice but to play by his rules.

At least for a while.

In my first attempt to get back on his good side, I manage to get up and go downstairs to help Mom with dinner.

Being alone with her is the closest I've felt to normal since this all began. That doesn't mean things *are* normal, of course. I know that. But it's as close as I can get. It's like the dash of water they give prisoners in movies to keep them alive.

"How are you, Mom?"

"I'm fine, dear."

74

I set the plates on the counter and face her, staring her up and down. I can see her much better now than when she came into my room with the soup.

She's thinner. Sadder. But she seems OK. Better than me. At least on the outside.

"I miss you," I whisper, like it's some forbidden, shameful secret.

She stiffens.

I wait for her to say she misses me, too, to hug me and tell me everything will be OK. But she doesn't. She just continues making dinner.

I need her reassurance so badly, though, that I decide to create it myself. So as I carry the plates out to the table, I have a fake conversation in my mind: *I miss you, too, Jessy*, she'll say. *So much.* Then she'll hug me, and we'll cry. We'll cry harsh, ugly tears for the hell we've been through. Then she'll straighten up, and in true Smith fashion, she'll fix our hair and makeup before walking us out the door and driving to the police station.

Even though I know it's a lie, this little fantasy still helps. It helps so much that I turn and march into the kitchen, ready to demand that we make the fantasy real. I'm going to tell Mom it's time to leave. I'm going to get us both out of here before it's too late.

Before I can open my mouth, I hear tires crunching on the driveway.

I freeze.

Someone's here.

I don't know who—Blake, his family, Cassie, the cops, someone who just happened to drive by and notice something suspicious. It doesn't matter. By some miracle, someone is here at exactly the moment Mom and I are ready to escape.

We're saved!

"Mom!" I shout. "This is it. This is our chance. Someone's here. Let's go!"

Something floods me and sets my muscles in motion. It's hope. I rush to the door, thinking she's right behind me. I rip open the door—and stop.

He's getting out of the car.

I glance around at the yard, at my home, desperately searching for someone else. Anyone else. Another vehicle. Someone out for a walk. A hunter. But it's just him.

My parents bought this farm for the privacy, but now it's our tomb. We're the only house on a dead end. The only reason people would be on this road would be to come here. The highway—salvation—is several miles away. Thick groves of trees shield us from view.

No one will ever see us. No one can hear us. We're all alone.

Worst yet, when I turn back, I see Mom still standing in the kitchen, fussing with the table settings. She didn't even try to escape with me.

Whatever hope I'd found shrivels up until I can no longer feel it.

The man stares at me, the car door wide open. "Jessy," he says, his voice wary, "you're not trying to run, are you?"

"No," I say instantly. "I was just . . . coming to tell you that dinner's ready. And to see if you needed help."

He grabs a bag from the car. It looks like a laptop case. "Good," he says. "I appreciate that, but I don't have much. Go back inside and help your mother. I'll be there in a minute."

I nod, then shut the door. I lean against it, slowly releasing my breath. I don't understand. I thought that after the talk Mom and I had in my room, things would be different. But they're not. We had a chance to run. A chance to finally escape. Sure, it ended up being him, but she didn't know that. She didn't even try. . . She'll never leave. No one is ever coming. It's hopeless.

Dad, please help.

‡

By dinnertime, we're back to the perfect-family charade, with Charles Manson playing the part of Dad. When we're done and I'm clearing the dinner plates, he stops me.

"I picked you up something while I was out," he says. He grabs an item from a bag on the counter and hands it to me.

It's a box of brown hair dye.

"What is this?" My heart trembles as soon as the words are out. He won't like that I'm questioning him.

He frowns, and he's silent for a moment. Then he says, "I thought it would look good on you. Why don't you and your mother go figure it out? Go have some girl time—or whatever. And after, we'll watch TV."

"That will be lovely," Mom says, smiling.

My mind races. Why does he want me to color my hair? He's changing my appearance.

He made Mom change hers right away. Her hair is a different color, her makeup is plain, and her clothes are simple. He's changed everything about her. Is he now doing the same to me?

Why? What does hair color have to do with anything? He wouldn't go to such lengths if he were planning to kill us. So what *is* he planning?

This is insane.

Yet I make sure to smile too. "Thank you." Then I add, "Dad."

I finish cleaning up and head upstairs with Mom. She's silent as she works the dye into my hair. But I don't want to be silent. I need to hear her voice. Her real voice. Like this afternoon.

That interaction wasn't enough. It was like giving a grape to someone starving. It wasn't even enough to sustain me. I need more.

But now that he's home, the danger is more prevalent.

We have to watch what we say and do.

I peek around Mom to make sure my door is still closed. It is. And since we're in the bathroom, there's no cameras. This room has become my sanctuary. Maybe hanging out with Mom here—alone—could become a routine thing? A small thing we could do together to conserve our sanity?

Although, that doesn't mean he isn't right outside the door, giving us the illusion of privacy.

"Mom," I whisper. "Why is he doing this? Who is he? What did he do with Dad? How does he know us?"

She sighs, shaking her head. "I knew you were stubborn, Jessica, but I didn't think it was this bad."

She seems frustrated with me. Angry. She sounds like *him*. Having her upset with me hurts. I can't recall the last time I disappointed her or Dad. Or when she was seriously angry with me. It hurts, and the fact that she's taking *his* side makes it so much worse.

"He is your father," she continues sternly. "We are a family. His reasons are his own, and it's not our place to question him. It's time you accept that."

"Knock, knock," we suddenly hear.

My body tenses as my eyes widen. He *was* outside the door. He heard her. Which must mean he knows I've disobeyed him again.

He walks into the bathroom. "How are my two favorite ladies doing?"

"We're great," Mom says. "This just needs to sit for a bit." She nods toward the kitchen timer she brought upstairs. "Then she'll be ready to wash."

I stare at the tiles, waiting and ready for the pain. Will it be a punch? A slap? Kick?

"I think she can handle that part on her own, right?" he says.

The normalcy of his tone has my head popping up. I'm relieved but confused. Did he not overhear us, then?

I study him closely for clues. He's grinning as he places

78

his arm around Mom.

My previous worries of him eavesdropping disappear. I don't like him touching her.

Mom nods, and she obediently follows him downstairs.

I sit, unsure of what else to do, waiting for the timer to go off. When it does, I rinse my hair and then style it.

The reflection in the mirror is a stranger. The chocolate coloring makes my normally tan complexion seem pale, and it draws attention to the dark circles under my pale blue eyes. As well as the green-and-yellow bruises.

I suppose this is a symbol for my new, unrecognizable life.

Not wanting to spend any more alone time with this strange version of myself, I head downstairs. As I walk into the living room, shock hits me hard, like a blindside sack on a quarterback. And then betrayal and revulsion hit me right behind it, piling on top.

They're on the couch. He's kissing her. And she's kissing him back. Like in a full-out, groping, make-out session. Like two horny teens at a party.

Why?

Why would she do this?

How can she stand it?

He spots me out of the corner of his eye. "Jessy!" he says.

They instantly jump apart. He's grinning sheepishly, like parents do when their kids catch them in the act. Mom is looking away, embarrassed?

Is she embarrassed that he kissed her? That she went along with it? Or is she just embarrassed that she got caught? Did he force her to kiss him?

Or did she want it?

She casts a timid, bashful look in his direction.

Do they know each other . . . ?

Is this why he came here—for *her*? Is that why he knows so much about us? Is that why she won't answer my questions and why she does whatever he wants, including letting him kiss her and share a bed with her? Is she doing this not because he's broken her, but because she actually wants to?

Is that why he murdered my dad? Because he and Mom are having an affair?

Or is it something more, something deeper? He says I'm his daughter and that I was "taken" from him.

Oh my God—is it true?

He clears his throat and pats the seat beside him. "Come here, Jessy."

Suddenly I hate my name. I hate the way he says it. I hate how often he says it. I want to choke him until he can't say it again.

Instead, I sit beside him.

He wraps his arm around me, just as he did Christmas Day. He then turns on the TV to the celebration in Times Square. It's New Year's Eve.

He's been here for ten days. Ten days, and no one has called. Ten days, and no one stopped by. Ten days living in hell, and no one knows. And ten days since he killed my father.

When the ball drops, he gives me a quick kiss on the head before leaning over and locking lips with Mom. To my relief, it only lasts a few seconds. Then he wraps his arms around us both, squeezing in an awkward hug.

"So far, this year is off to a fantastic start. I'm back home with my girls, where I belong. Nothing is going to separate us ever again."

My heart falls.

He'll never let us go . . .

‡

After breakfast, he surprises me by calling me into my dad's office. I've been in here countless times before, but this time it's different. He's moved things. Violated his space. On my father's desk, where pictures of me and Mom once sat, are six monitors. Each monitor displays eight tiny black-and-white video images. Forty-eight images total.

Looking at it all, I feel lightheaded. Overwhelmed. It's too much to take in at once. My eyes don't know where to look, so my brain doesn't know how to make sense of anything.

With all the cameras in the house, I knew he had a surveillance system of some kind. But this—this is far more advanced than I ever realized. In the blur of screens, I recognize some images are from our house. I see my bedroom, for example, as well as the room we're standing in. Two monitors, with sixteen cameras, are dedicated to home. But as my eyes dart over some of the other monitors and images . . . I get only a vague sense of recognition.

"Look at this one," he says, pointing at a video image marked as Camera 31. "Does that look familiar?"

It does. I lean closer, trying to figure out where this is. Then it hits me like a jolt of electricity. I can't look away. That's my *locker*.

I take a closer look at the other images on the remaining monitors. Classrooms, hallways, even the parking lot and common area outside. Just about every inch of my high school is on the screen.

"Did you know your school has cameras everywhere?" he asks, somewhat smugly.

I shake my head. I don't remember seeing them.

"Well, they do. There are cameras all over the city, in fact. I helped install them. And because of it, I'm able to remotely access them."

He clicks a few buttons, and the images change to street views of town. The buildings, stores, and restaurants are all ones I frequently visit. He even has cameras on my friends' houses.

A lump forms in my throat. Seeing this proves he's been watching me, but for how long? What has he seen?

He leans against the desk, smiling. "You've asked me why I'm here."

This is it. I don't move. I don't even breathe.

"I will tell you. But first, I want you to do something for me."

"Anything."

Even as I reply to him, my attention stays fixed on the video showing Cassie's home. She's out in the front yard, building a snowman with her little brother. With today being New Year's Day, her flight would have landed this morning. That means Blake and his family are home too. I search the monitors, and sure enough, I find his house all lit up.

A tear slips out, as I fear what the man plans to do with this surveillance. My home, my friends' homes, my school, my town.

"I'll do *anything*," I repeat.

And I mean it. I will do whatever he wants to keep my mom and friends safe.

"I want you to—"

Suddenly a horn honks from outside.

The hope I'd felt for days, the hope of a rescue, instantly returns. Someone is here—actually here. Our nightmare is over!

But just as quickly as it came, my hope is extinguished by terror as the man pulls the gun from his waistband. The gun that killed my father. The gun that nearly killed my mother as well. He hasn't brought it out since then, but my blood chills as I suddenly realize he's been carrying it all the time. At any moment, he's ready to use it.

"Don't say anything," he warns.

He presses some buttons on the computers, and the video scenes change to our house. One of the videos shows the front yard. A familiar SUV is parked out front.

Blake.

My pulse pounds like drums in my ears as I stare at the gun. I barely hear the man call for my mom.

"Yes, dear?" she asks, appearing in the doorway to the office.

"It's the boy." The man's voice is a growl. "Tell him she's sick. Get him to leave—or I'll kill him."

Blake came for me. And because of me, he could die.

"No!" I beg, tears instantly filling my eyes. "Please don't."

"Quiet," he snaps.

With terrified—but subservient—eyes, Mom leaves. I watch the screens, seeing her go outside.

The man moves between me and the doorway, blocking my only way to get to Blake.

"You've been doing so well the last few days, Jessy," he says. "Don't disappoint me. That boy isn't worth the pain it would cause you."

I look away from the monitor, trembling. I can't watch. Every time I blink, I see horrific images of Blake lying dead.

Since the moment this maniac entered our life, all I've wanted was to escape, to get away. But now that I finally have that chance, all I want is for Blake to go, to leave this place and never come back.

Please let him buy Mom's story about me being sick. Please let him leave.

A few moments later, the door opens again. When I open my eyes, one video shows Mom walking back inside the house. Another shows Blake's SUV driving away.

I'm both elated and heartbroken. He's gone. He's safe. And I'm still here.

Mom comes into the room, frowning with worry. "I did it—I said she was sick. But I'm not sure he believed me . . ."

As if on cue, I hear a familiar buzz from somewhere in the office. It's a phone. He pulls it out of his pocket, and I recognize the pink glittery case. It's mine. He's had it the whole time.

"Looks like the boy *didn't* believe you," the man says, glaring at Mom.

Blake's calling.

He flips the phone around in his hand and holds it out for me.

"Tell him you'll see him tomorrow. Do it, or your mother will be the one who pays the price."

To emphasize his point, he turns and points the gun at her. Her eyes widen just a fraction, but otherwise she stands there, doing his bidding—like always. He could end her life in seconds, yet she doesn't even defend herself. Does she trust him not to kill her? Does she think he's bluffing? Or does she not care if he pulls that trigger? Regardless, something inside her has broken.

Something inside me has broken as well.

"Answer it!" the man barks, pushing the phone at me again.

My throat dries. For a moment, I forget how to speak, how to form any words. All I can do is take the phone, answer the call, and hold the phone to my ear.

"Jessy!" Blake says.

I hold back a sob, hearing his voice. "H-hi."

"What gives? I just tried to stop by, but your mom wouldn't let me in."

In my mind, a vision flashes of what would have happened if he had come in. Of him lying in a pool of his own blood. Just like Dad.

I let out a shuddering breath and say, "Sorry. I'm sick."

"Yeah, that's what she said, but I didn't believe her. Now I do, though. You sound like crap, babe!" He laughs.

I laugh too. It feels so foreign.

"I missed you," he says. "I'm sorry I didn't call. I lost my phone skiing. I just picked up a new one."

My lips tremble as new tears rise. "It's OK. I missed you too."

Before Blake can say anything else, the murderer beside me clears his throat. "Tell him you'll see him tomorrow," he whispers.

"Blake, hey—I gotta go. B-but I'll see you tomorrow."
I hang up without even waiting for a reply.

I won't see him tomorrow. I'll probably never see him again. That very well could have been our last conversation ever—and it was full of lies.

The man holds out his hand for the phone. In a daze, I give it back.

"That was good, Jessy," he says, lowering the gun.

With a nod, he excuses Mom. She turns and leaves, acting as if she wasn't seconds away from dying. A part of me aches to see her leave me. Another part realizes that it doesn't make a difference. Even when she's standing just feet away from me, she's not here, *with* me.

"His presence and call were unexpected, but some good came out of it. Now I know you can be trusted to do as I ask."

"But I don't understand," I say, carefully choosing my words and tone, not wanting to upset him further while he's still holding a weapon. "I don't get why you had me say that I'd see him tomorrow. I won't. So now he'll call tomorrow, worried. He'll keep coming back until he can talk to me."

"No, he won't."

"Yes, he will," I stress. "You don't know Blake like I do."

His mouth twists into a sly grin. "You're wrong on multiple accounts. You *will* see that boy tomorrow. You're going back to school."

School.

Tomorrow.

Why?

My eyes flash to the gun, and my throat dries.

Is that his plan? Is he going to take me to school and force me to watch him hurt other people I care about—Blake, Cassie, and the rest of my friends? Force me to watch as punishment for yet another sin against him?

I stare at him, trying to read him. If that's his plan, I have to stop him. I can't let him go through with it.

"No. I can't—" I begin.

"Of course you'll go to school. Winter break is over. Tomorrow, school starts back up."

I'm caught off guard by his simple explanation. It almost sounds as though he wants me to *actually* go back to school. As in, to attend school as I would have if he hadn't destroyed everything.

But how will this ever work . . . ? Is this some sort of trap?

He seems to understand my shock and confusion.

"I want to have a normal life with you, Jessy," he says. "Be a normal family again. It's all I've ever wanted. Sending you back to school is part of that."

He smiles for a moment. Then his face hardens.

"But this will take a lot of trust—trust you haven't earned yet."

He isn't saying it outright, but I know what he means. Sending me to school will create opportunities for me to escape or get help.

"Until I can trust you, I'll need leverage." He pauses to make sure he has my full attention. "So while you're at school every day, your mother will be in the basement. I'll release her each day once you're home."

My freedom . . . at the price of hers.

"And that's not all," he continues. "I'll have other leverage as well."

To prove his point, he presses buttons to switch the video scenes back to the school. Then he sits on the edge of the desk, the gun still in his hand.

A chill flows up my back, and my spine stiffens.

"I will see everything. Hear everything. If something goes wrong, I'll know it. In an instant." He sighs. "I don't want to hurt you, Jessy. Not again. But if you try to run away or if you do anything to jeopardize our family, I will have no choice but to punish you."

My body shivers. Memories of his brand of punishment are literally etched into my skin, muscles, and bones. I'm just starting to heal. The pain is constant and felt with every movement. If he were to hit me again right now . . . I don't think my body could take another hit. I don't think I'd survive.

"I'd prefer to not hurt anyone else either. I don't like doing that. But if necessary, I will come to your school and kill anyone who tries to separate us again. Is that what you want?"

I shake my head frantically.

No matter how tempted I might feel to escape or get help, I won't risk it. Not just to spare myself from days of pain, not just to keep Mom safe, but to save everyone else too. I know how easy it would be for him to hurt or kill my friends, my teachers.

I can't handle the thought of losing anyone else.

"*Is that what you want?*" he repeats, more sternly.

"N-no, Dad." I force myself to say it.

He narrows his eyes, trying to read me. "I hope that's true." He takes a big breath, and his grip on the gun relaxes. "Now, I want you to understand that tomorrow will be a difficult day for you. It's not just time to return to school. It's also time to fix this mess of a life you've gotten yourself into. Tomorrow, I'll need you to do things you may not like, but you need to understand that they are for the best."

Now my eyes are narrowing. I don't understand. Fix this mess of my life? My life is ruined. Because of *him*. What is he talking about?

"First," he says, "I know how exciting it is when everyone goes back to school after break. Everyone asks how break went and what you did." He pauses. "Do I need to remind you not to breathe a word of what happened here?"

My mind is assaulted by visions of him hurting my friends, my peers, and my teachers. "N-no. I won't say anything. Not a word."

"Wrong."

I wince at this unexpected reply.

"Not saying *anything* will draw suspicion," he says. "Instead, you're going to tell them about how you stayed home with your mother while your *father*"—he spits the word out as if it were poison in his mouth—"has been in Cameroon with the charity organization. Since that boy showed up and forced us to improvise, we'll have to continue with the story about you being sick too. Can you do that, Jessy? Let me hear you practice it."

It takes a few moments to make my mouth move. "I stayed home with my mother while my father—"

"No!" he snaps. "No one will believe you if you sound like a robot."

I try again, reminding myself of the horrible reality that my friends' lives depend on my ability to sell these lies.

"My break was great," I say in a believably bright voice. "I had a wonderful time at home with Mom. We just relaxed and watched movies while Dad's been off in—"

"Good, good," he says, cutting me off.

He looks down and nods, as if mentally ticking that off his list of things to do.

"Next, you need to quit cheerleading."

My jaw drops. Telling his lies to protect people is one thing. But this . . .

After the accident, doctors told me I'd probably never be able to cheer again. I worked day and night on my stretches, put my body through all kinds of pain as I rebuilt my muscle strength. There were days when I would get so frustrated with my progress. Especially when I had setbacks.

But I was determined to return, and in six months, I was back on the squad. After ten months, I could do flips and jumps.

I did not go through all of that just for him to strip it all away now.

After the accident, I couldn't imagine a life without

cheerleading. I can't imagine a life without it now either.

It's not just the routines or outfits. And unlike what many people think, it's not about popularity. It's about the comradery. We train for hours multiple times a week. Some of us have been cheering together for years. We see more of each other than we do our families. Many of us are like sisters.

I'm the captain. I have responsibilities. Expectations. I can't just quit.

"I know you enjoy it," he says. "And I know you work very hard, creating the routines and keeping the other girls in line. You're a born leader."

The way he says this . . . Has he watched my practices? The games? Was it through the cameras, or was he actually there, watching me in person? How close did he get to me without me realizing?

"But cheerleading is just an unnecessary distraction, taking you away from your studies and, most importantly, from your family. I won't allow it to distract you and ruin your life—*our* life."

I can't stand it anymore. "No! You can't make—"

"Careful, Jessy," he interrupts. Veins pop in his hand as it tightens around the gun. "You wouldn't want to be punished right before you go back to school, would you?"

"No," I say, taking a step back. I look away so he can't see the fear in my eyes. He won't kill me. At least I'm pretty sure of that. But there are places to shoot people that aren't fatal. I prefer to never experience that, though.

He sits there in smug silence for a moment. Then he says, "Look at me, Jessy." He stops, waiting for me to do as he said.

I take a breath and then look up.

"You're going to quit cheerleading," he says, very slowly. "Or *else*. I mean it when I say I will not let anything or anyone get in our way of being a family."

And there it is. The final straw. It's not just about me.

89

It's about my squad. My friends. I love cheerleading, but I won't put the squad in danger. I won't let him hurt them.

"OK," I say, even though it kills me.

"That's my girl. Next, you will break up with Blake."

I gasp as if he had just punched me, cracking another rib. Of all the things this man has said and done, I was not prepared for this.

"Blake isn't right for you," the man says, a bitter scowl on his face. "I won't have him in your life."

"*In* my life? He *is* my life!" I stare at the lights, fighting my tears. I don't want to cry in front of him.

"And that's the problem!" the man snaps. "Don't you see that?"

He sounds like a dad lecturing a daughter. In his twisted, messed-up mind, he *is* a dad lecturing his daughter.

"Here's the thing, Jessy—the 'future' you have planned for yourself is all about Blake. We discussed this on Christmas Eve, remember? You have this ridiculous plan to just follow him, going wherever he goes."

I grit my teeth. Yes, I do remember. I remember how the man refused to answer me when I asked how he knows this private information.

"How do you know about that?" I ask, pressing the issue once again.

In frustration, he uses his free hand to rub his forehead. Then he sighs and opens a laptop I hadn't noticed before. I watch as he opens a folder labeled Jessy.

There are pictures. So many pictures.

Pictures of me doing everyday things. Some are at school, practice, the mall. Even a few of me kissing Blake when he dropped me off when break started and this nightmare began. There are thousands of them.

But that's not all. There are also videos and audio files. He plays an audio file. It takes me a moment to recognize my own voice. It's a recording of me and Blake talking over the phone. The audio clip is two hours—the whole time we talked—but he plays only a minute of it.

How does he have this? How did he do this?

"Jessy," the man says. "You're so smart. So talented. Being with Blake—you're holding yourself back. If you do nothing more than follow after him, he'll be the star. He'll get the fans and endorsements and make millions while you'll be just some trophy wife on the sidelines, barely making enough to survive. Can't you understand that I want better than that for my baby girl?"

There's a strange tenderness to his voice. I hate this murderer with every ounce of my being. He killed my father. Yet here he is, acting as if *he* is my father and as if he truly cares about me. I hate it. But something about it hits deep.

Is he right? Am I holding myself back with this dream about my future with Blake . . . ? It hurts to even ask myself that question. I shake my head to clear it away.

"I know you think you care for Blake," the man says, "but he doesn't feel the same way."

I keep shaking my head, trying to rid myself of his lies. "No. You're wrong."

He pulls out my phone again and opens my call log. "Do you see, Jessy?" He holds the phone out. "Blake never texted or called you from Aspen. Not once. No messages saying he missed you. No 'Merry Christmas' or 'Happy New Year.' Nothing. And I heard his excuse of losing his phone, but he had access to his parents' phones. Plus, you can't tell me he didn't have access to laptops and tablets. Same for Cassie. They had ample opportunities to reach out to you, yet they *chose* not to."

"I don't believe you," I say. "You're lying."

Really, though, I know it's the truth. I know he had many ways to reach out. Why didn't he?

Why didn't Cassie?

"Jessy, I'm your father—I will never lie to you." He sounds sincere.

"I don't understand why you're doing this," I whisper.

"I only want what's best for you. And that boy and those friends aren't it."

He places the gun back in his waistband, then looks at me for a long moment.

"So," he finally says, "can I trust you to go back to school and do everything I say?"

I want to scream at him. I want to tell him to go to hell. I want to fight.

But I don't. Too much is at stake for me to refuse.

"Yes," is all I can say.

SEVEN

FORTY-THREE SETS OF EYES BURN INTO ME. They're all staring.

It's horrible—and school hasn't even officially started yet. All I'm doing is riding the bus.

I knew this would happen—the staring. It might be my hair. It's so unlike me. Or it might be the bruises, which maybe I didn't cover up as well as I should have. The bruises from the black eye are hidden, thanks to the heavier makeup I use for cheerleading and pageants, but I forgot to put it on the rest of my body. I pull down the sleeves of my light-gray cowl-neck sweater, covering my battered hands and wrists. It used to fit perfectly, but now I'm drowning in it.

Most likely, though, they're staring because I've never ridden the bus. Ever. I usually drive myself or have Blake pick me up. But that monster doesn't trust me to drive my car. I haven't *earned* that privilege, he said. Once I gain more of his trust, maybe I can have my car back.

The staring gets more intense with every minute, it seems. It takes all my effort not to hyperventilate. This isn't going to work. They'll see the bruises. They'll see right through me. They'll know something is wrong—and then he'll come. He'll drag me away. And if anyone tries to stop him, they'll die.

Once I realized I had no choice but to attend school, I actually talked myself into the idea. When I woke up this morning, I told myself it would be good to go to school, get out of the house, act normal. Have a change of scenery and be away from him for a couple hours. But now, looking at all the innocent people who could get hurt because of me, I just want to go home.

As we arrive at school, I follow the underclassmen off the bus. I adjust my bag and try to ignore the additional stares and whispers as I walk up the steps. Even two teachers join in, gawking.

I can't take it. I push through the crowd, heading for the nearest bathroom. I lock myself in a stall.

I can't do this. They *know*. Somehow, they all know something is wrong. They're going to ask. I know someone will.

As much as I'd like to scream the truth from the rooftops, what good would it do? What would they do if I told them? Would they even believe me?

And then what would *he* do to them?

My phone buzzes in my pocket. After weeks of not having it, the once-familiar buzz now feels foreign. My heart clenches. I pull out my phone. The screen says "Daddy." My heart flutters, thinking of the last time I spoke to Dad over the phone. I want to hear his voice so bad. But it's not my dad.

It's *him*.

"H-hello," I say.

"What's wrong, Jessy?" he asks.

My lips tremble. How does he know something's wrong?

Of course—he's watching. Always watching. And listening. Did he have cameras on the bus? Did he see me walk in here? I scan the bathroom ceiling for cameras, relieved when I find none.

I don't know what to tell him. I decide to be honest.

"I can't do this. It's too hard. School hasn't even started, and everyone has me under a microscope. I just want to come home."

He's silent. Each passing second only worsens my fears.

I know he'll punish me for this, but I don't care. I'd rather be in the box than out there. Either way, I'm in a cage. But here, people are watching my every move. It's different from the way he watches me. With him, it's just one set of eyes. Here it's many. I feel like an animal at the zoo. And if anything goes wrong, they're the ones who will suffer the most.

"Jessy," he says. Surprisingly, the tenderness of his voice curls around me like a blanket on a cold night. "I wouldn't have let you go to school if I didn't think you could handle it. I have faith in you. So does your mother. Now take a deep breath." He pauses, waiting for me to do as instructed.

My breath trembles both on the way in and out.

"Good," he praises. "Now do another and another until you can feel yourself calm down."

Again, I do as I'm told.

"Better?" he asks.

Amazingly, I am. "Yes," I say. "Thank you."

"Excellent. Now wash your face, dry your tears, and go to class. And remember, I'm right here if you need me. I'm watching out for you, Jessy. And I'll do what's necessary to keep our family together. Remember that."

A strange feeling twists in my gut. I don't want to need *him*. He murdered my father in cold blood. Threatened my mother's life. Beat me. Locked me in a tiny room for days, depriving me of food and water. And now he's locked up my mom and is threatening the lives of all my friends.

Despite all that, some of what he said on the phone was . . . a comfort. All I've ever known from him was anger, manipulation, and aggression. But this . . . calming me down and encouraging me . . . it reminds me of conversations I had with Dad—my real dad.

LAURIE WETZEL ‡ PICTURE PERFECT

He told me I can do this. He has faith in me.

As strange as it sounds, I want to prove him right. I want to make him proud of me. Is it because his words bring me closer to the real father I lost? Or is it because making this man "proud" of me is the best way to keep myself and everyone I love safe?

I wash my face as instructed, pat down the tear streaks, and take several more deep breaths.

When I make it to my locker, relief flows through me. I made it. And this time, the gawking doesn't seem that bad. People have always stared at me. I never used to care. I guess now I have a reason to.

I let out another long exhale. Only six hours and fifty-four minutes to go.

Heat crawls along my skin. I can sense Nick before I see him. I turn, and sure enough, he's watching me as he walks over to his locker.

"Why did you do that?" he asks, glaring at me.

The venom in his voice has me instantly stepping back, dropping my shoulders, and closing my eyes. I'm preparing to be hit. When a strike doesn't come, though, I risk a peek.

Nick's still as a statue, staring at me.

I suppose my reaction was a bit over-the-top. But I couldn't help it. It's like it was instinctual.

"Why did I do what?" I ask. I straighten up and arch a brow, indicating that I'm waiting for his reply.

He points to my head, and his scowl returns. "Your hair."

My hand automatically reaches up. I don't like my hair, and I know people have been gawking at it. But I didn't think anyone would be so harsh about it. Especially someone who barely knows me.

"I—" I begin.

"Babe!" an all-too-familiar voice hollers.

As Blake rushes up and wraps his arms around me, panic flares inside.

"Don't touch me!" I cry out as I push him back.

Blake recoils.

Even Nick takes a step back.

Blake's strong arms used to feel like home—warm, safe, and inviting. Now . . . ? I don't know. The moment he touched me, every nerve ending in my body tensed, expecting pain.

What's happening to me? Why did his touch terrify me? Blake's never hurt me. Not once. He's always been perfect. He *loves* me.

So why did I freak out?

Is it because we haven't seen each other in weeks? Is it because I'm still recovering and sore? Or is my body trying to protect itself, knowing I have to break his heart today?

Blake's still staring. They both are.

My chest tightens. As fight-or-flight kicks in, I quickly search for the nearest exits, ready to bolt. Just as quickly, though, my panic does a one-eighty as I notice the cameras tucked near the ceiling. He's watching . . .

"What the hell, babe?" Blake asks.

"Sorry, it's just . . . it's just I don't want to get you sick," I say, remembering one of the many lies I'll tell today.

His shock dissolves, and he seems to buy the excuse, but he places an arm around me anyway. "Sick or not, I'll take my chances," he says.

I flinch and grit my teeth, trying to ignore the discomfort of his touch once again. Was he always this physically affectionate? I don't remember.

My skin is on pins and needles. I feel like I'm waiting—waiting for any indication that he's upset or that he's going to suddenly hurt me.

That's the third time in less than five minutes. Neither Blake nor Nick have ever threatened or hurt me in the past, yet my body doesn't care.

For two weeks, my body has endured intense pain and abuse. I thought coming to school would bring some relief. But instead, I'm practically paralyzed with fear. Every sight, sound, and touch is perceived as a threat.

What has *he* done to me? Is that what my life is now?

Blake reaches up, playing with my hair, and I fight not to react. I have it up in a messy bun, but a few shorter pieces have fallen out.

"I love this color, by the way," he says.

I brush my hair back behind my ear just as I see Nick shake his head at me. He's clearly staring at my hair too. In disgust.

I understand that there will always be an uncomfortable dynamic between us. How could there not be? But I don't understand why he's so upset today—about my new hair color, of all things.

Some of the panic I felt earlier is returning. Unable to stand it any longer, I shrug out of Blake's embrace. To avoid any more awkwardness or questions, I make it seem as though I did it just so I could take off my coat. I keep the charade going, putting my coat in my locker and grabbing my things for class. All the while, he's watching me carefully. Studying.

"Did you lose weight, babe?"

I stiffen. Yes, I did. I know I did. My clothes are loose. And under my sweater, my ribs show. But given that I spent most of the holiday break either unconscious or in the box, it was bound to happen.

Now Nick's eyes are on me. Scrutinizing.

I whirl around to face Blake, crossing my arms to cover my rail-thin torso, making sure to keep my damaged, ugly hands hidden.

"I told you—I was sick." Words start coming fast now. "Actually, I was sick over the entire break. Maybe it was a good thing I didn't go to Aspen after all."

My heart is racing. This isn't the lie *he* told me to tell. I'm supposed to say I lounged around with Mom. But I need something, anything, to explain my shocking appearance. I need Blake to stop asking questions. And the lie of being sick is proving to be quite convenient.

I quickly change the subject. "How was Aspen, anyway? Was it fun?"

He grimaces and looks away. "It was . . . it was fine."

He's lying. Of course it wasn't fine. I can only imagine how miserable he was without me, but he can't bring himself to admit that. He loves me so much, which only makes it harder to do what I'm supposed to do today.

"Did Cassie at least have fun?" I ask.

He licks his bottom lip, another move he always does when he's not being fully honest. "Yeah. I guess."

"Why didn't you call or text me on someone else's phone?" The words blurt out before I even realize it.

"What?" Blake asks, confused.

"You said your phone got lost skiing. But you could have used someone else's phone. Or your tablet. Why didn't you call or text me even just once?"

I have to know. Part of me just wants to prove *him* wrong about Blake. Another part of me just wants reassurance that Blake cares about me—even though I have to end it.

Nick scratches his head and looks at Blake as if waiting for his response to my question. I glare, annoyed that he's still listening in on everything.

For a second, worry and guilt flashes in Blake's eyes. But then he crosses his arms defensively.

"I was pissed, all right? I mean, you guys canceled at the last minute. I get it—stuff comes up. But c'mon. And the only way I hear about it is from my dad, after your dad leaves him a voicemail? I can't believe *you* didn't call *me*. Not once. Not even on Christmas. Last I checked, phones work two ways."

His reaction stings. It's the last thing I expected.

I turn around and slam my locker shut. "How many times do I have to tell you? I was sick! The entire time. You have *no idea* what I went through," I add with more sincerity than he will ever realize.

Blake sighs, then sticks his hands up in surrender. "Shit. Babe, I'm sorry. I'm an ass, OK? I'm so sorry you were sick. I'm so sorry about everything. You're right—I should have called you."

Then it hits me: He should have called, yes—but it wouldn't have mattered. *He* never would have let me talk to Blake anyway.

I rest back against the locker, facing Blake. "It's fine. Just forget it."

"Hey," he says, suddenly looking down at my neckline. "Why aren't you wearing the necklace I got you?"

I cringe. "I lost it . . ."

It's not a lie. I did lose it. And I wish I knew what that man did with it. I doubt I'll ever see it again.

His usually calm demeanor evaporates, and a harshness overtakes him like a bitter wind on a summer day. "Seriously? You lost a *diamond* necklace? What the—"

"Hey, guys!"

It's Cassie, running up to us, joined by Nevaeh and Rebecca, two of our other friends from the squad. They swarm in to hug me, but I duck behind Blake to avoid them.

"Careful," Blake says with more than a hint of sarcasm. "She's 'sick.'" He shakes his head and runs his fingers through his wavy, black hair.

He's still upset over the necklace. And he should be. *I* am.

"You were sick all break?" Rebecca asks. Her eyes go up and down like an elevator as she inspects me.

I nod.

"That's awful," Neveah says.

"Mm-hm," Cassie says flatly.

I can tell she's already changing the subject.

"But anyway," she says, "you will not *believe* what this loser said when I—oh my gosh!" She stops herself midsentence, staring at me. "Cute hair!"

"Thanks," I mumble.

"Anyway, what were you saying about the loser, Cass?" Blake asks.

Even though he still seems upset about the necklace, he steps closer to me and throws his arm around my shoulder again. It's heavy. So heavy. His muscles ripple underneath his sweater, reminding me just how strong he is. He's never hurt me before, but he easily could. I do my best to ignore my body's reaction, wanting to stay close to him while I still can.

With his arm over me, I notice Cassie flinch. She looks everywhere but at him.

Something is off here. Did they get into a fight in Aspen? I know she's never been his favorite among my friends. Maybe this is why he was dodging my questions about the trip. Maybe he hated every moment with her.

After a second, Cassie shakes her head, snapping out of whatever her issue was. "Oh! Yeah. As I was saying, some moron said they saw you on the bus this morning, Jessy. As if!"

I bite my lip. "I did ride the bus."

They gasp. Blake drops his arm and moves to stand beside Cassie. Even Nick stops pretending to rummage through his locker.

I shrug. "My car isn't working."

"Babe," Blake begins. "You could have called me."

"Or me," my friends say in unison.

For a second, their quick offers warm my heart. But then that warmth cools quickly when I remember that none of them reached out to me over break. Not once.

I try to shrug it off. "It's fine."

"Well, I'll give you a ride home after practice, then," Cassie says.

There it is. Practice.

"Um, actually, I won't need a ride then either." I turn to my girlfriends, tears already pooling in my eyes. "I need you guys to gather the squad and meet me in the gym at the beginning of lunch. I'm calling an emergency meeting."

They blanch.

"What's wrong?" Cassie asks, holding her hand to her throat.

I have no words. And thankfully, the first bell rings, saving me from speaking anyway.

Neveah and Rebecca wave, still looking worried, then I head off to gym with Blake and Cassie.

Sometime today, I have to break Blake's heart. Cassie's heart. All my friends' hearts. But I'm not ready. Even though it's a little awkward being here, and we aren't off to a great start, I need Blake and my friends. I'm not ready to lose them just yet.

Without them, I'm completely alone.

†
‡

In gym, we're running. Normally, I'm fine with that. But today, with my ribs, I'm already struggling on the first lap. Breathing deep causes intense pain, so all I can manage is short pants. Muscles all over my body cry out in protest from the exertion. Between practices and games, I worked out at least fifteen hours a week. But after two weeks of limited movement—and brutal abuse—it's like all of that has been erased.

Am I this weak because of the box? The beatings? Both?

"Come on, babe," Blake says, jogging beside me.

"Jeez," Cassie says. "How sick were you?"

"Just go ahead without me," I wheeze. "I'll be fine."

"You're sure?" he asks.

"Yes."

I put on another fake smile. This time, it's easier. Is that how Mom perfected it? She just kept doing it over and over, and now it's automatic?

Everyone continues to lap me, even the nonathletic kids. Some even laugh as they go by.

But not Nick. Each time he passes me, he seems upset. Or maybe worried.

So does his friend. I'm not sure what his name is. All I know is that he's the only person I've ever seen Nick hang out with. He's from South River High too.

The rest of the morning speeds by. Before I'm ready, it's lunch. The whole squad is waiting in the gym, just as I asked. Blake takes a seat on the bench as well. Maybe he's just waiting to head to lunch with me afterward. Or maybe he's as concerned about this emergency meeting as the girls are.

I take a deep, trembling breath, preparing to end the social life I've spent the last twelve years perfecting. But I need to do whatever I can to stay on that man's good side and to keep my friends safe. And that means following through with today's agenda.

"Thanks for coming, everyone," I begin. "I have an announcement, but before I say it, I just want you to know that my decision is final."

I stop and take another deep breath, but my ribs instantly let me know that was a stupid move. I have to bite my tongue to keep from vocalizing the pain. A pain that I will do whatever it takes to keep all my friends from ever experiencing. I blink up at the lights as tears well up. I try to hold them back as I continue.

"Effective immediately, I am stepping down as captain and leaving the squad."

Shocked cries ring out. I hear many of them asking if this is a joke.

I wait for them to calm down before I add, "And I'm naming Cassie as my successor."

"No way!" she shouts, hopping up from the bench. She starts to do a little dance, twirling to the victory party she's throwing herself in her head. But then she quickly turns her grin to a frown. "Don't get me wrong, hun. I'm super sad you're leaving . . . But *me*? Captain? *Eek!*"

The frown disappears as quickly as it came. She's

LAURIE WETZEL ‡ PICTURE PERFECT

screeching and hopping with glee, clapping her hands. She reminds me of a toy monkey with cymbals. The crowd splits, half going over to congratulate her, the other half still sitting in shock.

No one is coming over to me, though.

Except Blake. Suddenly, he's by my side. Deep lines of worry and confusion are etched into his perfect face.

"Why are you doing this, Jessy? Cheering is your life."

"I had a lot of alone time to think about things during break," I say, hoping this fake excuse will work as well as my fake smiles seem to be working.

In truth, it's not fake at all. I did, in fact, have a lot of "alone time." That's one way to describe being locked up in a box in the basement for hours on end.

He leans in closer, dropping his voice. "What about our future—you cheering for me on the sidelines at NFL games?"

My chest tightens. I wanted that future so bad. So did Blake. Now I have to throw it all away.

But then my thoughts spiral, and I'm reminded of what the man said. The future we had planned was all about Blake, while I would be literally on the sidelines.

I shake my head at that thought. I don't care what *he* thinks. Blake loves me. I know it. And I don't care what cheerleaders make. I know it's not much. Blake was going to support us while we both did what we loved.

But that can't happen now.

"You're not mad at me, are you . . . ?" Blake continues. His voice is tight and nervous, even though he's trying to hide it. He studies me, too, as if looking for something in my eyes or reaction.

"No," I reply. It's the truth.

Relief floods his face. "OK. Well then, let's get some food in you, and then let's talk about not making rash decisions that affect the both of us."

I should just end it all now. Get it over with. But I can't.

Not yet.

Instead, I let him place his hand at the small of my back and lead me out of the gym. No one even notices. The squad is still in a frenzy over my decision.

Blake and I grab our food, then make our way to our usual table. But my appetite is nonexistent. I pick at my fruit and salad. How can I eat when I have to crush his heart sometime in the next three hours?

Blake notices. "I know you're sick and all," he says, "but you should at least try to eat a little."

I nod, taking a bite here and there. But even then, I can't taste the food. I eventually just put my fork down.

"Everything OK?" Blake asks.

I shrug. "I'm just not hungry."

With a frown, he slides closer to me and raises his hand to my face.

I flinch.

"Babe, chill," he says, pulling his hand back. "I was just going to check if you have a fever."

I scooch away, not wanting to feel his touch—even for something so normal and caring.

"I—I don't have a fever." I have to think quick. "This isn't an infection. It's more of a stomach thing."

Not getting the hint, he erases the distance between us again. But now I'm at the end of the bench. I have nowhere else to go.

He leans in, putting his lips beside my ear. "How sick were you? Was it because of your missing spleen or something . . . worse? Because with the weight loss and how strange you're acting . . . Babe, I gotta be honest here— you're starting to freak me out. It's like you're delirious or something."

This is not good. I'm messing this up. The lies are eating at my empty gut, compiling the guilt.

"Tell you what," he continues. "I'll talk to Cassie and smooth things over about this whole quitting-the-squad thing. I'll let her know you're still sick and aren't thinking clear. Then I'll take you home so you can rest and—"

"No!" I shout.

Multiple tables look our way.

I quickly lower my voice. "No. I'm staying here. And I'm not delirious. I'm serious about quitting."

"Damn it, Jessy!"

His voice carries, echoing through the cafeteria. Several students look our way again, including Nick and his friend.

"I don't know if you're pissed at me or your parents or what," Blake says. Noticing our audience, his tone changes. He replaces his anger with forced concern. "Whatever it is, you don't want to tell me yet. And I get that. But I just want you to know that I'm here."

He reaches over, taking my covered hand. I know I should pull it away, just like I have to pull away from everything that he means to me. But I can't.

"I'm not going anywhere," he continues. "I'm going to be here every day. Forever. Cheerleading or not."

I stare up at the ceiling, holding back more tears. Why? Why do we have to break up? I don't understand why that man is making me do this.

"After school, I'm driving you home," Blake says. "If you want to talk, great. If not, that's fine too. Tomorrow I'll pick you up—same deal applies. I'll keep driving you, and I'll keep waiting, without pushing you, until you're ready to tell me what's wrong."

No.

I yank my hand away as a jolt of electric chills go through my whole body. It's suddenly clear now. I have to end this. That way, he won't get hurt.

I release my shaky breath, stare deadpan into his eyes, and say, "We're over."

"What's over, babe?"

"*We* are."

"What?" He stands, staggering back from the table.

"What are you talking about? Why would you say that?"

I look around the room. All tables are silent. Watching. Waiting. Gobbling this up and hanging on every word and expression.

And then I spot a camera tucked high up in the corner. *He's* watching too.

I can't tell Blake the truth—that I'm sparing him from the nightmare that is my life. That I'm saving his life.

Just then, the squad walks into the cafeteria, stopping as they notice the tension. Cassie looks at me, then at Blake, then back at me. Her eyes go wide.

"Jessy, I'm sorry!" she exclaims. "It was a mistake! And it was just the one time—"

"Cass, shut up!" Blake yells. His voice is angry—but also desperate.

Somehow the room becomes even more silent.

My head is on a swivel. I take in Cassie's shocked and guilty expression, then Blake's furious one. I have no idea what's happening. I feel as confused as everyone else in the cafeteria. Only I'm not some gawking onlooker. I'm somehow in the middle of this mess.

"Cassie, what are you talking about?" I say slowly. "What was a mistake?"

She shakes her head rapidly. "Nothing. I—" She looks to Blake, silently pleading with him to help her.

Oh God . . .

I wait for either of them to say it. To admit it.

They won't.

I guess I will.

"Was it just a kiss?" I ask. "Or worse?"

Shame drips off them like sweat in a locker room.

Suddenly I can't breathe. My lungs won't expand enough for me to catch my breath.

This can't be happening.

I shove past them and race for the bathroom. I lock myself in the same stall again and collapse as the tears flow.

How could he do this to me? How could she? Was it in Aspen?

Yes. Something had to have happened in Aspen. *Had* to. Before, Blake could barely tolerate hanging around her. But once I was out of the picture and they had time to themselves . . .

The signs all start piecing together. Neither of them texted or called me. He claimed he "lost" his phone. There was that strange "tension" between them this morning.

How could I have been so blind?

Knowing only makes it worse. The whole reason I even invited Cassie to Aspen was because her boyfriend had cheated on her. How could she turn around and do it to me knowing how shitty it feels?

And Blake . . . That's why he was so nervous earlier, eyeing me carefully. He was looking for any sign that I knew.

My body shakes as violent sobs rack through me.

Blake was my future. We had it all planned out. Now I have nothing. A part of me hoped that when I pushed them all away today, they'd realize something was really wrong, and they'd get me help. And then once that murderer was out of my life, we'd all go back to the way it was before.

But this—Blake and Cassie have betrayed me. There's no going back now. Even if I could somehow manage to be free of that man and his grip on my life.

Which maybe I'll never be.

My world has fallen apart. Mom has snapped. Dad is dead. Blake, Cassie, and all my friends are gone. I'm alone.

Maybe that's what *he* wanted. To destroy my support system so all I have is him.

My phone suddenly buzzes in my pocket.

It's a text from "Daddy." From *him*.

I told you he wasn't right for you, the text reads.

He knew? He knew they cheated?

Another text bubble from him pops up.

Go to class.

I lean my head back against the tiles and let out a choked laugh. Here I am, crying my eyes out as my world crumbles; meanwhile, he's sitting behind the screens at home, watching it all unfold live and unscripted. Is he happy with my performance? Does it live up to his expectations?

Unfortunately, I'm not finished yet. The show must go on.

Fearing what he'd do if I disobeyed him, I get up, dry my tears, and go to class. My face is still red from crying when I enter sixth period. No one says anything, but eyes dart in my direction. Some are sympathetic. Some are not.

I know they know. If they didn't witness it live in the cafeteria, then they heard about it from someone who did. Blake and I are royalty to this school. Our very public demise will be talked about long after we leave here.

Nick stiffens as I take my assigned seat beside him.

"All right, class," Mr. Hubert calls. "I want you to break up into groups of two and discuss what you did over winter break. I will be walking around, listening to your Spanish."

Nick leans over. "Are you OK?" he whispers.

Twice in one day he's talked to me. That's more than he's done all year. He usually sticks with staring.

Every time someone says my name, he looks up, searching for her. His sister. But he only finds me. That's why he stares. That's why he hates me. Because I'm here and she's not. I've thought about telling him how sorry I am, but sorry doesn't seem good enough.

Because he didn't just lose his sister. When the drunk driver appeared in court a few days after the accident, Nick's father attacked him and was arrested. That night, Nick's mom committed suicide.

The trials lasted for months. Nick's father was sentenced to two years in jail, while the drunk driver got only three years for the accident.

Nick lost everyone he loved. If anyone knows how I'm

feeling, it's him.

His world fell apart too. Yet somehow, he's still standing.

"No, Nick," I reply. "I'm not OK."

Nick gives a small, wry smile. "Gotta say, I wasn't expecting Blake to be such a jackass."

I snort. "Me either." For some reason, I want to keep going. I want to tell him more. "Blake and I have been together since seventh grade—friends since birth. Cassie for forever as well. I don't understand. How could I have not seen it? How could I have been so stupid?"

He places his hand on top of mine just as Blake did not even ten minutes ago. I wince from the contact, pulling my hand back and hugging myself. He stares at my covered hands but thankfully doesn't say anything.

"You're not stupid, Jessy. I'll admit that when I first met you, I wasn't sure—the whole blond-cheerleader thing, you know? But you're different. And I mean that in a good way."

"*En español, por favor,*" Mr. Hubert says as he strolls by.

"*Estás mejor sin él,*" Nick says loudly enough for Mr. Hubert to hear.

I want to argue and tell him he's wrong. I'm not better off without Blake. Blake's better off without me and that murderer threatening my whole world.

But Blake cheated . . . He cheated with my best friend while I was trapped in a nightmare.

"*Gracias,* Nick," I finally say.

"*De nada,* Jessy."

"*Bien!*" Mr. Hubert says, then keeps walking.

"Um," Nick begins, scratching the back of his neck, "if your car is in the shop and you need a ride to and from school, I could give you one."

"No." It comes out quickly.

He frowns and looks away.

"It's not that I don't appreciate the offer. I do. It's just—"

I pause, not knowing what to tell him. But I can't stand lying to him or hurting him. I've done enough of that for one day. My emotions can't take any more.

"It's just that I lied earlier," I admit. "My car's fine. My . . . parents want me to take the bus." I hate calling *him* my parent, but it's as close to the truth as I dare say.

"Harsh."

I shrug. "It's not that bad. I've actually never taken the bus before, so I suppose it was time I did. Get the whole high school experience."

He snorts. "Only you would call riding the bus an *experience*."

"What's that supposed to mean?"

"Most kids hate the bus and have no shame saying so," he says. "But you, Princess Jessy, were 'raised better' than that. Instead, you have to put that positive spin on it, like all rich people do."

I stare at him for several seconds, trying to wrap my mind around this discussion. "Wow. You really hate me, don't you?"

He falls silent, eyeing me as if I were some science experiment. "Who said I hate you?"

I lean back, stunned. As if someone would have to tell me that he hates me. As if it's not written all over his face every time he looks at me.

"Never mind." I sigh. "Forget I said anything."

If I were in his position, I'd hate me too.

Nick gives me a polite smile, and I know he wants me to think it's all smoothed over. Hopefully it is. It's not like we can suddenly become friends.

I'm not even allowed to keep the ones I had.

EIGHT

BEFORE I TAKE MY SEAT IN THE LAST CLASS of the day, Mrs. Perkins stops me. "Jessica, Ms. Shueller would like to see you."

Utter terror fills me. Ms. Shueller is my counselor.

It was stupid to think I could go the whole day without anyone seeing through my charade. I thought I was being so careful, but I did something wrong. Of course I did. Why else would she ask to see me?

As much as I want to pretend I didn't hear Mrs. Perkins—and pretend like none of this is happening—I know that would only make things worse. So I clutch my notebook and calculus textbook to my chest as if they were shields capable of sparing me from further pain, then I head back out into the hallway, toward the offices.

Before I make it more than one classroom away, my phone buzzes in my pocket. The vibrations ripple through me. My jaw clenches, my muscles tighten, and my nerves go into a frenzy. It's him. It has to be.

I pull out my phone, and sure enough, the screen flashes with a new message from "Daddy."

Who's Ms. Shueller? it says.

My feet become rooted to the spot. My blood freezes.

How does he know? How many microphones and cameras does he have?

My fingers tremble as I type back: *My counselor. She wants to see me. What do I do?*

I stare at the screen, not breathing, as I wait for his reply.

Talk to her.

That's it? That's his only response?

But what if she knows something is wrong? I type.

Wrong?

His one-word message makes the knots in my belly tighten even further, to the point where I'm barely able to stand upright.

Shit.

A few seconds later, another message comes in from him.

You are finally with your real father, who loves you unconditionally and isn't afraid to do whatever it takes to raise you into a lovely, respectable young woman. There is nothing "wrong" with that. Now go.

My "real father."

Once again, I picture him and Mom making out on the couch. Them sharing a bed at night. What if he *is* my biological father? What if I actually share DNA with that murderer?

No. I can't bring myself to explore the possibilities. It's too messed up.

What's even more messed up is that even if I am his daughter, it obviously doesn't guarantee my safety. He's adamant he's my father yet has no remorse about the things he's done to me.

I tuck my phone back into my pocket and finish the lonely walk. For a split second, I consider telling Ms. Shueller everything. All the horrid details.

But he'll kill her. Or my friends. Or Mom. Or all of them. There's no telling how many people he'd kill just to punish me.

I barely manage a wave at the elderly receptionist as I head toward the counselors' offices in the back. The tiny waiting area is filled with college brochures. I spent many weeks here last spring, narrowing my choices for schools. Ms. Shueller spent nearly every second of it with me. Having just graduated from college a few years back herself, she's eager to help students with their college searches.

She also helped me a lot when I came back to school after my accident. She listened. She helped me find the words to describe the fear, pain, and guilt I felt from that night. And even though schoolwork was the last thing on my mind during recovery, she made it her mission to make sure my grades didn't suffer. She told me that the drunk driver had taken so much from me already—she wouldn't let him take my future too. She knew that if my grades slipped too much, I could kiss all my top-choice colleges goodbye.

"Jessy—hi!"

Ms. Shueller's cheerful tone breaks up my grim thoughts. She's standing in her office doorway. Although it's the dead of winter, with two feet of snow outside, she's dressed in a bright floral skirt with a yellow sweater. Her long blond hair falls in perfect waves to her chest. As she smiles at me, her light-brown eyes are just as bright as her sweater and hair.

"Thank you for coming," she says. "Shall we talk in here?" She moves out of the doorway and gestures to her office.

Her office is small, but she somehow manages to squeeze in three different seating areas. Students can chat with her at her desk, at a table with swivel chairs, or in two plush armchairs.

I take a seat in one of the red armchairs, where I typically sit when I visit her. She shuts the door and takes a seat in the other armchair.

As soon she sits, I stand up. Today, the armchairs suddenly feel too personal. She's too close. I wish I'd chosen to sit at her desk instead.

Ms. Shueller watches as I pretend I'm interested in the various flyers and brochures tacked to her bulletin board.

"I've heard some troubling things today," she begins. "I thought it best to come directly to the source."

"OK," I say, concentrating hard on a random brochure. It's for depression.

"One of the many responsibilities a counselor has is to watch for major changes in their students. Some are easier to detect than others. Changes in appearance—such as different hairstyles and weight loss—can be red flags. Sudden changes in social activities and withdrawing from peer groups can be too."

She makes an obvious show of looking me up and down. She might as well be looking right *through* me.

"Jessy, you've checked all four red-flag boxes today. Is there something going on I should know about?"

My fingers tighten around my arms, as if they can literally keep myself together. "Blake and I broke up. He cheated on me with Cassie."

Ms. Shueller sucks in her breath. "I'm very sorry, Jessy. That has to hurt a great deal."

I nod, biting my lips to stop them from shaking.

"And then what happened in the gym before lunch?"

I clear my throat and whisper, "I quit the squad."

She doesn't reply.

After nearly a minute of silence, I glance back at her. Her chin rests on her fist as she stares at me. The sympathy in her eyes has me fighting to hold back my tears. One leaks through. I wipe the traitor away.

"Was that because of Cassie too?" she finally asks.

"What?"

"Did you quit the squad to distance yourself from her?"

"No. Not at all." I shake my head. "I quit because—"

But then the whole room begins to spin as I realize that I handed Cassie the squad—*my* squad—moments before I learned that she had betrayed me. That they both had betrayed me.

"I quit for other reasons," I say, leaving it vague. "And actually, I made Cassie"—I steady myself by grabbing her bookshelf—"I made Cassie captain."

I rest my head in my hands, stunned.

"But you love cheering," Ms. Shueller says. "An excellent cheerleading program was a must on the list of colleges you applied to."

"I know," I whisper.

"Your whole future was set around it," she presses.

Hearing her say this breaks my heart even more. Because it's true. My future—not Blake's future, not "our" future—was set around cheering. I love it. I've loved it for years. Long before Blake and I were an item. It's who I am.

But that man *forced* me to give it up. And worse yet, he tried to make me believe I was a cheerleader only because I was some mindless sheep following Blake. Did he somehow know Blake cheated? He was adamant that Blake wasn't good enough for me. Is that the real reason he made me break things off with him?

"Why don't you take a couple of days to reconsider your decision," Ms. Shueller says. "I'm sure the squad will understand if you decide you want to come back."

I nod, even though there's no point in thinking it over. I can't change my mind. I can't go back. Not just because I don't want to be around Cassie.

He won't let me.

"And I know it may not seem like it right now, but this—the hurt you're feeling about Blake—will get easier," she adds. "You are a remarkable young woman, and you will find someone worthy of you."

"OK." It's all I can say.

"Is there anything else going on I should know about? Something at home?"

I quickly turn back to the bulletin board, steeling my

emotions and putting on my invisible mask of normalcy. She can't know about that. No one can. As much as I wish I could tell her—tell anyone—so I wouldn't feel like I'm drowning, I can't. He's made it very clear what will happen if I do.

"No," I say with my back still to her.

"You're sure?" she asks.

I nod.

"OK, then. I should let you get back to class." She stands. "No matter what you need, Jessy, please know I'm here."

Without another word or even a glance at her, I leave.

‡

By the time the bus stops at the end of my mile-long driveway, my whole body is shaking. I rub my arms, pretending I'm cold. In reality, I'm terrified. I don't know what I'm coming home to.

Home.

It used to be warm and welcoming. A constant place of comfort.

Now it's synonymous with hell.

My fear is amplified when I see he's standing on the porch, waiting for me.

I stand in the snow, less than twenty yards away, unable to move.

"I have to admit," he begins, "I thought I'd have to spend my whole afternoon tracking you down. But you came home. I'm proud of you."

A floodgate of relief rushes through me, and I damn near collapse. This feeling—knowing I managed to escape his wrath—is the greatest I've felt in a very long time.

And with that, I realize I want to keep making him proud. I want to do whatever I can to escape his wrath.

"Come inside. I want to hear all about your day."

I guess I should have known he'd grill me, but I'm still caught off guard. With all the cameras, doesn't he know everything anyway?

We sit in his office. A quick glance at the monitors has my body stiffening. There's an image of an apartment building. On the walkway is Ms. Shueller.

"What did you discuss with your counselor?" he asks, giving the slightest nod toward the monitor. "Leave nothing out—and don't for a second lie to me."

So that's it. He didn't have a camera in her office.

A realization strikes me: I *could* have told her everything. She would have immediately called the cops. I'm sure of it.

I could have been free.

Perhaps.

Or perhaps he would have started a shoot-out, killing every cop who swarmed our house. Perhaps he would have shot Mom. Perhaps he would have run, taking Mom with him—and planning to return for me at the first moment my guard is down.

Something tells me that unless he's dead, I'll never be free.

And then another realization strikes me even harder than the first: for all he knows, I *did* tell Ms. Shueller everything. Or if not everything, then enough.

I didn't tell her a thing, yet her life is still in danger because of me.

Last night, he made it clear that this was all about trust. And leverage. So, I have to earn his trust in order to stop him from using that leverage against me.

"She was concerned about my appearance and how I was cutting myself off from my social ties," I say with utter honesty.

"And is she still concerned now?"

He doesn't come right out and say it, but I know if I tell him yes, he will go to her house and kill her. I just . . . I can't allow her to die because she cares about me.

"Please. Please don't hurt her. She doesn't suspect

anything. She was concerned—that's all."

"So are you saying she was just doing her job . . ." he says slowly, trying to follow my logic. "Nothing more? Is that it?"

I look up, meeting his gaze. Challenging him, even though there's no reason to. He seems to believe me. I don't need to make this point—yet I do.

"No. It's much more than that. She's much more than that. Without her, I don't know how I would have overcome what happened to me from the accident. She's one of the reasons I'm OK today."

He turns to the monitors, watching as Ms. Shueller walks through the halls and to her door. Apartment 4408.

"If she's that important to you, then I trust you won't put her life in jeopardy by doing something stupid."

"I won't. I promise."

He nods, though now I'm not sure I've convinced him of all of this.

"Well, I suppose we should see your mom," he says. "She's been *dying* to know how your day went." He winks.

Is that a *dad joke* about *murdering* my mother?

Stunned to silence, I follow him into the basement. He makes a big production of undoing the three locks.

I can't help but wonder what state she'll be in. Did she fight when the walls seemed to cave in? Did she break nails? Bruise herself? Did she feel suffocated by the pure darkness and loss of time?

He finally opens the door to reveal Mom, standing in the entryway with a bright smile, like we'd just opened the front door.

"Hello, Jessy dear. How was your day?"

I blink several times, not believing my eyes. She's OK. How is she OK?

I feel his gaze skate to me, nudging me to respond. The last thing I want is for him to shove me in there for being *rude* to her.

"Fine," I murmur.

We head upstairs—as a family.

And then the rest of the evening is a blur. I have a vague sense that I'm helping with dinner, eating, cleaning the table, and doing my homework. I'm present for all of it, but none of it registers.

It's autopilot. Survival mode. Call it whatever you want. With all the stresses and emotions of returning to school, I'm tapped out.

I'm thinking of heading to bed early—asking for permission to do so—but then I hear something. He's calling my name from the office. Something in his voice snaps me out of my foggy haze and throws me back into hypervigilance.

I thought I'd neutralized all the threats earlier. I thought I'd calmed him down and made it so everyone was safe. What else does he want?

Knowing I have no choice but to obey, I cross my arms against my chest and head to the office.

He's sitting in my father's chair. Again. On each of the monitors is a frozen frame of me walking to the counselors' office. I'm looking down at my phone. That was when I was texting him.

My skin prickles. My throat dries. I thought we covered this . . .

"I've been thinking—going over your day," he begins. "While I am proud of how you handled yourself, I keep coming back to one moment. I'm concerned about this idea that you think something is 'wrong.'"

He reaches for his cell phone, opens our text thread, and holds it out for me—as if presenting exhibit A for evidence.

But what if she knows something is wrong? it says.

Those were my words to him.

"The only thing that has been wrong lately is your attitude," he says. "You should be happy. You're free from Blake, Cassie, and all those other so-called friends. They were toxic. I trust you can see that now."

My head tilts as if staring at him from this angle will somehow bring clarity to the utter nonsense he just said.

My attitude is wrong? I should be happy? My friends are toxic?

What in the what?

"More importantly . . ." he continues.

His voice becomes eerily calm. It's strange, and for reasons I can't explain, I don't like it. My hairs stand on end. I feel as if he's backed me into a corner, though he's still sitting down.

". . . You should be happy because we're finally together again as a family. Things are good, Jessy."

"*Good*? Are you *serious*?"

The moment the words are out, I know I made a mistake.

"Sorry," I say, looking down and hoping against all hope that he didn't hear me.

But it's too late.

He stands and raises his hand. I clamp my eyes shut, waiting for him to hit me. Instead, he places his hand against my cheek, stroking it.

"I wish you could trust that I have your best interests at heart. I wish we could have an open and honest relationship. I wish you could stop fighting me long enough to see how good your life is now that we're back together."

I open my eyes slowly. His own eyes are cold and hard.

"But we aren't at that point in our relationship yet. So tonight you'll sleep downstairs. You'll continue to sleep there until your attitude improves."

"No!" I gasp, backing away. "Please don't put me back in there. I'm doing what you want! Please! I'll do anything!"

Silent tears fall as he roughly seizes my arm and leads me down to the box. Right before he shuts the door and locks me in, he says, "I love you, Jessy."

Once again, I'm left alone with only the darkness to share my pain and keep me company.

I quit the squad. I broke up with Blake. I lied to Ms. Shueller. I lied to them all. I went from class to class, pretending as though my body isn't covered in bruises and my whole world isn't in shambles.

But it wasn't enough. He wants me to do the impossible. Now he wants me to be happy.

NINE

THE BUS IS LATE ARRIVING TO SCHOOL. THE first-period bell has already rung. I'm kind of glad, though. It means the hallways are empty—which in turn means I don't have to walk through the whispered conversations, hostile glares, and snickers that follow me.

I've been back in school for a week now. Each day, the hours tick away, taunting me. I've learned how to plaster on a smile, even though I face animosity from students I barely know, and even though I'm shunned by my former friends.

Sometimes I want to grab each one of them by the shoulders and shake them as I scream in their face.

I'm saving your life. I'm the only thing standing between you and a psycho killer.

If they knew all I'm doing, all I'm sacrificing, they wouldn't treat me like this. They wouldn't shun me. They'd still love me. Idolize me. Maybe even think that I was a hero or something.

But they can't know.

They'll never know.

Instead I'm forced to play the role of the fading star here and the dutiful daughter at home. There isn't a single place where I can be myself anymore. The dual roles are exhausting. I'm not sure how much longer I can keep it up.

But as hellish as it is here at school, it's still better than my life at home. Mom's still playing her part as a Stepford Wife. I'm still sleeping on the cold, unforgiving cement. I hate every second of it. The dark, the cold floor, the tiny space, the knowledge that I'm locked in and can't get out . . . There is no getting used to that.

I've started dreaming of their faces—my mother's and friends'. My friends' families'. Even the faces of random people from town. Anyone and everyone I can think of, just to remind myself of why I can't give up. To remind myself of what I stand to lose if I give in.

And *he's* still behind it all. No matter if I'm home or at school, he's always there.

At lunch, my gaze roams the cafeteria. Every time I notice an empty seat, I have to calculate how hostile the other students at the table might be to me.

Then I see an open spot near Nick. I lock eyes with him.

He frowns but otherwise doesn't indicate that I can't come over.

Suddenly my view is blocked as someone steps in front of me. It's Blake.

"Can we talk?" he asks.

I glance around Blake. Now Nick is looking at his phone.

"Didn't you do enough of that last week?" I reply as I try to move by.

"Please," Blake says. He grabs my arm.

On reflex, my body panics. My tray falls to the floor, clattering over the hundreds of conversations.

I can feel everyone watching, staring. Waiting for another show like the one I gave them last week.

I break away and glare at Blake. "Don't ever touch me."

I turn and march out of the cafeteria. The moment I step into the hallway, confusion overtakes me. What just happened? Why did I react like that? Blake's never *hurt* me. Not once. But the second his hand touches me, every nerve flares up, waiting for the pain.

I take a deep breath. On the exhale, I realize this has nothing to do with Blake. There's only one reason—one person—to blame for this.

What has *he* done to me?

"Jessy!" Blake calls, chasing after me.

I cringe, wishing he would just go away. Better yet, maybe I'll just go away. I start heading down the hall, but he stops in front of me, blocking my path again.

"What just happened?" he asks. "Are you OK? I know this isn't from being sick or being pissed at me."

I cross my arms, trying to keep it together. "Am I *OK*?" I repeat. "How can I possibly be OK right now?"

"You're right. That was a stupid question."

His shoulders drop, and he frowns. He stares down, then his eyes widen. He grabs my right hand, gripping it tight enough that I can't pull away.

"Jesus, Jessy! What happened to your hands?"

My nails, like everything else about my old life, used to be perfect. I always had French manicures. Even on my toes. Now my broken fingernails are scabbed over and starting to regrow, but they still look awful. Tiny cuts from the broken glass mar my fingers.

I'm a wreck. And that's even without him seeing the bruises hidden underneath my clothes.

"What is going on with you?" he implores.

"Maybe if you weren't screwing my ex–best friend, you would know!"

In his shock, I'm able to yank my hand back. I cross my arms again, this time hiding my hands.

His expression hardens. His eyes are like ice. Then he punches a locker; the *clang* echoes through me.

I stagger back, expecting fury. But when he looks at me, his expression shows more remorse than anger.

"Dammit, Jessy! I was so pissed that you couldn't come to Aspen with us. I got super drunk one night and . . . things happened. It was a mistake. That's why I didn't call or message you—I felt so guilty. Cassie doesn't mean anything. It's just . . . I was drunk and lonely and—"

"I don't want to hear this," I interrupt.

I turn and nearly smack into Nick and his friend—Dan, I think. Have they been standing behind me the whole time? I huff and march past them too.

Even though there's still ten minutes left of lunch, I head to Spanish class, sit in my chair, and lay my head in my arms on my desk. As I hear someone sit beside me, I rise up, expecting it to be Blake. But instead, I find Nick.

"Are you OK, Jessy?"

My lips twist into a humorless smile. Here we are again. Last time he asked me this question, my whole world had just crumbled, thanks to Blake and Cassie. I could understand Nick's concern that day. Heck, most of the school pitied me then too.

But why is he still acting like he cares?

It's such a guy thing to want to rush in and *fix* what's wrong. I might literally be a damsel in distress who gets locked in a dungeon, but this is no fairy tale. This is a horror story. If he tries to "save" me, he'll wind up with a bullet in his head. Just like Dad. So I can't let anyone play the part of my hero. Especially Nick.

"Why do you even care if I'm OK or not?" I ask with more bite than I intend.

Surprise and maybe a little hurt flicker in his eyes before he turns away, muttering under his breath.

Crap.

"Look, Nick, I'm sorry. I just . . . I can't handle talking about it right now."

He nods in that way guys do. It's just a head tilt. As if that's somehow an acceptable form of communication.

I shouldn't care about giving him the brush-off. It's what I wanted—for him to just stop. Stop being there every time I look up. Stop asking questions. If anything, it'd be safer for him to stay as far away from my crazy life as possible.

Then again, I'm not sure I can stand to lose the one person left here who doesn't hate me. At least . . . doesn't hate me yet.

Switching tactics, I opt for a neutral topic. "Have any plans for the weekend?"

Even to my own ears, it sounds forced and lame.

Nick keys right in on that awkwardness and desperate attempt to keep the lines of communication going. He shifts his whole body toward me. Even though we're both sitting, he still manages to tower over me. He stares at me, searching for something. I worry those stormy eyes will see through me. That they'll see everything.

As if on reflex, my eyes flick to the cameras in the corners of the classroom. Nick's eyes aren't the only ones seeing everything.

When he finally turns away, I release my breath.

"I'm working," he finally answers.

"You work?"

My parents always told me that school is my job. I'll have my whole life to work, but right now, my grades and my extracurriculars are my only priorities. Scratch that. I no longer have extracurricular activities, so I guess it's just school. And staying alive.

"Someone has to pay the bills," Nick gripes.

"Bills? What bills?"

What teenager has their own bills? My parents pay for everything. Same for my friends' parents.

But then suddenly I remember that Nick's mom is dead and his dad's in jail. He's alone.

In a way, I'm alone too.

My dad was murdered. My mom is in some sort of altered reality, thinking she's the murderer's wife.

I know it's not exactly the same as Nick's situation. And he's been dealing with his hell for way longer than I've been dealing with mine. But out of everyone here, he's come the closest to understanding what I'm going through.

Not that I can ever tell him about it, though.

Nick snorts. "What? Didn't it ever dawn on you that the rest of the world doesn't have everything handed to them?"

I flinch.

"Sorry," he says, looking away. "That was rude."

"It's fine." I brush some hair behind my ear, taking a moment to compose myself. "So, you don't live with relatives or a foster family or something?"

He sighs, leaning his head on his bent arm. Those stormy eyes burrow deep into me.

"No relatives in town," he says. "Foster system is a joke. I lived with Dan and his family for a while. But I hated taking advantage of their generosity, so I emancipated this summer and got a place of my own."

"Wow," I respond.

I envision myself living entirely on my own, like Nick. Finding a place to live, paying rent, buying groceries, and doing a million other things I don't even understand because I've never had to.

Tears threaten to ruin my facade. My mom may not be protecting me from that monster at home, but she's still providing for me. She's still my mother.

She's still *alive*.

Nick and I refocus our attention as the teacher and other students trickle in. After listening to the teacher go over our assignment for the day, we get to work, quizzing each other on the vocabulary list.

The room is full of chatter, some in Spanish and some in English. Nick and I finish early. He flips ahead in the textbook, starting on tonight's homework. I find myself wanting to take advantage of the moment so I can learn more about Nick.

"So, what do you do for fun?" I whisper.

He stills, glaring at me from the corner of his eye.

For a moment, I fear he won't answer me. Maybe I'm

coming on too strong. Too pushy. I have talked to him more in the last half hour than I have in the four months we've been in school together.

But talking about him is so much easier than talking about me. And it almost feels normal—chatting with him like this. Learning about his life and plans.

I'm kind of envious of him. Not his situation per se, but that he can make his own choices. He doesn't have to run every decision through a parent, waiting and hoping they'd agree. Most importantly, he doesn't have to deal with an abuser, like the one I have controlling my life.

Nick surprises me by saying, "I play drums."

"Really? That's pretty cool."

I'm genuinely surprised. And intrigued. I'm learning so much. More than I ever knew about him. It's not that hard talking to him. I don't even have to fake that I'm enjoying it.

I didn't realize until now how much I miss normal human interactions. I even miss the trivial conversations that used to bore me to tears—like "Lovely weather we're having" or "Did you catch the game last night?"

Nick slams his book closed and barely spares me a parting glance. "Glad I have your approval."

The bell rings, and Nick is through the classroom door before the echo fades. And just like that, I'm alone again.

As the final hours of the day tick by, anxiety creeps ahold of me. Even though practically no one likes me here anymore, no one yells at me. No one locks me up. No one hits me.

But once I'm home, I will spend every minute walking on eggshells, constantly waiting and watching for any sign that I've upset or displeased *him*. I face this dread at the end of every school day, but it's especially hard to face it on Fridays. I have the entire weekend ahead of me.

What will he want to do? Watching television as a family after homework and dinner seems to be his go-to ritual. The three of us sit on the couch together, watching his favorite

shows. It all sounds so perfectly normal. But it's torture.
Pure hell.

He always has an arm around me, keeping me close. I'm
sure he does it because he can tell I hate it. It's especially
nauseating when he's eating chips, chomping away at them
like a damned cow.

I'd love to tune it all out and let my mind wander to some
happy place. But I'm expected to pay attention. To laugh or
gasp at the right moments in whatever we're watching.

I'm even expected to share in his outrage during football
games. Those are the worst—the games go on forever. I
enjoyed sports before. Now I hate them. So that's what I'm
sure Sunday will consist of. Back-to-back football games as
he yells at the referees. If he ever attended a game, he'd
probably end up shooting someone.

Nick and I reach our lockers at the same time. I pack my
things silently beside him.

With my anxiety in full force now, I don't have the
energy to start up another conversation and pretend like
everything is fine.

Nothing is.

"Yoo-hoo, Jess?" someone says.

I turn, and Nick and his friend are staring at me.

When did Dan get here?

I wince, clearing my head. They're still staring. They're
waiting for me to say something. Did they say something to
me?

Did *Dan* say something to me?

"Yoo-hoo," Dan repeats, confirming my guess. "Earth to
Jess."

Jess?

No one has ever called me Jess before. I'm not entirely
sure how I feel about it. But I do know that I don't hate it the
way I hate *him* saying my name in any way. And after a week
of being ridiculed and ignored by anyone I used to consider
a friend, it feels kind of good to have someone give me a

nickname.

"I'm sorry—what?" I ask, trying to focus.

"I said, 'What are you doing this weekend?'" Dan forms each word loudly and slowly. I think he's teasing me, but I'm not really sure.

"You did?" I balk. "Why?"

He smiles, amused. "Last time I checked, it was considered polite to inquire about someone's plans."

"Oh."

I sling my bag over my shoulder as I consider how to answer his question. It's funny, because it's the same question I asked Nick. And I feel as discombobulated by it as Nick felt when I asked.

I glance over at Nick, wondering if he notices it too. But as usual, he's now hanging back, assuming his stance as the silent observer, overhearing my conversation.

"I don't have any plans," I finally reply. I doubt Dan would find my itinerary of hanging out with a murderer and being locked up at night humorous.

"I don't believe that," Dan says. "You probably have galas to attend with champagne and caviar and tennis lessons with your private instructor."

I grimace. "Is that really what you think of me?"

He freezes. Even Nick stills.

"You know what," I begin, "it doesn't matter."

I push past them and head for the bus.

His words hurt, whether he meant them to or not. Either way, he spoke the truth. That *was* my life—minus tennis. And I think that's what bothers me the most. But now . . . after everything . . . it seems so shallow. So empty.

"Jess, wait," Dan calls behind me.

As much as I want to keep going, my body rebels. I stop, my back still to him.

"I'm sorry," he says, coming around to face me.

I instantly tense up, expecting him to reach out and grab me. But he doesn't. He doesn't even invade my space.

There's a safe yet comfortable distance between us.

"In my head, that didn't sound crass," he says sheepishly. "I was going for"—he waves his hand in the air as if trying to pull words from it—"charmingly sarcastic. Apparently, I failed miserably. Let's try it again."

He smiles again, and something relaxes inside me. He has a really nice smile. Genuine. And it makes his brown eyes warm like caramel.

"I'm going to the Grotto tonight to listen to the band Melophobia. Ever heard of them?" he asks.

"No. Are they any good?"

He scratches the back of his neck. "They're getting better. Anyway, I was wondering . . . if you aren't busy . . ." He trails off.

I don't know him. This is probably the first conversation we've ever had. I don't know how to read this.

Is he halfheartedly asking, just to be nice? Or does he seriously want to go out with me? If so, why? What about my current status could be so appealing?

But even with the doubt, my stomach flutters.

"So . . . would you like to go?" he finishes.

Spend Friday night out of the house? Away from *him*? Do something blissfully normal?

"Yes!" I say instantly.

My face lights up, and so does Dan's.

But then my excitement dies. Dan can tell.

If I were a normal teen, I could simply say yes to this cute boy asking me out on a Friday night. But nothing about my life is normal. If I want to go to the Grotto with Dan, I have to check with *him* first.

Just thinking about that is enough to send me into a spiral. In his twisted fatherly role, he claims I can ask him anything, but I doubt he was thinking of situations like this. He forced me to break up with Blake—what if this throws him into a rage?

Dan is still watching me intently, holding his breath and

trying to read my face. I have to say something.

"What I mean is—yes, I would like to go, but I don't think I can," I say, trying to avoid his eyes.

"Oh!" he says, failing to hide his surprise. "Shoot. Really? That's too bad."

Even without looking up, I can see him shuffling his feet and lifting his hand to rub his neck. His disappointment seems genuine, which only increases my guilt.

"Well," he says, "if you change your mind, the band starts at nine."

If only it were that simple . . .

I wait for him to wander away, but he doesn't. He's still here. Still lingering.

"If I don't see you," he says, "have a great weekend, Jess."

He's serious. He truly does want me to go. But he isn't pressing me to justify my decision, like Blake and my friends would. He accepts my refusal point-blank. Without the theatrics or guilt.

Is it a trick? Some kind of mental game to get me to bend to his will?

No.

No. Not everyone is like the monster I live with.

Dan is not.

I can't help it. I smile. A real, genuine smile. I lift my head and meet Dan's gaze, getting caught up by how bright his hazel eyes are when he smiles.

"I'll try to make it, Dan," I say.

And I mean it.

For the first time in a long time, I'm excited to go home. I know it's risky to tell *him* about Dan and ask permission to go out. I hate everything about it. But I have to try.

I remember that he keeps saying I'm supposed to be "happy." So maybe he'll let me go out tonight when he sees how happy this really does make me.

The bus ride seems to take forever. As soon as it drops

me off, I all but jog through the snow, up the driveway, to the house.

He's waiting on the porch, as usual. As he takes in my ear-to-ear grin, he arches his brows and smiles back.

"Well, you must have had a great day."

"I did," I say.

"Join me in the office, and we'll go over it." He places his hand on my shoulder and leads me inside.

As excited as I am to tell him about Dan, a lump forms in my throat. For a week now, this has been my least favorite part of the day. Every day after school, we go into the office and review the recordings from my day. Sometimes he asks questions, but mostly he lectures me on things I could improve. Like how I can do a better job of looking like a daughter who's happy to have her "father back."

"Your gym teacher called your mother today," he begins.

That lump feeling gets worse. I sit silently, knowing that's what he wants me to do.

"If you don't start participating, he's going to fail you."

I could tell him it's *his* fault I'm not participating, but that would just add more bruises to my collection.

"I'll try to do better on Monday," I say.

"Trying isn't good enough. You *will* do better. You *will* participate. Failing grades are unacceptable."

He points next to a screen that shows a frozen clip of Blake grabbing me. "What did the footballer do to you? Let me see your arm, Jessy."

"I'm fine," I say. "It's nothing."

"Let me see your arm," he repeats with intensity.

He holds out his hand, and I know he won't drop it until I show him. I pull up my sweater, revealing the faint markings of Blake's fingers.

In a flash, he's out of his chair, gun in hand. "I'm going to kill that boy!"

"No!" I shout.

I instantly regret it.

Furious, he glares at me, his breath coming in quick pants. I picture him as a bull, readying to charge at me.

"I'm sorry—I shouldn't have raised my voice like that," I say, dropping my head. "But please, don't hurt Blake. I'm fine. I swear. I don't even feel it."

His nostrils flare, but thankfully, he takes his seat.

I don't understand him. It's just a light mark from Blake's hand—most likely because my skin is already so bruised and fragile from what *he's* done to me.

He points now at another screen. "You were whispering with this boy when you should have been paying attention." Anger is still present in his clipped tone.

I glance at the monitors, seeing a shot of Nick and me during Spanish. My gaze drops to the gun, then flickers back to Nick. He was being nice. Showing me a moment of common decency. And because of it, his life is now in danger.

"You're close to failing gym, and now you're not paying attention in Spanish! It's only been a week, and already you're slipping into old habits, Jessica."

The use of my full name sets my spine ramrod straight.

"What was so 'important' that it trumped your studies?"

At first I assume it's a rhetorical question. But he keeps staring at me, waiting for an answer. Does he honestly want to know what Nick and I talked about? I scramble to think back.

"It was nothing. I just asked him his plans for the weekend and what he does for fun. I—"

"And what about this after school?" he asks before I can finish.

He points to an image of Dan and me outside. My stomach plummets.

"He followed you outside. Why? What did he want?"

Oh God. What have I done?

This horrible man just threatened to kill Blake, and now he's asking about Dan. I was so foolish to think this would work, that I could just simply ask *him* for permission go out with some boy from school that I barely know. Or that he would actually agree.

Because of me, Dan is now in a murderer's sights.

"What did he say to you?" he presses.

He plays the video, and all I can hear are muffled voices drowned out by the wind.

I open my mouth, but nothing comes out. I want nothing more than to lie. To say Dan and I were just talking about our weekend plans. But lying could have consequences. Deadly ones.

"Jessica." He taps Dan's chest on the monitor. "Who is that boy?"

My heart pounds against my ribs, wanting to leap out and run for cover. Me too, heart. Me too.

"Dan," I finally say. "I don't know his last name. He's a friend of Nick—"

"Your smile is more genuine around him."

My mouth drops open. I can't believe he noticed that. What does that mean? Does that make Dan a bigger target than even Blake? Just because I smiled at him?

He crosses his arms and leans back in his chair, examining me.

"You've been at school for over a week now, and this is the first day you've come home smiling like you used to. Only thing different is that boy. So I'll ask again, what were you talking about?"

There's something different in his tone. It's lost most of its edge. He seems . . . curious? Less hostile. I don't know what it is, but I feel like I can answer honestly without fearing for Dan's life.

"He invited me to go watch a band tonight at the Grotto."

He makes a face, but it's not a frown. "And what did you tell him?"

"That I couldn't go."

He turns back to the screens, tapping on the keyboards to

bring up more videos. It's a highlight reel staring me, Nick, and Dan.

"School is for learning, not flirting with boys," he says in that fatherly tone. "They're a distraction. It's why I had you break up with that footballer."

"I know." The words are barely a whisper, but I know he hears them.

He's not letting me go. I feel my shoulders slump. With sadness but also with relief. Maybe it's better this way . . .

He watches me, then lets out a sigh. "I'm not an unreasonable man, Jessy. Going out with friends—with boys—is something we can work toward. I'm just not sure you're ready—"

"I am!" I can't help but interject. "I mean, please. Please let me go. Even just for a little bit."

Two seconds ago, I didn't think there was a chance in hell. But now that there is, I want it. I want it so badly.

"It could be another way for me to earn more of your trust," I continue. "Please. Please, Dad," I add knowingly.

He stares at me for so long that I'm certain he'll say no.

"Fine," he says.

I'm so stunned that my body and emotions are frozen, waiting for him to say "Just kidding."

"I'll allow you to go," he begins, "but know I'll be watching." He points to the screens. "And I expect to see an improvement in your attitude at school and at home from now on. No more moping or self-pity. You should be happy. You're a wonderful girl, Jessy. The world needs more smiles like yours."

He stands and hastily leaves the room.

It takes several minutes for the shock to dissolve, then I rush upstairs to get ready.

TEN

H E LETS ME DRIVE MY CAR.
The instant I sit in the driver's seat, I feel a rush of
peace and freedom I've never felt before. That
feeling keeps flowing through me as I start driving, getting
farther and farther away from home. From *him*.

But even as that wonderful feeling flows through me, I
know it's superficial.

He has cameras, mics, and trackers everywhere. He also
made a point to tell me there will be consequences if I don't
make it home by my 11:00 curfew. The way he said it led
me to believe he was referring to more than another night in
the box . . .

Mom is currently keeping it warm for me. You'd think
spending the evening in there after every day this week
would finally crack her, but it doesn't.

It's not resiliency, though. It's not some reserve of
strength. No.

I'm beginning to realize that when you're broken—truly,
deeply broken—you get to a point where the horrors stop
affecting you. That's where Mom is now. She just accepts it.
Accepts that this is our life.

I can't.

I won't.

It's why I have to get out tonight. Even at the cost of her standing in that box.

I'm not free. This isn't freedom. I'm like a pet bird that's been allowed to go outside—though still in its cage. I can see, smell, and touch freedom, but I can't have it.

I never will.

To be honest, I'm surprised he agreed to this—letting me go to some club I've never been to on the other side of town, to listen to some band I've never heard of, and to hang out with some guy I essentially just met.

Considering that he forced me to destroy my old relationships, I don't know why he's allowing me to build new ones. It can't just be because of a smile, right? Perhaps giving me permission to go out tonight fits into his twisted delusion that we're a normal family, living a normal life.

Underneath it all, though, I have to admit that this is as close to freedom as I've experienced since that horrible man came into my life. At least I get to escape him for a few hours, and not just to attend school. So I'll take this chance for what it's worth.

My phone says my destination is up ahead. I slowly release my breath as I park along the side street close to the club.

The Grotto is three blocks from the river that separates the two sides of town. On the other side of the river, stores and businesses are tucked into quaint little brick buildings all connected together. But here, things are more industrial— a few shops and warehouses. Some places are closed for the night, while others sustained too much damage from the tornado and have closed permanently.

Other than about a dozen parked cars, the street is empty. It's only a half block to the Grotto, but out in the wind and snow, the walk seems longer. It doesn't help that several of the streetlights aren't working. I'm half tempted to return to my car, lock the doors, then drive home. But who knows when or if I will ever get another opportunity like this again? The bitter wind picks up, and instantly, I'm freezing. I hold my jacket tighter around me, but it doesn't do much.

It took a while to figure out what to wear—it's been so long since I've gone out on a Friday night. Thankfully, the bruises are gone, so I didn't have to worry about maximum coverage. Wanting to appear casual, I opted for a gray cable-knit sweater with skinny jeans. Even though it's a club the old me never would have been caught dead in, I wanted to get all dolled up tonight. I missed it.

I miss me.

Doing my hair and makeup and getting all dressed up . . . it felt good. For a few brief moments, I almost forgot what my life is like now. I feel normal.

Maybe I'm the delusional one now.

The band is already playing when I come in. The singer is screaming something incomprehensible as the band rocks out behind him. Even though the place is small and doesn't have a true dance floor, a crowd of people are out there, mashed together and jamming along.

But I don't care. I'm not really here for the music.

I walk through the crowd, keeping an eye out for Dan. Instead of the friendly welcomes I used to get whenever I went to a hangout, I get a mix of disbelief and hostile glares. It's as if everyone here knows who I am and wants me to know that I don't belong.

Maybe they're right.

I don't fit in anywhere anymore.

"Hey, Jess!" someone says, pulling me out of my head.

I turn and find Dan staring at me from over near the pool tables.

What was I thinking?

School is getting easier—everyone ignores me now. But here . . . he invited me. That means he'll want to talk to me. Get to know me.

I should go. I should definitely leave.

But then I see a camera near the ceiling.

Plastering on that fake smile I've gotten so used to, I walk over to him, my skin prickling the whole time with a new awareness.

"You actually came," he says, leaning against the pool table.

I take my coat off and set it on a nearby chair, catching him checking me out from the corner of my eye. I straighten, and it takes him a moment to lift his gaze.

"I said I would try," I remind him, trying to keep things light so he can't tell how close I am to freaking out. "Did you think I wouldn't?"

"Honestly . . ."

He pauses midsentence. With each millisecond of the pause, my heart begins to race.

"Honestly," he continues, "I had no idea. I don't know you well enough yet to say what you'll do."

Yet.

He said *yet*.

"I'd like to, though—get to know you more, that is," he adds.

Does that mean he wants to hang out again beyond just tonight? My lips shift as my smile becomes real. Who would have thought that I—Jessica Smith—would be so dang happy over possibly making a new friend.

The old me had countless friends. I'm not proud to admit it, but most of those friendships were shallow. Convenient. I'm starting to wonder if any of my relationships had depth. Even with Blake and Cassie. Because if those relationships were real and genuine, then Blake and Cassie never would have done what they did to me.

"You wanna play?" he asks, holding out a pool cue for me.

"Sure." As a joke, I ask, "What are the stakes?"

He cocks his head, thinking for a moment. "Well, how about this: whenever someone knocks a ball in, they get to ask a question. We have to answer truthfully—and no passing."

My fingers tighten around the cue. Suddenly the room is like a sauna. I can't do this. There are so many questions I can't answer.

"I know," he says in my silence. His eyes shine with mirth. "Pretty steep stakes, right? But you and I know very little about each other, so maybe this will change that."

I couldn't release my grip on the cue even if I wanted to. Waves of anxiety wash over me. Once again, I want to run straight back to my car.

But then what? Head home? To a murderer posing as my father and holding us hostage? He said there would be consequences for breaking curfew. What if there are consequences for ditching out on this opportunity to be "happy" and "normal"?

More importantly, shouldn't I actually want to be here? I don't know if I can let my guard down enough to be "happy," but I can try to seize this rare chance to interact with someone who isn't psychotic.

So maybe there's a way to make this work. I've been figuring out how to avoid the "truth" for a week now at school. This won't be too different.

"Deal," I say. "But I break first."

He grins and bows. "Of course. Ladies first."

I take my time lining up my shot, and it pays off as I sink two solids.

Dan whistles. "I think I've been hustled."

I can't help but let a little smile escape. "OK, first question: Why did you ask me to come here tonight?"

He shrugs. "Figured you could use a fun night."

Now *that* is the truth.

I nod toward the band. "Second question: Is this your favorite type of music?"

He tries not to grimace. "No. I mean, they're good. But I'm more of a classic-rock guy."

LAURIE WETZEL ‡ PICTURE PERFECT

I move around the table for my next shot. I notice that as I move, Dan does too. Not in an awkward way, though. He's just comfortably, naturally keeping at least a foot between us the whole time. It makes me think he's noticed all those times I've reacted whenever someone has touched me or gotten too close.

It suddenly dawns on me that Dan doesn't make me feel nervous. I do still feel nervous, yes. But it's not *because* of him. The anxiety that's threatened to overtake me all night— all week, for that matter—has one source: that murderer in my home. Identifying that key aspect helps. It doesn't make things better. But it does help.

I sink one into the far corner pocket. That's three.

"So why are we here if you don't really like them?" I ask.

"You don't know?" He smiles in that way someone does when they know an inside joke but you don't.

I frown, waiting for my anxiety to spike like it does at home. It doesn't.

He points to the stage. "Nick's the drummer."

I whip around. Sure enough, there he is behind the drum set, banging away. How did I not see him the first time? The bright stage lights practically form a beacon on him.

I'm shocked. I guess he did tell me he played drums, but I had no idea he meant like this.

He's in his element. Totally focused and totally loving it.

I can feel Dan watching me watch Nick. He seems amused. With a little laugh, I resume our game and take my next shot. This time, I scratch. Damn.

Dan retrieves the cue ball. "For a minute there," he says, "I was worried you were going to clear the table and I wouldn't get to learn a single thing about you. Of course, if that had happened, I would have switched to darts. You can't be perfect at *everything*."

As he takes his shot, I pray the ball won't go in.

It does.

"All right, then," he says, rubbing his chin as if in deep

thought about what to ask. "Who taught you to play pool?"

I let out a relieved breath. This question is OK. Until I realize it isn't.

"My d-dad."

It's the truth. And it's the first time I've talked about him to anyone since . . . well . . .

The memory of him teaching me plays out in my mind. I was four. Mom had bought him a pool table for his birthday—the same one that's still in the basement, beside the prison I now sleep in most nights.

Dad loved pool.

I miss him. *So much.*

"Well, he must have been a great teacher," Dan says, lining up his next shot.

"He was," I agree.

The memories of my father get shoved aside as I hear the familiar sound of a ball sinking into a pocket. Here comes another question.

I'm suddenly terrified. I'm trying to hold back the intense sadness about Dad, but what if Dan can see right through me? What if he asks something else about Dad? Does he know Dad used to be the governor? Everyone knows that, don't they? What if he asks what Dad is doing now? What if—

"What do you want to drink?"

"What?"

"That's my next question," Dan says, laughing. "I'm thirsty, and I thought I'd get you a soda too. What would you like?"

"Ginger ale."

He smiles. "Coming right up."

He heads to the bar, and I feel the knots inside me loosen. Dan could be asking me about anything—why I quit cheerleading, why I broke up with Blake, how I act like a spaz every time someone touches me. But he hasn't. Maybe because he can tell I'm nervous? Or maybe he's just

144

naturally this easygoing?

I suddenly notice the music has stopped. I turn to look over at the stage. It's empty. The band must be on a break.

When I turn back around, I smack into Nick.

I back away.

He stands there, staring at me with mild annoyance. "Having fun?"

"Yes." And for the most part, it's the truth.

I clear my throat as he continues to stare.

"You're really good, by the way," I say, pointing to the stage, where his drum set sits. "Incredible, actually."

"If you say so." He rolls his eyes, then very deliberately moves his stare out into the crowd.

I frown, taking the hint. He doesn't want me here. Why? I know our conversation in Spanish class wasn't the greatest this afternoon. But it wasn't *that* bad, was it?

I decide to go straight at it. "Have I done something to upset you, Nick?"

He huffs and turns to face me. "Why are you here, Jessy?"

"Dan invited—"

"No," he interrupts. "Why are you *really* here? This isn't exactly your crowd or even your part of town. Since you've been back from winter break, you've been an entirely different person."

I suck in a breath, stunned. His words attack like daggers. But he's right. I am an entirely different person. And the fact that he's picked up on it is something I need to shut down right now. For his sake, for Dan's, and for mine.

"You don't know a thing about me, Nick," I finally say. It's not a lie.

Nick rears his head back and laughs. It's loud and obnoxious. I grind my teeth as I wait for him to finish. His stormy eyes are vibrant as they stare down at me once more.

"Then please—tell me more about you, Jessy." The words are covered in sarcasm. "What specifically brought you out here? Was it this club, where you've never set foot in before? My band, which you've never heard of? Or was it my best friend, who you didn't know existed until today?"

He's mere inches from me now.

"I'm sure you had dozens of other offers from guys just dying to take Blake's place. Why *Dan*? He isn't like those other guys."

My insides tighten and nerves flutter at his closeness. Still, I won't let him get to me. I won't let him ruin this.

"You answered your own question. Because Dan *isn't* like them. He didn't invite me here as a date. We're just hanging out. Getting to know each other. He's nice and kind. And I have to say, I'm actually having a really good—"

"You're 'actually' having a really good time? You say that like you're surprised."

"What? No. I didn't mean—"

"Dan is my best friend, Jessy," Nick interrupts again. "And I won't let you hurt him. So why don't you do everyone a favor and leave."

With that, he marches off in the other direction.

"Hold on!" I snap, following him and blocking his way.

My boldness shocks the heck out of me. I'd never ever consider doing something like this at home. Yet even as I realize this, nothing in my body is screaming out to stand down and back away.

I'm not afraid of Nick.

The realization is both liberating and humiliating. It's liberating to know I can stand up for myself around both Dan and Nick without fear of retaliation. But it's humiliating to admit that my life has fallen so much that I'm celebrating the fact that I feel safe—something that I and everyone should inherently always feel.

Not ready to give up my newfound spark of courage, I continue with my tirade. "You don't get to tell me what to do. And as far as Dan goes, he invited me. He wants to get to know me. So like it or not, I'm not leaving!"

He laughs again, shaking his head. "Dan asked you to come because he pitied you."

I balk.

"Dan and I watched you all week as your so-called friends and that dumbass boyfriend of yours ditched you. And yeah, that sucked. But maybe you needed to tumble off your pedestal. And for some reason, Dan—being the class act he is—wanted to step in and save the day, even though I told him not to."

That meager shred of bravery I'd found burns to ashes in the wake of his revelations.

No one has ever pitied me before.

Is it true? Is this whole night because Dan felt *sorry* for me?

"So that's it," Nick continues, his voice loud now. "Dan doesn't *like* you. Whatever you think this is between you two—it isn't going to happen. So once again, why don't you do us all a favor and take yourself back to your castle in the country."

"What the hell, Nick?" Dan barks, suddenly standing behind me.

The moment he sees Dan, guilt flashes in Nick's eyes.

"Whatever," Nick mutters.

As he stalks off, I just stand there, unmoving, barely blinking.

"Jess," Dan says, coming around to face me, "what he said . . . it isn't—"

"Save it," I rasp. "I don't need your pity."

I grab my coat and run out as he calls after me. I keep running all the way to the car.

Nick's words play on a loop, haunting me with each dark road I pass as I drive.

I should have seen it. I should have known.

I'm a laughingstock.

Is it just Nick and Dan? Our classmates? Or the whole school?

It's just too much. The shame. The humiliation. Every word Nick said echoes in my mind like a worn-out recording. My vision blurs as I lose my grip on my emotions.

As I'm wiping away tears, the car suddenly hits a patch of ice. Without thinking, I lock the brakes, and the car whips around like a carnival ride.

I scream.

Flashbacks of the accident on that fateful night flare.

When it's finally over, the car is in the middle of the bridge, facing the guardrail.

My body trembles. I can't even drive a car right.

Then I notice the cameras all around me in the car.

He saw it all. He saw me crying. He saw me spin out. He's going to be so upset. He said I wasn't ready to go out tonight. But I practically begged him. And look what happened. He put his faith and trust in me, and I let him down.

Banishing me to the box won't be good enough.

He'll punish me. Worse than he's ever done before. And it will be my fault.

No.

No, wait.

It's *his* fault—not mine. None of this would have happened if he weren't here ruining everything.

I can't breathe.

I get out of the car, gasping for air in the middle of the snowy, lonely street. After several moments, my breathing steadies. But I don't want to get back in the car. I can't. I won't. I don't want to be where he can see me. I don't want to be anywhere near him.

But his cameras aren't just in the car. He's shown me the city ones. Somehow he has access to them. My attention zaps to the streetlamps. Sure enough, I spot the little black camera near the light.

As I stare up at the camera, something cold and wet lands on my cheek.

Snow.

The snowflakes scatter around me, falling on me, the car, the bridge, the guardrails. The flakes fall wherever they want. No one tells them where to go or what to do. And they certainly don't get punished for things they can't control.

I move to the guardrail as I watch them, transfixed. Looking out over the railing, I see thousands more fall onto the frozen river. It's breathtakingly beautiful.

The snowflakes fall into darkness—but it's different than the darkness in the box. It isn't oppressive. There's no pain. No walls or locks. No fear. No one pitying them. Here, the snowflakes are free.

I glance back at the car. It's too close. He's too close. I glance down the road, seeing more lampposts, wondering if he has access to those cameras too. If I move closer to them, he'd see me. And if I go back in the car, he'll see me there too. Even if I stay right here, he'll see. He's everywhere.

Everywhere *but* the darkness.

The darkness is his blind spot. My mittens grip the guardrail as I climb over it. The ledge on the other side is small and icy. There's only enough room for my feet to fit sideways. It doesn't matter, though. Not right now.

In this moment, the only thing that matters is that for once, he can't see me. I could cry. Shout. Even flip him off. And he would never know.

I never want this moment to end. But it will. Eventually, I'll have to go back to him. If I don't, he'll come. He'll always find me.

In a daze, I watch the snowflakes fall. I wish I could join them in the darkness. All I'd have to do is step off the ledge . . . and I'd fall.

One step, and I'd be free.

Free of the pressure.

The fear.

The grief.

Would anyone care? Would anyone even know? Would

they believe I was off somewhere in another country, like Dad, while my body just disappeared?

Like Dad's did.

I dip my foot off the ledge, testing to see what it's like.

My heart beats faster. Excited more than scared. It's a rush.

I do it again just to see if it feels the same way. This time it's *exhilarating*.

I bite my lips, holding back a smile.

Can I do this?

Can I just let go?

Suddenly, bright lights shine around me. A car speeds onto the bridge, then screams to a stop with the headlights fixed on me. Red and blue flashing lights illuminate the snow.

It takes me a moment to realize it's a cop.

ELEVEN

I STIFFEN, NOT WANTING TO TURN AROUND.
"Miss, stay where you are!" the male officer calls
out. His voice is urgent, though he's trying to remain
calm. "Don't move. Let's talk."

I glance back, and he's slowly moving toward me. Our
eyes connect, and he stops.

"You're Bob Smith's daughter," he says. "Jessica, isn't
it?"

I gulp. He knows me.

This is bad. This is really bad.

"Whatever happened, Jessica, we can fix it." His brown
eyes are brimming with concern. "Nothing is worth ending
your life."

"No! You can't fix it!" I shout. "It will never get better.
Only worse."

I turn back to the river, watching more snowflakes
disappear.

He's quiet for a moment, then he speaks. "My first night
on the force, we got a call—a multivehicle accident on the
highway. I responded. It was horrific. Cars were mangled. I
helped pull survivors out of the vehicles and load them into
ambulances. They were mostly teens. All coming back from

a football game."

I close my eyes and suck in my breath. He was there. He was at my accident.

"I went to the hospital too. So many parents were terrified, not knowing where their kids were or what had happened to them. One poor family was told that their sixteen-year-old daughter was dead. I will never forget the sound of their grief."

He pauses until I turn and look at him.

"Jessica, they were your parents," he says. "They thought you were dead."

My lips tremble as a tear falls.

"And when your parents found out you were actually alive, it was like a miracle. It was a tragedy for the other Jessica Smith, yes. But a miracle for you and your family."

He takes a step closer to me.

"You were given a gift that night. The gift of life. So please—please don't throw it away."

He's right. He's so right. I should have died that night. But I didn't. I lived.

I'm not going to let that psychopath take that away from me.

I look back over my shoulder at the cop. He's two feet from me now. Steel determination comes over me as I meet his gaze, preparing to do what I've dreamed of doing countless times since this whole nightmare began.

I'm going to save myself.

I've never felt so strong yet so weak at the same time.

"I don't want to jump . . . but I can't go home. He'll kill me," I add, barely above a whisper.

His concerned face twists, and his eyes darken. "Who will, Jessica? Your father? I thought he was in Africa."

I quickly look away. Oh God. No. What am I doing? I shouldn't have said that. I can't do this.

"Whatever's happened," he says, "I promise I'll help you. I'll protect you."

It isn't true. He can't help me. But I want to believe that he could. I'm so tired of fighting this alone.

"*I can help you,*" he repeats.

There's something in his voice. Sincerity. Determination. Whatever it is, it's pushing past my doubt and fears.

I lock eyes with him, daring to believe him.

"There's a man," I whisper. "He has my mom. And me."

He straightens, not expecting that. "Has he hurt you? What's he doing? Has he contacted your father?"

A sob racks through me. "D-Dad's not in Cameroon. H-he's . . ."

"Shit," he mumbles, eyes wide. "I'm so sorry, Jessica. I really am. I promise you—I will help you. I will get justice for your dad and get you and your mom to safety." He stops and holds out his hand for me. "But first, I need you to step back over the rail. Let me get you into my squad, get you warmed up. And then you can tell me everything while we wait for backup."

All the fear, pain, and anguish slides down my body and into the slumbering river below. Everything I've carried since that man destroyed my life. It's gone.

It's finally over. My nightmare is over.

I smile as I reach out to grab him.

Right before we touch, a loud bang erupts. Something splatters on my face. Numbly, I watch as he falls to his knees, then crumples onto the ground, blood running from a hole in his head.

Standing to his right is my father's killer, holding a gun.

Oh God. He shot the officer. *Killed* him. We were just talking, and now he's dead.

The murderer is wearing a pair of Dad's pajamas and slippers. His coat is unzipped. Everything about him is haphazard. It's how someone looks when they suddenly bolt out of the house and rush out at night.

But how? When? With how far away we live, it had to

have been when I spun out. He must have been watching the camera feed, and he came running the moment he saw me lose control.

But what else did he see? What did he hear?

He steps toward me.

I instinctively take a step back but find only air behind me. I jolt and reach out for the railing, stopping myself from falling off the ledge.

"Don't come any closer," I scream at him. "Don't—or I'll let go!"

I will. I don't want to, but it's better than going back with him. I was so close to this finally being over . . .

Instantly, he stops. His eyes are wide, fearful, pleading. He tucks the gun behind his waist, then stretches his hands out, ready to reach for me.

He's acting as if he cares—but how can he? How can he stand there and act like my life has value when, just moments before, he so effortlessly ended someone else's?

"It's OK, Jessy," he says. He's trying to sound calm, but there's a tremor in his voice. "I'm not mad about the car. The roads are bad. Just like the night of the accident."

This takes me so aback that I nearly lose my grip on the railing.

From the moment this man kicked in our front door, my mind has never stopped trying to put the puzzle pieces together: Why me? Why him? Who is he?

It's clear that he's been following me for a while. Weeks. A few months.

But this . . . He knows about the accident too. How many *years* has he been following me?

"H-how do you know about that night?" I ask.

He grimaces. "That was the worst night of my life, thinking I'd lost you. I prayed to God that he wouldn't take you away from me. I told him that if he saved you, I wouldn't touch another drop of alcohol ever again. I used to be a drunk, Jessy. I admit it was bad. Alcohol almost stole you from me. In more ways than one. But then you survived. God heard my prayers. So while you got better, I got better too. Getting sober was hard—hardest thing I've ever done. Whenever I thought of giving up, though, I'd think of you and how easily I could've killed you on those nights I drove drunk." He pauses, his eyes full of regret and desperation. "Please, Jessy—after everything we've been through. Don't make it have been for nothing."

I feel stabbing pain in my temples as my mind struggles with what he just said. I don't understand a word of it. But it's too strange to not be true.

Who is he?

What *am* I to him?

I look away. Down at the dark, icy waters.

"Jessica—look at me, baby."

I don't. "Why did you kill him?" My eyes wander to the cop lying next to him.

"You know why."

The sudden glacial tone of his voice has my gaze snapping up to him. In his eyes is a look I've become all too familiar with. I've upset him. Disappointed him.

Something inside of me collapses. It's true, then. He saw everything, heard everything. He knows I told the officer the truth. And because of it, that innocent man is dead.

"I will never let anyone keep us apart ever again, Jessica," the murderer says. "I've told you that. And now I've shown you." He nods to the dead body. "If anyone else tries, they'll end up the same way."

How can he stand here, discussing murder so calmly?

With pleading eyes and a shaking lip, I beg this heartless monster for an ounce of compassion. "Please just leave me alone. Please just go."

"Never." He rubs his forehead in frustration. "Look. I know what happened tonight. But it's not your fault. It's Dan's. He let you down. He let us both down. I thought letting you go with him tonight would make you happy.

155

Clearly he's not the boy he once was."

The stabbing in my temples intensifies. *The boy he once was?* But before I can even respond to the confusion, he speaks.

"No boy is worth ending your life."

"No!" I shout. "*No!*" I can't stop myself. "It's not because of Dan! It's because of *you*! Don't you get it? It's because of you!"

He ignores every word. "Don't do this, Jessy. Come over onto this side of the railing. Come where it's *safe*."

It isn't safe over there. Not with him.

He steps toward me, stepping into the blood of the officer.

I don't want him near me. I move over. But my foot hits an icy patch, and it slips off the edge.

Bringing me down with it.

"*Jessy!*" he screams.

He catches my wrist through the bars of the railing, stopping my fall.

I sway fifteen feet above the frozen water. My left shoe dangles from the tip of my toe. I tilt my foot down, letting the shoe drop.

It falls with the snow. The darkness swallows it. It doesn't even make a sound when it hits the snow-covered river.

With one hand holding me, he reaches the other through the bars. "Give me your other hand, Jessy."

I pull my gaze away from the darkness below—away from freedom—and stare at him. My shoulder aches. I want to let go. I want to be free.

I look back at the frozen river. The water will be cold. I'll fight to get out of the ice, even though I was the one who let myself fall. I've heard finding the surface again is the hardest part.

It's not a peaceful death. I won't be like one of those blissful snowflakes, gently falling. It will be pure terror.

I live in terror—why would I want to die in it too? I guess I can't escape it.

I take a breath. When I look at the darkness this time, it doesn't seem inviting. It's cold, dark, and lonely. Just like the box.

I don't want to live with that murderer in my life. But I don't want to die.

I've got to get back up.

"Please," he begs. "I can't lose you again."

Incredibly, he's not lying. He's terrified too. You can't fake the desperation in his eyes.

I suddenly realize I can use that to my advantage. I may be dangling with nothing more than his grip keeping me from certain death—but I have the upper hand.

"I won't go back in the box," I declare.

"What?" He frowns, confused. "Is that what this is really about—the box?"

I glare at him, then deliberately look back down toward the river.

His other hand wraps around my wrist, holding tightly to my jacket.

"Jessy, look at me!"

The urgency in his voice instantly makes me comply.

"All right, all right," he says. "I only wanted what's best for you, and in my drive to do that, I pushed you too hard. So give me your hand, OK? We'll go home. Your mother is waiting for you. She knows you had an accident tonight. She's so worried about you."

Mom.

If I died, she'd be all alone. He could do whatever he wanted to her then. She wouldn't be safe. Now I have another reason to live.

"We'll have a fun weekend," he continues. "We can watch movies and order pizza and stay up late. You can sleep in your room. Not the box—all right? There will be no talk of school or Dan. You can just relax. You deserve a break."

Yes, I do. That does sound nice.

I'm ready now. I reach up with my free hand, and he grabs my wrist. Quicker than I thought possible, he pulls me to the other side of the railing. Before my feet have a chance to touch the ground, I'm in his arms. I don't want to be here, but his grip is so tight that I have no choice.

"Thank God," he whispers into my hair. "I thought I lost you. Don't ever scare me like that again."

He means it. He was honestly scared I was going to die. I still don't understand why. But it's becoming glaringly obvious that I'm important to him. Enough for him to have spent years watching over me. If I can figure out why, then maybe I can finally make some sense of all this.

He smiles and sets me on my feet. The cold snow burns my bare foot.

I glance down and see the slain officer. Red clashes against the peaceful snow as blood continues to pour out of him.

Seeing it up close like this . . . I cover my mouth to stifle my gasp.

"Shh," his killer whispers. "It's OK, Jessy. Everything's going to be OK."

A moment later, something stabs me in the neck. I stagger back, and he's holding an empty syringe.

"What did you do?"

The words come out of my mouth, yet they feel distant. My vision blurs. My eyelids become heavy. The ground tilts, coming closer.

Right before I hit, he scoops me up.

"It's OK. Daddy's got you."

TWELVE

FINGERS RUN THROUGH MY HAIR, PULLING me from the void.

On reflex, I turn away.

I open my eyes, but the space around me is dark. After a second, I realize I'm lying on a bed.

Where am I? What's happening to me?

"It's all right, sweetie," a voice says. A familiar voice. Mom's voice.

"You're safe now," she says, continuing to stroke my hair.

Tears run, unabashed, down my cheeks. Mom's here. She's OK.

I shift closer to her, her fingers now soothing.

"Is she awake?" a man's voice asks from somewhere behind me.

It's him.

"Yes," Mom replies.

Lights flicker on, and I clamp my eyes shut from the sudden brightness. I blink repeatedly as I try to adjust. Once my vision clears, I realize I'm in my room, lying on my bed. I'm on my side, facing away from the bathroom.

Why? What happened? I try to think back, but there's a

thick fog in my mind.

The bed dips behind me as he sits down.

All at once, images flood my mind: The Grotto. Dan's pity. The car. The bridge. The cop.

Oh God—the cop. *He* killed a cop.

And then . . . what . . . ?

I clamp my eyes shut, trying to concentrate. But my mind is so foggy.

He leans over me, staring at me with concern. My lips quiver.

"You really scared us last night, kiddo," he says.

It takes me a moment to figure out what he means.

I thought about killing myself.

Some of the fog clears. I came close to jumping, to ending it all. Doing the only thing I could think of to finally escape him. But I didn't. I climbed back up from the ledge, with his help. And then . . . something in my neck. It all went black . . .

He *drugged* me.

Mom caresses my hair again, but this time, she seems unsure. As if I'm too delicate to even touch. "I heard what happened last night—what you almost did. Why would you do that, honey?" Mom asks. "Please, help us understand."

"We love you so much," he adds. He places a hand on my cheek, tenderly stroking it.

It takes everything in my power to not recoil.

"Where is the cop?" I ask. "*What did you do?*"

He sighs, not liking my question. But I don't care.

"I did what I had to do to protect our family," he says, his tone firm. "I will always protect our family. Now promise me you will *never* do something like that again."

Never do what again? Not try to kill myself? Or not tell someone about him—someone he will then murder?

It doesn't matter. I won't do either of those things ever again. That cop is dead because of me.

So I nod.

"Words, Jessy," he says. "I need to hear you say you will never do that again."

"I promise I won't do that ever again." It's no lie.

He nods, satisfied. "So, why don't you relax in a bath while we make breakfast," he says. "Afterwards, if you're up for it, your mother would like to spend the day with you—take you shopping and have some mother-daughter time. Would you like that? Like we talked about last night, right?"

I remember that now. I made him promise last night that things would change. No more sleeping in the box. I refused to climb up from the ledge—literally and figuratively—until he agreed. *You deserve a break*, he said.

"Yes." I nod again. "I remember."

Mom places a kiss in my hair. "I'm glad you're safe, honey." She stands, waiting beside the bed.

He leans over me again, and I stiffen. He places a kiss in my hair too. "We're both glad. Love you, Jessy."

Then he stands, puts his arm around Mom, and walks out of my room.

I lie here in bed for a few minutes. My mind is swimming.

I thought I understood him. He's a monster. A murderer. Cold. Cruel. I knew what to expect.

But now . . . I'm clueless. It's like it's the first day all over again.

I know he's still a monster. He murdered that cop last night, just as he murdered my own father. That part hasn't changed.

Yet there's this other side to him that is so different. I saw it last night. I saw it here, now. When I'm honest with myself, I know I've seen flashes and moments of it since he's overtaken our life.

He has a caring—maybe even loving—side. Like a father.

I of course don't feel that way for him. I *never* will. But that's not the point.

161

LAURIE WETZEL ‡ PICTURE PERFECT

The point is, he feels that way for me. As twisted as it is, he loves me and cares for me as a father cares for his daughter. It isn't an act for him. It's real. It's second nature. After all, hasn't this idea been circling in my head from the very beginning? In between the abusive, cruel moments, I've seen the fatherly moments and wondered how in the world a monster like him could act that way.

But it's clear now. I know it.

He *is* a father. Specifically, he's the father of a daughter.

At one time, I considered whether he actually *is* my biological father, from some old tryst with Mom. But it doesn't add up. Simply getting a woman pregnant doesn't make a man a "father."

No, he's been a father in the fullest sense of the word. He's raised a daughter. He's cared for her. Loved her. Protected her.

He's had a wife too. Maybe other kids. He's had a family of his own.

So where are they? Are they alive? Or did he kill them too?

And the even bigger mystery still remains: Why me? If he has a family, if he is a father, then why is he here now? Why me? Why is he "loving" me like a real father loves his daughter—yet murdering people and abusing me?

My head hurts.

I don't want to get up—and I'm not entirely sure I can get up. But I have to. I have to get ready for my day with Mom. It does sound nice, I have to admit. And maybe getting out of the house will do her some good too. Show her that there's still some good in our life. It gives me the push I need to get up and head to the bathroom.

I draw myself a bath, then step in. The warm water begins to melt away some of my tension and relieves some of the lingering aches and pains.

But not all of it.

I keep thinking of the cop. Who was he? Did he have a

family? A wife? A daughter? A son? It's the second person I've seen die in this way. A gunshot exploding. Blood splattering. A face contorting in horror.

Both times, the brutal act of murder didn't faze the man who had forced his way into my life, my home, my family. Where did he come from? Who *is* he?

These thoughts circle on a never-ending loop.

After the bath, I do my hair and makeup. My reflection is even more of a stranger now. The girl on the other side of the glass is haunted. Her hair is limp and dull. Her skin has sunken in. Her light-blue eyes are dead.

No wonder Nick and Dan pity me. I'm a wreck. They can see it from miles away. Everyone can.

And now fresh bruises cover my wrists from where he gripped me last night. He was holding on so tight—I thought for sure my shoulder would pop out again.

I don't understand why I mean so much to him. Why does my life matter when no one else's does?

And what in the world did he mean when he said he changed his life and got sober after I nearly died in the accident two years ago? He said alcohol nearly stole me from him, in more ways than one . . .

‡

They've made my favorite breakfast: French toast. It's surprisingly good.

He and Mom talk animatedly about their plans for the day. The way they're acting, it's as if we were a perfectly normal family. He goes on and on about the errands he'll run while Mom and I shop and pamper ourselves.

He's letting us go alone . . . ?

After breakfast, we all get ready to leave. As we're about to head for the door, he stops to hug me and kiss me on the top of my head.

"Have a great time, Jessy."

Unsure of what to say or do, I fall back on what typically works: "Thank you."

He smiles, but the joy doesn't reach his eyes. They're still filled with emotions from last night.

We walk out to the cars together. He climbs into Dad's Land Rover, and Mom and I take the Enclave. He follows behind us as we head toward town. When we turn for the salon, he turns in a different direction.

I keep watching in the side mirror, expecting to suddenly see him reappear in the distance, tailing us. But after several minutes, there's no sign of him.

Is it true, then? Is he really running errands and letting us be by ourselves? I know that's what he'd said all along, but I didn't really believe it.

Perhaps that's because he's been so laid-back about it all. Usually, I can't take a step out the door without him first taking me into the office, showing me all the cameras he'd be watching me from, and threatening to kill the people I care about if I don't comply.

But this is different. How much, I don't know. That all depends on Mom.

Mom chats happily all the way to the salon. I wonder what's going through her head. There's a camera in her vehicle, just like in mine, though she doesn't seem bothered by it.

For all I know, she's grateful that psycho is watching over us.

As soon as that thought arrives in my head, I push it aside. I don't want to be bitter today. At least not against Mom. I know she's doing the best she can with this hell she's in too.

Mom parks in front of the salon. I'm thankful that the sidewalks have been shoveled and cleared out after last night's snow. There's an open walkway to the shop, so we don't have to trudge through snowbanks.

Before we get out, Mom grabs my arm and puts my

conviction to the test. "I know these last couple weeks have been difficult," she says. "But things will get better. You'll see. And a new makeover will be just the thing to perk you up again!"

In my old life, that used to be true. For years, she would bring me here to the salon whenever I had a bad day. Or a good day. Whatever the occasion, a day at the salon was the answer. I always felt so happy by the time we left.

I want to believe her. I want to feel happy, if only for a moment.

"OK, Mom."

She hops out, and I silently follow her into the salon. At the door, I abruptly stop and scan the area. There's no sign of him. Still.

"Hello, ladies!" Mai, the owner, greets us as we step inside. Over the years, we've come to know Mai well. She and her family opened the shop twenty years ago, when they emigrated from Vietnam. The majority of the employees are her relatives, and we know them well too. They make everyone feel like part of their family.

Then Mai says something that makes me freeze: "Is Bob still in Africa?"

I turn to watch Mom for her reaction. What did hearing Dad's name for the first time since his death do to her? What does she feel? How will she react?

To my shock, Mom smiles without even a flinch. "Yes, he is! Things are a real mess there. So, it's just us girls for a while, and I figured we could use a day of pampering."

She lied.

She lied right to Mai's face. And *he's* not even here to force her to do so.

How can she do it? How can she just stand there and talk about Dad as if he were still alive? He didn't deserve to die, and he sure as heck doesn't deserve to have his wife tell his murderer's lies about him.

I want so badly to scream from the rooftops at the

injustice of it all, but there are over a dozen people here right now. And he'd slaughter them all without even batting an eye.

Mai smiles and nods back, then I see her eyes go right to my hair—the box-dye brunette color has definitely caught her attention. From there, her eyes move down to my face and the rest of my body. When she lifts her gaze to meet my own, I see concern and kindness in her expression.

Mom's attention shifts from Mai to my hair, then back to Mai. "It's a new look Jessy's testing out," she says brightly. She reaches over and runs her fingers through my hair. "Jessy wanted to experiment with a wash-out before committing to the color. If she likes it, we'll set up an appointment with you to do it up right!"

Mai nods as if she hears that all the time. Maybe she does.

We start with pedicures. Mai works on Mom, while I have her sister, Lien. At first, I'm nervous about the fading bruises on my legs, but Lien doesn't say anything as she rubs my calves and feet, and neither does Mom. It puts me a bit more at ease, and I allow myself to give in to the moment.

Between Lien's massage and the chair kneading my back, I'm not sure I want to leave this place. Ever. I had no idea just how sore and tender my muscles were. But I suppose sleeping on a cement floor will do that.

But then we move on to nails, and my worry returns. Kim, the manicurist, visibly reacts with shock as she reaches for my hands and sees my nails.

"Oh my—what did you do?" she asks.

I pull my hands back, hiding them in my lap. I've been coming here since I was seven, and the worst they've ever seen is an occasional hangnail on me. I open my mouth to offer some explanation, but nothing comes out.

"She was in an accident," Mom says, quickly jumping in. "But hopefully you can help. That's why we're here. I thought it would help her feel more like herself."

Accidents might explain the nails, but not fingerprint bruises.

"All right, then," Kim says. "Let's see what we can do." She taps the desk for my hands. After a moment's hesitation, I place them on top. She frowns once more, then gets to work fixing the damage. If she knows this is more than an "accident," she doesn't say.

"Oh yeah," Kim says after a few moments. "I think we'll be able to fix you right up."

"You'll look so good, you'll drive your boyfriend crazy," Trina, Kim's sister, adds, before returning to Mom's nails.

Mom gently clears her throat and shakes her head.

Kim and Trina instantly know what she means.

"Well, he was no good for you anyway," Kim says with certainty—even though she barely knows Blake.

There's something funny—yet touching—about her remark. It makes me smile a bit.

"In fact, you're perfect for our nephew Johnny," Trina says. "He just moved here. You should come back tomorrow and meet him."

I don't know if she's joking or not, but it makes me smile even more.

But then the smile fades, and I feel myself zoning out. Vaguely, I'm aware of the three of them talking about other boys I should date. It doesn't matter. That murderer won't allow it, which is probably for the best anyway.

After nails, it's on to makeup. As an added treat, Mom asks them to condition my hair.

"Yep," Mai says. "We've got some great stuff that will bring the life right back to your hair."

Briefly, I wonder if I could bring my *whole* life back if I rubbed it all over like lotion.

Mom decides to get her makeup done, too, and they encourage her to do the conditioner as well. We sit as they get to work on us, bustling about.

A scene from *The Wizard of Oz* pops into my head. It's

the one where they're in Oz and the Cowardly Lion, Scarecrow, Tin Man, and Dorothy are getting ready to meet the Wizard. The Scarecrow gets new stuffing, the Tin Man is polished, and the Lion and Dorothy have their hair and nails done.

By the time they're done, it's the middle of the afternoon. This time, the girl staring back in the mirror isn't a stranger. I recognize that she's me—albeit a thinner, brown-haired version of me. My nails are back to pristine condition. Makeup and hair are flawless. Even my skin seems like it's glowing. They did a great job gussying me up. So good that even I'm having a hard time believing that the trauma I'm enduring is really happening to the face staring back at me.

For what, though? I do look better, yes. But this doesn't fix anything more than some split ends and cracked nails. It doesn't free me from the hell that is my life. It doesn't absolve me of the fears and guilt eating me alive. It's nothing more than a fresh coat of paint on a ramshackle house.

"So," Mom says cheerfully, "now that we look like a million bucks, who's up for a shopping spree at the mall?"

I nod and put on the best smile I can manage. Sadly, it's not hard to fool Mom. She's locked into one mode: trying to make me feel better. Not *actually* making me feel better. Just *trying*. In other words, she's going through the motions, thinking that's all that matters.

As we're walking out of the salon, someone calls my name.

It's Dan.

My heart is suddenly in my throat.

He rushes over to me from the sandwich shop a few doors down. "Hey! I'm so glad I ran into you. I wanted to call you and apologize, but I don't have your number. I messaged you online, but you haven't replied."

Even though I've had hours of beauty treatments that make me look fabulous and empowered, I certainly don't feel that way right now with Dan standing in front of me. I

feel weak. Exposed. Small.
Pitiful.
"What Nick said—" Dan continues.
"Just don't, OK?" I say, cutting him off. "I heard enough last night."
"You heard his side. You didn't hear mine."
"Like it matters." I wrap my arms around myself and turn my head as far away from him as my neck muscles allow. "I told you—I don't need your pity."
His shoulders drop, and he lets out a sigh. "Look. There's a difference between pitying someone and wanting to help them. What Blake and Cassie did to you sucks on a massive scale. My last girlfriend cheated on me, so I know how shitty it feels. I'm thankful to have a friend like Nick, who got me through that tough time. But you—your friends are the ones who did this to you."
Slowly, I turn my head back to him.
"Well, what I'm saying is, I didn't invite you out because I pitied you. I invited you out because you needed a friend. I wanted to take your mind off things for a little bit. I wanted you to have some fun. Be happy. Smile."
"Really . . . ?" I ask this quietly. It feels dangerous.
"Really. Because you have a gorgeous smile, and it pisses me off that that jackass broke your heart." He grins, revealing dimples as his eyes brighten.
I bite my lip and look away again. This time, I see Mom standing beside the Enclave, watching us intently from only a few feet away. It makes me realize that the moment I saw Dan, Mom and everything else in the world around me disappeared.
The look on Mom's face is hard to decipher. In one way, she looks a little nervous. Mom only knows what *he* told her about last night, and maybe he put all the blame on Dan.
But then again, Mom also looks curious and amused. Her eyes are twinkling in the same way they did when everyone was talking about the boys I should date. I think I even see

her nod with encouragement.

She wouldn't dare do that if that monster had blamed it all on Dan, would she?

"Hey," Dan continues. "What are you doing for the rest of the day?"

I turn away from Mom to look back to him. He's grinning even more. Excited.

"I don't know," I say. "Why?"

Immediately, I want to kick myself. I *do* know what I'm doing for the rest of the day—I'm shopping with Mom. It's our "special day." And it's been sort of nice. Sort of normal. It feels good to hang out with Mom.

Or does it . . . ? Maybe my answer to Dan is proof that I've been going through the motions all day too.

"Well, I'm going sledding with some people at South River Park," he says. "Wanna come?"

"Sledding?" I echo.

A funny expression crosses my face. I haven't gone sledding since . . . I can't even remember. Honestly, it sounds fun.

But then I remember I'm dressed for a girls' day, not tromping around in the snow.

"Well, I'm not dressed for sledding."

He glances down, seeing my Uggs, leggings, and light jacket. "That's no problem," he says. "I have stuff you can borrow."

"I don't know . . ." I hear myself saying out loud.

I frown, torn.

What if Dan's lying? He seems sincere, and I want to believe him. But what if this is just another opportunity for him to kick me while I'm already down? Or what if Dan isn't the one I should be worried about?

"Will Nick be there?" I ask pointedly.

Dan scowls. "No. I'm not hanging out with him until he apologizes to you."

"Seriously?"

"Yeah. You were my guest last night, and he was rude, insulting, and, quite frankly, a prat."

"A *prat*?"

He shrugs sheepishly. "I watch a lot of BBC shows."

When he laughs, it takes me a moment to realize I'm laughing with him.

"Anyway," Dan continues, "he had no right to say any of that to you—and I'm very sorry he did. I meant what I said. I just wanted you to have fun. I still do."

I may not know much about Dan, but it's obvious the events of last night really upset him. "So what do you say? Will you come?"

What am I doing, considering Dan's offer? What am I even doing, standing here talking to him? I bet that monster is somehow seeing and listening to all of this.

Panic nearly overtakes me until I glance back at Mom. To my surprise, she's smiling, nodding, and giving me two thumbs-up.

"Say yes!" she whispers, though it's deliberately loud enough for both me and Dan to hear.

"Hang on," I tell Dan.

I run over to Mom and lean in so I can speak quietly to her. I have to be careful that Dan doesn't hear any of this.

"Are you sure?" I ask. "It's Dan . . ."

I watch her closely, scanning for any signs of that nervousness I saw before. It seems entirely gone now.

"I know you two had a little disagreement last night, but it's great that you're able to work it out like this. He seems really sincere—not that I mean to be eavesdropping!" she adds with a little laugh.

A little disagreement? Is that what *he* told her happened at the Grotto? Well, that's better than him leading her to believe Dan did something so horrible that I tried to kill myself because of it. I have to believe that if Mom still approves of Dan, then that means he still approves.

But then another worry pops into my mind.

"If I go with Dan, won't it ruin the plan for the day? He wanted us to have a girls' day. Won't he get mad?"

Mom smiles and rubs my arms. "Sweetie, all he wants is for you to be happy. While I would love nothing more than to spend the rest of the day with my favorite person, that's not fair to you. You've spent so much time at home in your room. Socializing with kids your age would be good for you. Plus, just in the few minutes you've interacted with him, you've already smiled and laughed more than you have all day with me."

Before I can answer, she pulls me in close, hugging me. "You go have your fun. We can have another girly day any time you want. And don't you worry about me. There are plenty of things for me to do back at home. Maybe your father and I can have a date night."

I lean back. "A date? With *him*? You can't be serious."

She frowns and glances at Dan. He's kicking the snow, waiting for me. When he sees us eyeing him—and no doubt sees the expression on Mom's face—he makes a little motion with his hand, pointing down the sidewalk. He awkwardly moves closer to the sandwich shop to give us more privacy.

"I know things got off to a bad start," Mom begins. She's still whispering, though Dan is out of earshot. "But I really think things are going to be better now. Your father and I both want that. Don't you?"

Father.

He's not even here, and she calls him that?

I have a father. He was *her husband.* And she's just going to act like he didn't exist? Pretend that he wasn't murdered by that psychopath?

No more.

"What I want, Mom, is for him to be gone."

She flinches at the force of my tone, but I ignore her reaction and keep going.

"He's not my father, and you know that. You know

because he murdered my *real* father right in front of us. Is that the 'bad start' you mentioned?"

I grab her hand. It's so soft from the manicure.

"Please—let's just get in the car and drive." I'm pleading now. "Let's keep going until we're far, far away from here. Someplace he'll never find us. It'll be just the two of us. I miss you so much!"

Tears would be streaming from my eyes if I had any left to cry.

Mom places her hand on my cheek. I lean into it.

"Oh, Jessy. My sweet, beautiful girl . . ."

This is it. It's happening. I cannot breathe as I await her next words.

"Go have fun with your friend—your father and I will be so happy to hear all about it later tonight."

As my heart shatters, she lets go of my face, pastes on a smile, then calls out to Dan, "Are you able to give her a ride home later?"

He turns around and rushes back to us, nodding. "It would be my pleasure, Mrs. Smith."

Mom climbs into her vehicle and refuses to look at me.

I stand there, in shock, watching her drive away.

We had a chance to run, and she didn't take it. I opened my heart to her, and she slammed the door in my face.

I see the truth now. All along, I'd been hoping that this is just an act on her part. That she's been playing along to keep him from hurting her. I've played that game too.

But I see it now. It's no act. He's brainwashed her. Turned her into his mouthpiece.

Today wasn't real. I wasn't here with my mom.

I was here with his toy.

THIRTEEN

DAN AND I HEAD FOR HIS BEAT-UP HONDA civic. We take the first few steps together, then he races ahead of me to the passenger side and opens the door for me.

I wrinkle my face. It's not quite a smile, not quite a frown, but it's all I can muster at the moment. "I can get my own door, you know."

"I know—it's just that the door kind of sticks a little." Then he shrugs apologetically. "Plus, my dad would have my ass if I didn't get the door for a lady." He winks.

I narrow my eyes, staring him up and down. Normally I wouldn't think twice about his comment, but now I am.

I used to think that abuse only happened in TV shows and movies, but then it happened to me. Maybe it happens to a lot of my classmates. Maybe their lives are hell and they're suffering in silence too. Maybe it's even happening to Dan. I hope not. He doesn't seem skittish like I am now. Only way to know for sure is to spend more time with him. Get to know him better.

After an awkward moment of us standing around like idiots, I get in the car. He shuts my door, runs around the front, and hops in.

We're quiet as he gets us on the road. On instinct, my gaze slides to the rearview mirror, looking for the tiny black camera, wondering what *he's* thinking as he watches me sitting in Dan's car.

Only, there's no camera. Nothing on the dash either. And no microphones.

Of course not, I remind myself. This is *Dan's* car. Not Mom's. Not mine. That monster may have eyes and ears all over our home and all over town, but he doesn't have them *everywhere*.

Right now, he can't see me or hear me. I'm in one of his blind spots.

But I was in a blind spot last night too. On the bridge.

Still-fresh memories rush at me. It was such a relief to be out from under his thumb last night, even for just a moment. But that temporary breathing space came with too heavy of a price—a man's life.

Will this new temporary breathing space come at a price as well? Is Dan in danger?

I'm sure Mom has called him to let him know I'm with Dan. Yet we're still here, still driving, without any trouble. I haven't gotten any threatening texts or demands to come home. So I don't think Dan's in danger. But just in case, I have to play it safe. I can't do or say anything else to increase the risks.

Maybe there truly is no "blind spot." No "safe." For all I know, *he'll* be there at the sledding hill, ready and waiting the moment Dan steps out of his car.

So I'll keep my secrets. And keep my guard up.

Dan shifts in the driver's seat. I think he can tell something heavy is on my mind.

"Would it be too much to ask for us to forget that last night ever happened?"

I freeze. He *knows*.

Somehow Dan knows about the bridge.

Dan shifts again. "I mean, it was great getting to know

you while we played pool. But afterwards—that was a disaster. That's the part we can maybe forget."

Oh. He meant what happened at the Grotto. Good. Because he can't know anything about the bridge.

He turns his head to give me a quick glance before refocusing on the road. "Maybe we can treat today like our first date instead."

I understand what point he's trying to make, but my brain locks in on only one word for it.

"*Date?*" I gulp.

"Um . . ." He scratches the back of his neck. Then his words come streaming out. "I mean a date as friends. Just us, as friends. Hanging out at a big hill. With some people I know. And a bunch of people I don't know. And wow—I'm already screwing this up. So just forget all this too."

He's nervous. Rambling. He shakes his head as if resetting himself.

"So, sledding, huh? Ever gone sledding at South River Park?"

He glances at me with this look that reminds me of a puppy, begging me to save him.

I decide to throw him a bone. "No, I haven't gone sledding there."

"Excellent! That's excellent." He slowly releases his breath. Then his lips twist into a slanted, shy grin.

My face suddenly feels funny. My cheeks are warm. I think I'm blushing. It's been a while since someone smiled at me like that.

Instantly, I chide myself. I shouldn't be thinking like this. Not about him. Not now. How can I sit here pretending like everything is normal when nothing is? Less than twenty hours ago, I watched a man—a cop—get murdered by the man my mother keeps calling my "father." By the man who murdered my own father.

I close my eyes for a moment, fighting back the emotions trying to overwhelm me. After a few deep breaths I open my eyes—to see that we're driving on the bridge from last night. My breath is ripped from my lungs.

"You want to hear something crazy . . . ?" I hear Dan ask in a quiet voice.

"What's that?" I automatically reply, unable to turn away from the sight of the bridge, the railing ledge, the frozen river below.

"Someone tried to jump off the bridge last night."

I freeze once again. It's a deeper, colder freeze this time.

"My dad told me about it. He's a cop. Charlie—Officer Adams, that is—called him last night for backup as he pulled up on the scene. Charlie said there was a woman on the bridge. She was about to jump."

Charlie Adams. That's his name. *Was* his name.

"The weird thing is, by the time my dad got there, everyone was gone. Charlie didn't report back in. He still hasn't. My dad says Charlie is like that sometimes. When there's an emotional case, he takes things hard, and he needs to be alone for a bit. But still . . ."

As Dan's words trail off, I can hear the concern hanging in the air.

"I guess they searched the river this morning," he says, "but they didn't turn up anything. They weren't even sure what—or who—they were looking for. The woman? Charlie? Both?"

He cleaned up. Again. Was it before he brought me home, or did he take me home then come back to the scene? I can't imagine he could have left the scene and come back. Not with how big of a mess he made.

So where's the officer? What did he do with his body? And where's his car?

"I'm sorry," I whisper. It's meant for Officer Adams and his family.

"Me too," he says. "I hope Charlie is OK. I hope the woman is too. They don't even know who she was. If she survived last night, I hope she can still get help before it's too late."

It's already too late. But I can't tell him that.

Dan frowns. "Suicide sucks. I don't know if you know this, but Nick's mom killed herself a few years back. He found her. The pain he feels from that . . . I wouldn't wish that on anyone."

"I knew about his mom," I say slowly. "But I didn't know he found her."

"Not many do. He doesn't like to talk about it."

Silence fills the car again, but this time it's weighted with Dan's pain and my guilt.

I can't tell him it was me out on that bridge last night. I can't tell him why I was out there, inches and seconds away from ending my life. I can't tell him how Charlie tried to help me before he was brutally murdered. I can't tell him how I'm still trapped with the man who's behind it all.

If I could, though . . . what would he say? I can tell he's a generally happy person and easy to please—as well as very compassionate. Basically, he's a giant teddy bear. He's not some shallow guy, unable to face emotions or understand how other people feel.

A part of me feels safe around him. If he did know the truth, I think he'd maybe help me. But another part of me can't help but worry that he'd freak out, pull over, kick me out of his car, and leave me in his rearview mirror.

Dan lets out a whistle. "So yeah . . . um, sorry that all got so dark," he says. He tries to laugh a little to lighten the mood.

I turn to face him. We exchange a meaningful look for a second, then he focuses back on driving.

"Anyway, I keep forgetting to tell you that Sadie, Amanda, and Julie will be sledding with us too."

I raise my eyebrows. I don't recognize these names. Other classmates . . . ? Three *girls*, though?

"My little sisters," he clarifies, seeing my look. "I'm keeping an eye on them for the afternoon while my parents work. I hope you don't mind."

Sisters. This makes me chuckle.

"That's fine with me," I say.

"I should have told you that they'd be hanging around with us, but I was afraid you'd say no. Who wants three rug rats around?" He pauses. "To be honest, I'm still a little surprised you're here." He glances over as if checking to make sure I'm actually sitting beside him.

"Dan," I say.

"Yeah?"

"You can relax. I'm here, and I'm not going anywhere."

He shrugs sheepishly. "I know. I just want things to be perfect—to make up for last night."

My lips shift into a small smile. "For the night that didn't happen, you mean?"

He snorts. "Yeah."

With that, the shy grin is back.

He pulls into the park and drives past a huge wooden play area, some baseball fields, and a grove of giant trees, all the way to the field that rests at the foot of the big hill.

Tons of cars are parked here along the side of the road, but none of them are *his*. He's not here. Dan grabs an open spot, then gets out. I follow him.

As he digs into the trunk, I immediately check for cameras. I see a few on the light poles on the street but none in the actual park. Which means I'm perhaps being watched right now, but as soon as we leave the road and head for the hill, I won't be in view. Everything I say and do won't be dissected and used against me, as it is while I'm at school.

It should feel freeing. Instead, it fills me with indecision that renders me temporarily immobile. What do I do? How do I act? Do I play this safe? Do I stay ever vigilant, watching over my shoulder for him? Just the thought has me twisting up inside.

Dan pulls out two inflatable tubes and hands one to me. Screams and laughter ring out from the snow hill. As Dan digs some more in his trunk, I watch the sledders, people our age, having fun. Being carefree.

I want that.

I want what they have.

I don't want to waste what little time I have here waiting for the other shoe to drop. Maybe he'll punish me later. Maybe he won't. What I do for the next hour or so won't change that. If this outing with Dan is supposed to make up for last night's botched date, then I'm going to do my part to be present and not overcome with fear.

"Here you go," Dan says, straightening as he pulls out a thick pair of gloves and a stocking hat. I start putting them on, but he stops me.

"Hang on—you'll need this too."

To my surprise, he takes off his own jacket and holds it out to me. He's down to just a zip-up hoodie.

"No way!" I say, refusing. "I can't take your jacket! Now you'll be cold."

"Nah. I have more built-in insulation than you." He pushes his jacket into my arms, insisting.

Not wanting to be rude, I put it on, along with the hat and gloves. The gloves fit, but the coat is about five sizes too big. I'm drowning in it. It's warm, though. And it smells good. Woodsy. Like walking through a forest.

It makes me blush a little.

"Better?" he asks.

I already feel warmer. "Much. Thank you."

"You're welcome. Ready?"

My lips shift into a smile. "Yes."

With one last glance at the cameras, I follow Dan across the snowy field to the big hill, keeping clear of the sleds at the bottom. On the far side is a wooden set of stairs. It has to be more stairs than we climb at school.

"The trip up kind of sucks," Dan says, "but it's worth it."

"*Danny!*" a high-pitched voice squeals.

We turn to see three girls dressed in blue, pink, and

purple snowsuits running through the snow toward us, dragging sleds behind them. They look to be between seven and thirteen.

When the girls reach us, they stop in their tracks and gawk. As they do, their smiles widen. Their cheeks are bright red from the cold.

Dan takes a big breath. "Jess, these are my sisters—Sadie, Amanda, and Julie." He points to each as he says their names. "Girls, this is—"

"I know who she is," the oldest one, Sadie, says. "That's Jessy Smith."

The younger girls' eyes widen.

"As in, 'Jessy's so hot' Jessy?" the middle one, Amanda, asks.

"And 'Hey, Nick—did you see what Jessy was wearing today' Jessy?" Julie adds.

Sadie nods. "Don't forget those pictures he has of her stashed in his—"

"So, you're an only child, Jess?" Dan deliberately interrupts, cutting her off. "That sounds *so great* right now."

For a moment, we're all silent as the awkwardness lingers over us.

And in this moment, I can't help but wonder how much worse my situation would be if I did have younger siblings—brothers or sisters I'd have to protect from the monster. Even in this hypothetical situation, I know I would do anything and everything to keep them safe. Would that mean I'd cave, like Mom?

Yes, being an only child does sound great right now.

Amanda and Julie burst out laughing. Next, Julie sticks out her tongue at him, which only makes her sisters laugh harder.

"That's it!" Dan says. "You little twerps are going to get it!" He lunges for them, and they shriek.

My heart plummets. I'm suddenly reliving how that murderer has lunged at me. The abuse and pain he's put me through.

Thankfully, the trigger lasts only a few seconds. My senses return, pulling me out of my past and into the present. When I listen closely, I can hear the delightful laughter in the girls' screams. When I look closely, I can see the grins on their faces.

I take a closer look at Dan too. His face is red with embarrassment, and he's pretending to look mad, but his smile is just under the surface as well. It's easy to tell he loves them.

They were just playing. That's all. He wasn't going to hurt them.

My panic lessens. I risk a peek at him, hoping he didn't notice how scared I had been for that moment. Judging by the light in his eyes and that relaxed smile, he didn't.

"Now, git!" Dan orders his sisters, pointing up the steps.

The girls take off, running up the steps while still laughing.

He chuckles as he watches them scramble. "Well, that will give us a few minutes alone anyway."

He reaches for my hand.

After a few seconds, I oblige. Instead of fear, butterflies erupt in my stomach as his fingers curl around mine. I stare at his hand, waiting for the fear that contact always brings, but it isn't there. The absence of it is nearly foreign, actually. My body is struggling to process *not* being terrified and on edge. It leaves me feeling . . . cautiously optimistic.

"Come on." He nods to the steps.

As we climb, I double-check the few lamp poles we walk past. When I don't find any cameras, some weight lifts. Not all of it, though. At any moment, he could show up. Threaten the lives of everyone here just to get me back in the car— back under his control. If he did that, if he came after me in public, we couldn't just go back home and resume pretending everything is perfect.

No.

We'd have to leave. And that—the thought of going on the run with him—is truly terrifying.

We're quiet for a bit, then Dan clears his throat.

"About what they said . . ." he begins. "They were joking. You know that, right? I mean, it's not like Nick and I sit around my house, talking about you all day."

"So you don't think I'm hot?" I joke.

He balks. But a half second later, that grin is back. It feels nice to be responsible for it. To joke around with him.

"I'm pretty sure even blind guys can tell you're hot. You're Jessica freakin' Smith. Even before my school closed, every guy in my class knew about you."

I make a face. "Really?"

He stops and stares.

"What?" I ask, confused.

He shakes his head.

"What?" I press.

"You. Just now, when you said 'Really?' You made this little crinkle along the bridge of your nose. I've never seen you do that before. It's kind of adorable."

"Kiss her!" someone in front of us says.

Our heads turn in unison. His sisters are standing a few steps above us, watching us. Sadie and Amanda begin making kissing noises while Julie sings "Kiss the Girl" from *The Little Mermaid*.

Dan's ears redden as his lips purse. Then he lunges for them again. Like before, they shriek and run away.

This time, the fear doesn't resurface. I'm filled with something else, though. A confusing array of emotions that encompasses everything from excitement to worry.

Kissing? I barely know him.

Hanging out and even holding his hand is one thing, while kissing would mean we were in some sort of "normal" relationship. But I can't have that with him. I'm not even sure we can be friends, let alone anything beyond that. He'd undoubtedly want to get to know me even more. Ask me things I can't answer. Meet my parents.

Plus, even if I could have a new relationship with him, I don't know if I'd be ready to jump into something like that. Not after everything with Blake and Cassie—how deeply they betrayed me.

My life is far too complicated to add relationship drama into the mix. If anything, what I really need is a friend.

And I could easily see myself being friends with Dan.

I want to be friends with him.

"So, you're probably never going to speak to me after this, right?" Dan asks as he straightens.

I flinch. "Why would you think that?"

He points after his sisters. "I'm not exactly having the best luck making a good impression."

"Relax, Dan. This is just a 'date as friends,' right?"

He nods and laughs, remembering his own words from earlier. "Sure, Jess."

"Besides," I say, my voice more serious now, "you don't need to worry about impressing me."

He meets my gaze, wide-eyed and hopeful. "Why's that?"

"Because you've already shown me how compassionate and kind you are. You barely know me—I'm practically a stranger to you—yet you invited me out when you knew I needed a friend. You stuck up for me, even against your own best friend. You went out of your way to make sure I was OK after everything that happened last night. Then you gave me the literal coat off your back! Not to mention, you've shown me how awesome and loving you are as a brother."

I pause and smile.

"I get that we barely know each other, but from the few moments we've been together, I can tell you're a kind person, Dan. There's just something about you that puts me at ease in a way no one else can. I'm glad we ran into each other today."

None of it is a lie.

We climb the rest of the way, holding hands still. When we get to the top, he positions our tubes so they're next to each other. He gets in his and grabs the handle on mine, holding it steady for me.

"We're going to go down together, OK? Are you ready?" The way he asks the question, I know he's actually waiting for my answer. He's waiting for me to decide if I am, indeed, ready.

If he only knew . . .

Part of me still feels it's wrong to be here. I shouldn't be laughing and having fun. Two people—a police officer and my own father—are dead. But no one can know that. I hold this horrible secret, and I can't tell anyone—not unless I want them to die too.

These three weeks have been hell. Is it really so wrong for me to step outside that? To breathe? To pretend for just a few hours that I'm not scared out of my mind? Is it possible that giving myself this momentary reprieve will help strengthen me when my fear undoubtedly returns?

Yes.

Yes, I can have some fun. I can act my age rather than react to a situation that is so far beyond something a teenager should have to handle.

I bite my lip, nod, then say, "Yes. I'm ready."

I sit down on the tube. Now that I'm pushing away all thoughts of my current life and focusing solely on this experience with Dan, I can feel excitement percolate inside me. It's just sledding, something that has had no appeal to me whatsoever since elementary school. But right now, it feels like I'm about to ride on a roller coaster. It feels like the greatest thrill in my life.

He slides us closer to the edge. "Here we go. Three . . . two . . . one!"

With that, he gives us a shove. A frozen wind whips my face as we fly down the hill. With the uneven weight, though, our tubes begin to twist. Next thing I know, we've spun around so we're sliding down backward, completely unable to see.

"Oh crap!" Dan calls out.

I can't help but scream and laugh.

We keep going, all the way down the hill—and then some. We keep sliding and eventually crash into the hay bales strategically placed to keep the sleds from going into the road. The impact flings me from the tube, and I land on my back in the snow on the other side of the hay.

"Jess!" Dan cries. A moment later he's leaning over me. "Are you OK?"

A laugh bursts out of me. I cover my mouth to stop it. But it feels *so good* to laugh. A real laugh. One that isn't forced. When's the last time I did this? I don't remember.

I decide to let it go. I take my hand off my mouth as I lay there, in the snow, laughing at myself.

Dan smiles and grabs my hand. He means to pull me up, but instead I playfully yank him down. He lands in a heap beside me. A moment later, he starts laughing too.

When he faces me, he reaches out to brush a few strands of hair from my face. His gloved hand lingers on my cheek.

The laughter dies down, but we're both still smiling. Being this close to him, I pick out the earthy tones of green and brown that swirl together in his hazel eyes. His gaze flickers to my lips.

He wants to kiss me.

Mixed emotions flood me again. Can I kiss Dan? Should I kiss him?

Right before his lips press in, I turn away, leaving his lips to meet the corner of my mouth and cheek. His lips are cold. But soft. Gentle.

Instantly, his eyes pop open, surprised that I'd turned my head. He pulls away.

I can feel his eyes on me. I look down, ashamed and embarrassed.

LAURIE WETZEL ‡ PICTURE PERFECT

I hurt him. I hadn't meant to. To him, it was a kiss, our first kiss. That's a big deal. But I couldn't do it. I couldn't kiss him. I can't allow whatever this is to become a relationship. Not only am I not ready, but it's just too risky. And now that I've turned him down, I've ruined my second chance at having a friendship with him.

"I'm sorry," I whisper. "It just surprised me."

He leans down, putting himself in my line of sight instead of forcing me to meet his. I expect to find something akin to anger or disappointment on his face. Instead, it's a mix of understanding and guilt.

"Don't apologize, Jess. I'm the one who needs to apologize. I wasn't thinking. You've been through hell this week. The last thing you need is to jump into another relationship." He frowns, pushing himself up to sit beside me. "You know, maybe we should just call it a day. Maybe I should bring you home."

No.

I'm not ready for the day to end. I'm not ready to be plunged back into the chaos. I need Dan. I need his friendship and kindness. In these few moments we've had together, I'm free from my living nightmare.

He makes me happy. But I screwed it up. I didn't kiss him when he wanted me to. And because of that, I've ruined the one shot I had at having an ally in all this. Someone to turn to in my darkest hour.

"Or," he continues, "we could stay and go down the hill again. Only if you want to, though."

My eyes pop open, and my gaze fixes on him, checking repeatedly to see if this is some kind of trick or test.

"I don't understand," I say. "I didn't kiss you . . ."

His hazel eyes soften, and a tender smile lights up his face. "That's on me, Jess. And again, I'm really sorry. I shouldn't have done that." His expression curls into a sheepish grin. "Would I love to kiss you? Sure. One day—*if* our friendship heads that direction, and *if* we're both ready.

Then yeah, absolutely. But in the meantime, I'd be over the moon if I could still call you my friend."

Friend.

Even though I know I shouldn't, I want his friendship. Even though I know it isn't safe. It's just . . . being here with him . . . I finally see just how dark and desperate my life has become.

I look back up at the hill, at all the people sledding on this beautiful winter day, at all their joy. There's no pain here. There's no fear here. That's because *he's* not here.

I hadn't realized until now how easy it is to breathe when I'm away from him and his surveillance. I had no idea how suffocating it was to constantly walk on eggshells. But now I can suddenly feel the blissful weightlessness of being away from home.

The blissful weightlessness of being with Dan.

I look at him, seeing him in a new light beyond just our budding friendship. If I let him, Dan can be a source of refuge. He can be the place—the only place—where I can breathe. Where I can be me. With no expectations. No punishments. No walking on eggshells. He can be my escape. As long as I have him, I can hold on to hope and keep fighting.

I squeeze his hand, suddenly grateful for him.

"Sure. Let's do it."

Grinning, I let him pull me to my feet. We grab our tubes and start the long trek back to the top. We slide down the hill five more times before his sisters want to leave.

I should have Dan bring me home, but I'm not ready for this to end. I'm not ready to be away from Dan just yet.

He makes it really easy to like him. He's so funny and kind and sweet. I don't think there's a single mean bone in his body.

Plus, the longer I'm here, the more the old me—the me who laughed easily and was fearless and fun—has come out of hiding. I didn't realize how much I've missed her. How much of me *he'd* stolen.

His sisters pile in the back of his car and spend the entire drive to their home whispering and giggling about us. Dan tries to take it all in stride, but by the time we pull into their driveway, he's visibly irritated with them. It doesn't last long, though, before he's back in caring-older-brother mode. When we get in the house, he tells them, "Take your wet stuff off, and put on warm, dry clothes. I'll make you some hot chocolate."

"Don't forget the marshmallows!" Julie calls as they race up the stairs to the second story.

He shakes his head, then fills a tea kettle and turns on the stove. As the water heats, he turns to me. "Sorry about them."

I shrug and smile. "It's fine."

He drops his gaze, frowning as he stares at my leggings. "You're soaked! You must be freezing. Come on—I'll get you some dry clothes."

He holds out his hand for me. Again.

And I take it. Again.

FOURTEEN

D AN TAKES ME UPSTAIRS AND KNOCKS ON a white door with purple flowers. It's cute, girlie, and innocent. I love it.

I make a vow right then and there to protect Dan and his family from the darkness in my life.

"What's the password?" one of his sisters asks from the other side of the door.

It's probably Amanda. But I can hear other footsteps too. I think they're all standing by the door together.

"Open up, or I'll kick your butt."

His sisters whisper, then one of them says, "Wrong answer. Go away."

Dan rolls his eyes and finally just pushes the door open. "Jess needs to borrow some clothes."

Their faces light up.

"Ooh! Why didn't you say so?" Sadie says.

"I tried," he grumbles.

"Well, we'll take it from here," Amanda says, grabbing my arm and yanking me into the room.

"Yeah, get!" Julie adds to him.

He glances over their heads at me. "You sure you'll be all right with them?"

I smile. "I'll be fine."

"OK, then. Hot chocolate will be ready in five."

"Eep!" Amanda says. "That doesn't leave us much time."

Suddenly, all three of them race around their room, tossing clothes at me from every direction. When my arms are full, they shove me into the bathroom across the hall and order me to get dressed.

I stare at the pile, doubting anything will fit. These are Sadie's clothes, and she's almost five years younger than me. The tags on the jeans reveal them to be a size 0. I wear size 4. Granted, my own jeans are a little baggy these days. But still. There's no way I'll get in Sadie's jeans.

I think I would have better luck with something from his mom's closet. Or even his. I could have worn his sweats or something.

"Hey, guys?" I call out through the bathroom door. "Do you think you can get me something closer to my size?"

"Really? Those don't fit?" Amanda asks. I don't need to see her face to know she's raising an eyebrow at me.

"Well . . . I haven't tried them on . . ." I admit.

"Then try them on, silly!" she replies.

Apparently, I can't get other clothes until I prove these don't fit. With a little shake of my head, I slip one leg, then the other, into the jeans. Then I pull them right over my hips, and I zip and button with ease.

My stomach twists. Not in a giddy, happy, oh-wow-I-fit-a-size-0 way. But in a horrible, sickening, oh-God-I-fit-a-size-0 way.

How much weight have I lost? I knew it was some, but I didn't realize it was this much.

I've never longed to be waifish thin or wear a certain size. Sure, I worked out a lot for cheerleading. But I did it because I loved it. Because it made me strong. Because it made me happy. I was comfortable in my skin. Now . . . I barely recognize myself. I hate this.

He's killing me. Slowly. Day by day. If he doesn't finish whatever his plans are soon, there will be nothing left of me.

Just as I finish putting on a shirt, someone knocks on the door.

"Are you coming out or what?" Julie asks.

I sigh, gather my wet clothes, then open the door.

They scrutinize my outfit—Sadie's jeans and a small teal long-sleeved shirt with a large purple unicorn on it. I'm not thrilled with the character, but all the other shirts are short-sleeved and would show the bruises. The nods and smiles confirm that it meets their approval.

"Hot chocolate's done," Dan calls.

All three girls bolt forward, pushing and shoving in a race to get to the kitchen.

When I enter behind them, Dan smiles at the My Little Pony shirt as he hands me a mug. Thankfully, he doesn't comment on my wardrobe. Instead, he just asks, "Better?"

"Much." I take a sip of the hot chocolate. It's delicious, all warm and extra chocolatey. "Thank you."

"You're most welcome." He too takes a sip. "When do you need to be home by?"

Instantly, my happy bubble bursts and dread fills me. I don't want to answer that. I don't want to go home. I don't want this moment to end.

My fingers rub along the outside of the cup, as if trying to savor the warmth. Everything is perfect here. And Dan is easy to be around. No expectations. No pressure. Just . . . contentment. I can't remember the last time I felt this way.

"If something was going on with you, you'd tell me, right?"

When I look up, Dan's staring at me. "Why do you ask that?"

He walks around the counter, stopping in front of me. "I would think that's obvious—I like you, Jess."

I flinch and turn away.

"I know we're just starting to get to know each other, but

there's something about you, Jess. Something special."

I can feel emotions I'd long thought dead bubbling to the surface. My stomach fills with butterflies, my cheeks heat, and my heart pumps with hope. It has little to do with Dan "liking" me, and everything to do with him *seeing* me. Not the glitz and glamour everyone else sees—or at least used to. He sees *me*.

But these bubbling feelings are dangerous. Everything about this is dangerous. Dan truly sees me, enough to suspect something might be wrong in my life. And I can't have that.

This was a mistake—coming here, being with Dan, thinking I could have a normal life for even a few moments. My life's too messy. Too complicated.

To keep my tears at bay, I focus on the pictures on the wall. There are some of Dan and his sisters at various ages. A few photos of a man and woman who I assume are his parents. In one of them, his father is in a uniform.

He's a cop.

I knew that. Dan said that in the car earlier. At the time, it didn't sink in. But now it has.

Dan's father is a police officer. Yet here I am, standing in his kitchen, when not twenty hours earlier I was standing in front of one of his fellow officers, watching the life fade from his eyes.

Charlie. His name was Charlie. He was their friend.

And I watched a psychotic murderer take his life. Isn't Charlie's blood on my hands as well? For not being able to stop it? For not reporting it? For not reporting my own father's murder? For not reporting anything that maniac has done?

Will anyone understand that he's forcing me—both literally and figuratively—into silence, threatening my life and the lives of those I love? Or will they stick to the letter of the law, lock me up in a different cell, and throw away the key?

When I open my eyes, I can barely look at Dan. "How

long has your dad been a cop?"

"My whole life. He's the chief, actually."

Chief. Oh my God. That makes this so much worse.

But then, slowly, a new idea dawns on me: Dad used to say that knowledge is one of the most valuable assets. With Dan's dad being the chief of police, he has access to all kinds of valuable knowledge. Perhaps even Dan has access to it.

The monster living in my home kills with such ease that I don't doubt he's done it before. And the surveillance and stalking—it's likely an MO. Most criminals have several run-ins with the police before they're ultimately caught for their most heinous crimes. What if that murderer is already on Dan's dad's radar? Maybe then I can finally learn something about my devil.

"So . . ." I begin, trying to keep my tone casual, "I bet your dad's dealt with some pretty awful criminals and wackos, huh?"

Dan takes a sip of hot chocolate. "Probably."

"Does he share the stories with you? Like, does he talk about some of the crazier ones?"

"I don't know. Why are you so interested in my dad all the sudden? I mean, you've met him."

I whip around. "I have? When?"

"Your dad was the governor. My dad is the chief of police. They've been to a lot of functions together, especially while your dad was in office. Some of them even families went to. That's when I first saw you—we were eight."

I try to think back to those days. The days when Dad was governor. Things were so much simpler then. So simple that I barely paid any attention to them. True, we went to tons of functions, but all I had to do was stand next to my parents and smile for the cameras. I treated it like an extension of my beauty pageants.

"I'm sorry. I don't remember that. I should."

"It's OK." He shrugs, then gives me a cocky grin. "But just so you know, you're even cuter now than you were back then."

I smile, but it's not as big as earlier. My joy is overshadowed by my grief and guilt.

When will this nightmare be over? What will finally satisfy that man? What is he even doing, pretending he's my father and that we're some picture-perfect family? We can't keep up this charade forever. Especially if he keeps going around killing people. So when this does come to the end, what happens to me and Mom?

Will we even live to see the end?

"You want to watch TV while I toss your clothes in the dryer?" Dan says, contrasting my surreal, morbid thoughts with a mundane yet sweet question.

He watches me closely while I consider his offer.

I should say no. We've only spent a handful of hours together, and already it's enough for Dan to pick up that something is not right in my world. How can he see so clearly what others—Blake, Cassie, the squad—have missed? Is Dan more compassionate than them? Or does the proverbial apple not fall far from the tree, and he just has the same investigative instincts as his dad? That's all the more reason for me to go home and stay as far away from Dan as possible.

But . . . I can't leave yet. My clothes do need to dry, and it probably wouldn't be a good idea for me to go home wearing something other than what I left in. It would raise too many questions I don't want to answer.

I suppose I should be ashamed that wet clothes are all it takes to convince me to stay when I know I shouldn't. I should feel horrible.

But I don't. Especially since there's no curfew or rules set for today. Mom said it would all be OK. It's supposed to be a day of fun—and staying here with Dan is way more fun than what I would be doing if I went home.

I follow Dan into the living room, only to discover that his sisters have claimed the space. One is on the couch, another on the love seat, and the third in the chair. The TV pauses.

"Beat it," he says. "Jess and I are going to watch TV."

All three of them look over, swiveling their heads in perfect synchronicity.

"How about no," Sadie says.

The screen is paused right as some guy is about to stab someone. The victim is strapped down on a table with plastic wrap. The entire room is covered in it.

I cringe and look away. This isn't something I want to see, paused or otherwise.

"What the hell are you—is that *Dexter*?" Dan exclaims. Then he sighs. "You know you're not supposed to be watching that."

"Duh," Amanda says. "Which is why you need to leave, so we can get in two episodes before Mom gets home."

"Plus," Sadie adds, "*you're* not supposed to have your girlfriend over either."

I suck in a breath, not prepared for them to slap that kind of label on us. I know they're just kids, but still. Is that what they think we are? Is that what everyone at the park thought, too, watching us together? Is that what Dan thinks?

"She's my *friend*," Dan corrects, stunning me once again. "And for the record, I'm allowed to have friends over. You, however, are not allowed to watch this show. It'll give you nightmares."

"Nuh-uh," Amanda says, sticking her tongue out.

"OK, how about this—you don't squeal on us," Julie begins, "and we won't squeal on you. Deal?"

Dan scratches his head. I can tell he's seriously considering this.

"I can leave," I say. "I don't want to get you in trouble."

"Nah," he says. "The vultures are good at keeping their word." He turns back to his sisters. "Deal. Jess and I will just watch TV in my room."

Before I can say a word, he grabs my hand again and

leads me upstairs. As we enter the last room on the left, he lets go.

I stand in the center of his bedroom, taking it all in. It's neat. Organized. Above his desk are two hanging shelves overloaded with trophies from various sports, most of them basketball. His full-size bed is in the corner opposite the door. In the other corner is a tall dresser. On top of it is the TV—it's an older box-style set.

None of the furniture matches, and yet somehow it all fits him. Simple. Classic. Comfortable. Dan to a T.

Compared to my old room, this is tiny. But compared to my new *room*, this is perfect.

Dan shuts the door, and an all-too-familiar clicking sound echoes through me.

He locked the door.

I whirl around and unlock it, yanking the door open. "Don't do that! Leave it open, please."

He stares down at me. I cringe, knowing he must think I'm nuts. But then he nods.

"Claustrophobic, huh? My mom is a little too. Anyway, it's fine with the door open. I only closed it to keep my sisters out, but I'm sure they'll be glued to their show anyway. Come on." He takes my hand again and pulls me to his bed.

Now a new panic rises in me.

The couch was one thing. But this—his bed—is completely different. As much as I like Dan and enjoy hanging out with him, I'm not ready for this.

He releases my hand once he reaches the bed. He plops himself down with his back against the headboard and stacked-up pillows, legs stretched out. He looks comfortable. Natural. Like it's no big deal to watch TV with a friend. In your room. On your bed.

Well, maybe it's not a big deal. Other than the small folding chair tucked under his desk, the bed is the only furniture in the room that can be sat on. In a way, watching TV on his bed is no different than watching TV on his couch out in the living room.

So I slide onto the far edge of the bed, keeping as much space between us as possible.

He snorts. "I don't bite." He pats the vacant space between us. "You're gonna fall off!"

After a second, I shift over. As I do, my hand brushes against his arm. He yanks his arm back and rubs it in dramatic fashion.

"Jeez! You're freezing!"

I am cold—I hadn't noticed. It's glaringly obvious now, though. Even just brushing up against him, I could feel how warm he was. He's like a furnace.

He reaches down to snatch a blanket from the foot of the bed. With meticulous care, he wraps me up in the blanket so only my head is exposed. I bite my lip, fighting a grin. I feel like a burrito. As silly as it sounds, it's the nicest thing anyone has done for me in a while.

He slides back into position beside me, with one arm tucked casually behind his head. With the other hand, he grabs the remote, turning on the TV.

"So, why'd you change your hair?" he asks.

I pull back, suddenly self-conscious. "You don't like it?"

He takes a breath, wanting to choose his words carefully. "It's just that your hair was one of the first things I noticed about you when we were kids. It's golden—the color of wheat. Ever since then, I think of you every time I pass a wheat field. So I was a little sad when we came back from winter break and you'd changed it. You still look beautiful," he adds quickly. "But . . ."

"But you prefer the blond," I finish for him, with a small smile.

He shrugs, and his lips shift into a sympathetic grin. "I'm sorry. I hope I haven't offended you."

"You haven't. This color isn't really me." It feels good to say it.

"So why keep it?"

That good feeling vanishes. I tilt my head back, staring at the ceiling, wondering what I'm supposed to say now. He can't know the truth. Yet I don't want to lie to him.

"I just haven't been able to change it back yet," I finally say.

He smiles, satisfied, and nods toward the TV. "What do you want to watch?"

"Anything—as long as it's not scary."

"Not a horror fan?"

I grimace. "I used to be, but not anymore."

He closes one eye, scrunches his face, and cocks his head as he considers this. "What changed your mind?"

I consider again how truthful I should be. The answer comes quickly this time. "Life is scary enough."

Dan nods and lets out a long exhale. "Very true." His eyes meet mine, and there's understanding reflected in them.

No, Dan doesn't *truly* understand. No one could. Not even if I were free to open up and tell him everything.

But just the fact that he's listening and trying to understand me on some basic level is everything. It's easy talking to him, being with him. While he wants to know me and has many questions, he doesn't badger me. He takes my answers at face value. I like that. He's very calming.

He flips through Netflix, stopping on some action-adventure movie with Kevin Hart and the Rock. I appreciate that he didn't try to do some kind of romance or drama.

The movie is full of witty one-liners and mishaps that has Dan cracking up. His joy is infectious. After a while, I join in, laughing like my world isn't imploding around me. It's strange, but nice. Perhaps hanging out with him won't be so hard after all.

"Do you want to stay for dinner?" he asks. "There's always tons of food, so it wouldn't be a problem."

Just thinking about Dan's family gathered for dinner fills me with a warm feeling. But then I glance out the window, seeing the setting sun, and dread fills me.

Family meals are always a big production back home. We eat in the formal dining room with the fancy china every night at six, like clockwork. It's never a simple meal. Always something elaborate that Mom must have spent hours on.

There's no way I can just skip dinner. If I want to eat with Dan, I'll need to call and ask permission. And I'm not sure I could handle *him* saying no.

"I should probably get home . . ."

Dan nudges me with an elbow. "Why do I sense there's a 'but' there?"

Panic flares, as I think about the hell I'll be walking into.

"You don't want to go home, do you?" he says, matter-of-fact.

The truth is dangerous. Deadly. But I choose it anyway.

"No," I say.

Blue meets hazel. For a moment, we sit there, unmoving, silently staring at each other. We don't even blink.

Can he sense it? Can he read it written all over my face? Does he know why I don't want to go home? Does he know my horrible secret, despite how hard I'm trying to hide it from him, to keep him safe?

Then he smiles. It's a sweet smile. Shy. "Not ready to be rid of me yet, huh? Good. Because I'm really glad we got to hang out today. Hopefully we can do it again soon?"

A tiny breath releases from my lungs. No, he doesn't know my secret. He simply thinks I don't want to go home because I'd rather just hang out with him.

His assumption is far better than the truth.

My phone suddenly buzzes, making us both jump and pull away. I pull it out of my pocket. It's *him*, telling me to come home now.

"I have to go."

"I wish you didn't have to."

I lean my head back and sigh, wishing like hell that this moment didn't have to end. Fighting to please *him*, to appease *him*, is exhausting.

"Me too."

A moment later, his strong, warm arms wrap around me. For the first time in a long time, I lean into human touch, not fearing it, but instead embracing it. Accepting the comfort it brings. A sensation rushes through me. It takes me a few seconds to even realize what it is.

In his arms, I feel safe.

Dan grabs my stuff from the dryer. After I change, we walk out to the car. I glance back at the house and see his sisters in the living room window, giggling at us.

It makes me smile so wide that my cheeks hurt. It's as if those particular facial muscles are weak and out of shape. It feels like the burn you get from a new workout routine. I like this burn, though. And that thought only makes me smile more.

"Do they always gang up on you like that?" I ask.

He shrugs. "They're less annoying when—"

He stops. He's staring over my shoulder, behind me.

I whirl around.

Nick's standing halfway up the driveway.

"So I guess my feelings mean dick to you," Nick says, glaring at Dan.

His words take me aback. I don't know what he's talking about.

Dan runs a hand through his hair and releases his breath. "Come on, man. You know that's not true."

Nick's only response is a huff.

"Just—" Dan begins, only to stop, groan, and squeezes his eyes shut for a moment. When he opens his eyes, he holds them fast on Nick.

"Listen—let me take Jess home, then you and I can talk."

Obviously, this isn't what Nick wants to hear. "Screw you," he spits. He begins to turn away, but he stops for a second to throw a look of disgust at me.

That's it. This is about me. They're fighting over me. Just like at the club Friday. Nick doesn't want me and Dan to be friends.

"Why do you hate me so much?" I suddenly shout at him.

The instant the words are out, I wish I could take them back. I don't need to ask why he hates me.

I already know the reason. And because of it, I'm too ashamed to meet his gaze when he looks back at me.

"Forget this," he says, marching away.

I move to chase after him, but Dan gently grabs my arm to stop me. "Let him go. It's not you. It's him."

"No. It *is* me."

My eyes are heavy with guilt as I look up at Dan. He looks back down at me in confusion.

"Why would you say that?"

"Because I lived."

FIFTEEN

AS DAN DRIVES ME HOME, I SHARE MY story about the accident, Nick's sister, the horrible mistake over our identities, the tension between me and Nick. All of it.

Dan doesn't say a word the whole time. He just sits there and listens while I share my soul without interrupting—something I'm realizing Blake struggled with.

By the time I'm finished, we're parked at the end of my driveway. I watch Dan for a moment, giving him space with his thoughts. I sense that he doesn't even know where to begin, so I offer something.

"You must have known his sister well, considering how close you and Nick are . . ."

He leans forward, resting his forehead in his hands. "I did." Then he looks at me from the corner of his eye. "We were dating when she died—we'd just started going out."

I slump back against my seat, shocked. I hadn't expected that. I had no idea.

Yet strangely, I don't feel awkward or jealous or upset. If anything, I'm happy they had each other—and heartbroken about how it had tragically ended.

So many questions and thoughts swirl in my head, but

it's my turn to sit and listen, giving him space.

"The thing is, she and I'd been around each other for years—for as long as Nick and I have been friends. Their homelife wasn't great, so Nick always brought her along whenever he and I hung out. I never minded it—my sisters were always around too. And Jessica was so quiet—always just reading or taking pictures—that I sometimes totally forgot she was even with us."

A little smile curls his mouth.

"Eventually, she started coming over without Nick. I just thought it was to hang out. Then one day she finally came out and told me she had a crush on me. Man, it pulled the rug right out from under me. But then I stopped and realized that I had feelings for her too. So we started going out . . . though we kept it on the down-low from almost everyone."

I can't help but shake my head in confusion at this last part. "Why?"

He snorts. "Nick. When I told him about us, he gave me a black eye."

My hand flies to my mouth, covering a gasp. "He didn't!"

Dan nods. "Afterward, he felt worse about it than I did. He *hates* violence."

"So . . . why did he do it?"

Dan grimaces, not wanting to answer.

I don't want to pry. But I would like to understand. What happened between Dan, Nick, and Jessica adds a whole other level to what's playing out between Dan, Nick, and me.

More importantly, I want to be here for Dan. It's clear he's still carrying so much grief and guilt from her loss. Has he talked to Nick about this? Or has he been carrying it alone?

I place my hand on his arm. "Please. I just want to understand you and your friendship a little better. Why was he so against you dating Jessica?"

"It's a guy thing, you know?" he says quickly. "You're

not supposed to date your friend's sister."

He shrugs and rolls his eyes. But then he looks away quickly, out the window. He chews the inside of his cheek.

"And . . . well . . ." He pulls in a deep breath, then releases it, running his fingers through his long hair. "Don't tell him I said this, OK?"

"I promise."

"Well, Nick's dad was an alcoholic. A bad one. He used to hit them all. Nick took most of it, though. That's why he was so protective of Jessica. It was hard for him to trust anyone around her—even me."

My heart aches for Nick and his sister. I've lived in fear of an abuser for a few weeks. They dealt with it their whole lives.

"I'm so sorry," I say, even though my words can do nothing.

"My dad arrested their dad on a regular basis," Dan says. "Then the accident happened, and . . . well, you know the rest. Jessica is gone, their mom is gone, and that bastard got sent to prison. And through it all, Nick's somehow still Nick."

A hint of a smile crosses his lips, then it slips into a frown.

"What beef he has against *you*, though, I don't know." He shrugs, then lets out a huge sigh. "It has nothing to do with the accident—that much I do know. But we'll figure it out. I know this turned all depressing, so how about ending on a positive note?" He leans toward me. "Can I see you tomorrow?"

I glance down the driveway, toward my house. Though I can't see it clearly through the trees, I can feel the oppressive weight of *him*. I want to say yes to Dan. I wish I could. I would love to have another day like today. But I'm no longer in charge of my life, and something tells me *he's* not going to be OK with me spending another day away from the family.

"I don't know . . . I think we have plans."

"Can I call you, then? Text? Email? Send a handwritten letter via carrier pigeon?"

I can't hold back a laugh. "Carrier pigeon? Really?"

He shrugs and grins. "It got you to smile. Mission accomplished."

I suddenly realize that in all the many times Blake dropped me off, he never went out of his way to make me smile before leaving.

"Well, thanks for everything today—I'll see you later," I say, reaching for the door handle.

"Wait! Where are you going?" Dan blurts.

I glance over, and he's giving me a goofy look.

"I only stopped here at the end of the driveway so we could continue our conversation. Let me drive you up to the house and walk you to your door!"

"No!"

There's alarm in my voice—which, in turn, alarms him. He stares at me. "Why not?"

I can't tell him the truth: walking me to the door would be the last thing he'd do on this earth. I have to think fast.

"Our driveway sucks in winter," I say, settling my voice a bit. "That's why I'm not driving my car right now. I get stuck a lot. I don't want you to get stuck too."

Once again, it's not a complete lie. I don't know if his car could make it. His car is old, and I doubt it has four-wheel drive. It's quite possible that he'd get stuck in the high snow drifts.

"I'll just walk from here," I continue. "It's no problem. Really." I give a little wave of my hands as if to shoo away any worries.

Dan sighs, clearly not liking the idea. "Walk? In the snow? Are you sure? How much farther is it?" He cranes his neck to see around me, looking for the house.

"It's just past the trees. And I'm positive—it's no problem. I do this every day for the bus now."

206

Inside, I cringe. I never should have mentioned the bus. Sure enough, Dan is all over it.

"Why are you even riding the bus, anyway? I can give you a ride to school Monday, if you want."

I have to think fast yet again. "Nah. It's fine. You don't need to trek all the way out here for me."

"It's not a problem," he insists.

He would do it, if I let him. He'd drive all the way out here to pick me up every day for school just to help me—a friend—in need. And he'd drive me up to the house and walk me right to the door tonight. I wish life were as simple as saying yes.

Instead, his kindness would be repaid in violence and death.

"I'll be fine," I say. "I promise. Talk to you later?"

His brows narrow, and he frowns. But he doesn't push it anymore. "OK. Looking forward to it."

Then he opens his door and moves to get out.

"Wait! What are you doing?" I squeak as panic threatens to consume me.

"Your door sticks, remember?"

He walks around the car as if nothing is amiss while I work on calming the stampede that is my heart. He opens my door with that easy smile I'm starting to suspect is just his normal expression—as in he's just normally a happy guy. Which is one more reason to keep my darkness as far away from him as possible.

"Thanks again for today," I say. "I'll see you at school." I give him a quick smile and move to walk up the driveway, hoping that my dismissal will be a clear sign he can't follow.

"Jess!" he calls out.

I whirl around, relieved that he's still beside the car and not trudging through the snow behind me.

"Don't forget—carrier pigeons."

I grin at him, then rush through the snow toward the house.

I'm still smiling when I walk through the door. I actually had a great time. The smiles and laughs were genuine. So were the feelings. It was the first time in a long time that I felt like I could be myself and not what someone else expected me to be.

As I'm taking off my coat and boots, *he* steps into the hallway from the office. The man who murdered my father.

Sharp awareness zips through me, accompanied by anxiety and dread. They have been my constant companions for weeks. They'd disappeared for a few short hours today. But now they're back.

It's suffocating.

"H-hello," I say, stammering.

"Hello." His voice is clipped and laced with anger. He takes a step toward me.

Suddenly, my footing is unstable. My skin prickles, and my stomach tightens.

"A-are you mad at me?" My voice is small, like a child's.

He pauses, tilting his head. "What do you think, Jessy?"

I flinch, and my mind races. Is he mad because I changed his plans for the day? A day that was already tense after last night—when he murdered someone.

Panicking, I try to backpedal and take some of his focus off me. "But Mom said you'd be happy," I say, backing up. "She said you'd be OK with it . . ."

"I *know* what your mother said!" he shouts in rage.

I'm rooted to the floor, stunned to silence, still not really understanding what I've done to upset him.

His fists pound the wall. And before the force of the impact can even finish echoing through my body, he steps into the office, then reappears.

With Mom in his grip.

There's panic in her eyes that hasn't existed since the first night.

Why? Why is he so upset? I was gone for only a few hours . . .

"*What were you thinking!*" he screams at Mom, his face inches from hers.

She trembles as he continues screaming, spraying her in spittle.

"We almost lost our daughter the other day! Then she tells you she wants to drive away and leave us! Yet somehow, in your simple little mind, you think it's OK to let her go off with some strange boy, in her delicate state?!"

Realization dawns.

She told him what I said in the parking lot.

I'd all but forgotten that before going off with Dan, I'd pleaded with Mom. I'd told her that I wanted *him* gone. That he'd murdered Dad. That I wanted to drive away with her and escape this insanity.

But instead of turning his rage on me, he's turning it on her.

He's been upset with me before. He's punished me before. But not Mom. She's been so careful to placate him ever since that first day, when he murdered Dad and then aimed the gun at her. But even placating him isn't enough.

A slap echoes through the space, and Mom collapses.

"This is why *I* make the decisions and *you* stick to your place in the goddamn kitchen!"

Before I even think through my actions, I'm on him, tugging back his arm to keep him from hurting her again. I can't let him hurt her. I can't let him take her away too.

"Leave her alone!" I scream.

Mom places a hand on her cheek, gazing up with stunned, hurt eyes. She looks so small there on the floor.

My drive to protect her increases. Somehow I manage to pull him back a few feet away from her. The distance feels like a victory—until he turns it around on me, shoving me back.

I slam into the wall, my teeth clacking as the hit reverberates through me.

"I gave you freedom. I trusted you. And the moment I

do, you throw it in my face!"

I cringe. "Please . . . I'm sorry."

"Sorry? You're sorry? You're always sorry, Jessy. I used to believe you. But not anymore. Not after you tried to leave me."

And just like that, my courage evaporates. There's no fight left. Just flight. I look toward the front door, calculating the distance.

He knows exactly what I'm thinking. "Don't do it, Jessy. You'll only make things worse."

I know it's true, but I can't stop myself. I can't stay here. Not when he's looking at me like he wants to kill me. Not when he's hurt Mom. I have to get out of here. For the both of us.

I bolt forward, rip the door open, and run. I run faster and harder than I've ever run before. Maybe Dan is still there. Maybe if I hurry, I can catch him.

"Jessy!" he screams. His voice is close. He's so close. "Get back here, Jessica!"

My heart beats faster, fear fueling me on. It's so cold, but I don't care. I can't stop. I can never stop.

If I can just make it past the trees . . . Dan will be out on the road up ahead. He'll see me in his rearview mirror. He'll come back for me, and I'll tell him everything. Then his dad will arrest *him,* and Mom and I will finally be free.

Free.

Such a beautiful word.

Snow crunches behind me, and I glance over my shoulder. He's right behind me. I can hear his breath.

I can't outrun him.

"*Jessica, stop!*" he roars.

And just like that, my body listens. My mind wants to keep going, to escape, but my body refuses. Freezes. After all, when he dishes out his punishments, it's my body that suffers the most. And I will be punished for this.

Had I kept running, though, perhaps he would have

killed me . . .

He stops behind me, but I don't turn around. I don't want to see it.

Then, slowly, he moves toward me. Snow crunches underneath his feet. With each step, my body tightens, preparing itself for the pain.

The footsteps stop, and I clamp my eyes shut tighter, knowing he's right in front of me.

"Why do you keep making me do this?" he asks. His breath is still heavy from chasing me. "It hurts me to have to discipline you—I don't like it. I don't like being the bad guy. I just want you to be a good girl. Be my little Jessy. Is that so hard? Am I asking too much?"

He waits for a reply.

I open my eyes, staring out at him, not feeling anything. "Because you're a psychopath."

He backhands me. "*I am not crazy!*"

Blood fills my mouth; I bit my cheek. I spit, turning the snow red.

I place my hand against my cheek. I feel nothing other than the cold. My ears are ringing. But there is no pain.

I've reached the point where he's hurt me so much that I can't feel anything anymore.

It should break me. But instead, it steels me.

"What happened to your other family?" I hear myself say. "I know you were a father. Did your family leave you? Your wife? Your kids? Or did you kill them? Maybe you took one of your *punishments* a little too far?"

"Other family . . . ? What?" His shock and confusion sound surprisingly real.

My hands ball into fists at my side. Now I feel something. Rage. It galvanizes me even more.

"You're a monster. A heartless murderer."

"I'm a *victim!*" he shouts. "You don't know what happened to me. The things I've endured."

I scoff at him. Bile rises in my throat to hear this man

call himself a victim.

"Whatever happened to you, it doesn't excuse *anything* you've done to me and my family!"

"I *am* your family!"

I punch him.

I didn't think about it. I just did it. Hit him right in his lying mouth.

Oh God. I hit him.

His tongue rubs along his cheek and jaw, then he spits blood out onto the snow, beside mine.

Before I can react, he lunges for me, grabbing me by the neck, squeezing as he lifts me off the ground.

My hands wrap around his wrists in an attempt to pull him off me and to help support my weight.

He tilts his head as his eyes narrow, glaring at me. "Jessy, Jessy, Jessy," he says, shaking his head. "When will you ever learn? You're my family. I am your father. I have tried to be patient and understanding. I tried talking and rewarding and praising you. But it doesn't work. The only thing that works is the one thing I don't want to do, and that's hurt you. I'm sorry, Jessy, but I have to do what's best."

He lifts me higher. My toes dangle above the snow as I futilely struggle to free myself. Then he tosses me to the ground like a sack of potatoes. The snow does little to break my fall.

This time I feel the pain. This time it hurts.

Everywhere.

He kicks me, hard, in the gut, hitting my cracked ribs. Over and over and over again.

My body cries out in agony. I cry out too. I beg him to stop.

But he doesn't. Not for a long time.

When he does, things are blurry. Choppy. It hurts to blink. It hurts to move. It hurts to breathe.

Only when I succumb to the darkness do I find peace.

SIXTEEN

I'M IN THE BOX AGAIN.
  I don't know how long I've been here. A day, for sure. If not longer. It's so hard to tell when the only source of light is the tiny blinking red dot on the camera.

Thankfully, I've been unconscious for most of it. Most, but not all.

And in those lucid moments, I've been very aware of the pain. The cement has done its fair share of reminding me just how battered I am physically.

Emotionally too. I thought for sure he was going to kill me out there in the snow. He easily could have, seeing as I was in such a vulnerable state. Why didn't he? Why does he keep doing this? Why won't he let me go?

Not wanting to ponder such morbid thoughts or risk falling back asleep from either the pain or boredom, I count the blinks of the red light of his camera. When I reach 4,872, the locks on the door click open. I try to shuffle to my feet but stop when the pain flares. When the door swings open, I don't even have the strength to shield myself from the intrusive light.

He stops at my feet, towering over me. "Dan has been texting you."

My lips quiver, and I take a shaky breath. "Please don't hurt him."

"Hurt him?" he echoes, stunned. "Now, why would I do that? He didn't harm you. And he brought you home—though a proper gentleman would have escorted you to the door and waited to introduce himself to me. Kids these days."

My mind skips, momentarily choosing to ignore his outdated rules for dating his abductee daughter. What I focus on instead are his justifications regarding why he wouldn't have killed Dan. In a way, I guess it's good that he has *some* sort of code. Some rules that he follows, as opposed to just killing whomever he wants whenever he wants.

"In his text, Dan asked if you wanted to hang out today," he continues. "It's Sunday afternoon, by the way. I replied for you—I hope you don't mind. I said that you didn't feel well."

He crouches down, stroking his chin.

I lift my shoulders, not wanting to look away from him for one second. My abs and ribs scream out in agony, but I keep quiet.

"I don't think you're well enough to go to school either," he says. There's a different tone now. "Not for a while."

I pick up the cues. Not being able to return to school has nothing to do with my injuries. Well, very little to do with them, at least. Rather, he doesn't trust me to go back. I screwed up. And because of it, I lost what little freedom I did have.

I press my head against the plywood as violent sobs ripple through me. Tears spill down the sides of my face, falling into my shoulders and hair.

When my heartache numbs enough for the tears to slow, he gives me a small smile of reassurance. "There's my girl. Let's go upstairs—get you cleaned up and something decent to eat. Your mother should have dinner ready soon."

Knowing refusal would only bring more pain, I follow the monster upstairs.

‡

After a bath and a change of clothes, I head downstairs. He's sitting on the couch, watching hockey.

When he sees me, his face brightens. "Come sit and watch the game with me, Jessy."

I stand there like a deer in headlights.

How many more nights of playing pretend is he going to inflict on us? This can't go on forever.

He notices my hesitation. Something akin to disappointment flashes in his eyes, and he slumps back against the cushions.

"Actually," he says, "maybe you should go help your mother with dinner." He waves me away like a king would his subject.

I hightail it to the kitchen, my head spinning with his dismissal. It's never been that easy before.

Mom's pulling something out of the oven. She turns— and my heart sinks.

Her right eye is swollen shut, her left cheek is bruised, and her lip is split open.

He hit her. Repeatedly.

Was it while I was unconscious? It had to have been. So he tossed me in the box and then wailed on her? For how long?

I rush to her side. "What did he do to you?" I ask.

I catalog all her injuries. The ones I can see, anyway. Did she fight back against him? Did she even stand up for herself at all? Somehow, I don't think she did. I bet she would have let him kill her, if he wanted.

Somewhere in the back of my mind, I realize *she* should be the one cataloging *my* injuries and offering *me* comfort. At the very least, we should be comforting and supporting each other.

But no. The roles are reversed once again. She's simply not present in the way a mother should be. And we've done this song and dance often enough that it no longer surprises me or saddens me. It just simply is.

Her one good eye meets my gaze. "He didn't do this. *You* did. This is your fault, Jessy."

Each word is like a knife stabbing my gut.

Suddenly he appears behind me. "It's ugly, isn't it—the consequences of your actions?" he says. "It doesn't feel good, does it?"

My lips quiver. "No."

He slides his arm around Mom. She doesn't even flinch. So it's true. She doesn't blame him at all. She blames me. My fault. I'm the one who suggested we run, and she was punished for it.

I won't give him an excuse to hurt her. Not again. Never again.

Dinner is a silent affair.

As usual, Mom makes a big production of it. Linen tablecloth. China. Candles. Parmesan-encrusted porkchops, asparagus, and twice-baked potatoes, then crème brûlée for dessert.

I think it goes fine—as well as any other dinner with a killer can. But when he lets out a deep sigh and tosses his napkin on the table, my body goes tighter than a violin string about to snap. He pushes his chair back and stands. My heart beats like a drum, pounding so fast and ferociously I feel it in my eyes.

"Come on, Jessy," he says, holding out his hand for me. "There's something I'd like you to see."

I don't fight him. There's no point. I take his hand and let him lead me wherever he wants, though I'm a bit surprised when that turns out to be the basement. More specifically, the box.

He gestures for me to get back inside.

216

I'd rather spend the night recuperating in bed, but I guess I haven't earned that yet. I step over the threshold to my tiny plywood cell.

"I put a lot of work into rebuilding our family, Jessy. I didn't just show up here out of the blue. It took years and many sacrifices to get you back. But in all my planning and preparing, I never once imagined that you wouldn't remember me. That they *made* you forget me."

He says these words with such vehemence that it triggers something deep inside.

I suddenly remember the moment when I first saw him on the landing. It feels like ages ago, though it's only been a few weeks. The second I saw his face, I was hit with a spark of familiarity. I knew I'd seen him before. But try as I might, I couldn't place it. Still can't.

But now that spark has reignited. He's insisting that I *should* know him but have forgotten him.

My accident did cause some memory lapses, though it mostly only affects memories from shortly before and after the crash. If I had met him during the accident and its aftermath, it's highly possible I wouldn't recall him now.

But I don't believe that's the answer. I have the feeling that it's something more significant. Something that goes deep to the core of who I am.

No. What am I talking about? I'm not the crazy one here. He is. This is nothing but rambling figments of his lunatic brain.

"They made you forget me," he repeats. "So I'm going to fix that. I'm going to help you remember. And hopefully, we can finally move forward as a family. Heal. Make up for lost time."

He moves, reaching for something on the wall. Something I hadn't noticed earlier but now do. A small TV has been mounted near the ceiling of the box. Cables run up the wall and out through a hole drilled in the ceiling. Was that always there, or did he install it just now, while I was in the bath?

Blue light flickers as the screen comes to life. It's a picture of a young man holding a baby. The clothing style and photo quality suggest it's from at least a decade ago, possibly two. The man's hair is dark and well kept. His eyes are filled with happiness as he stares at the bundle wrapped in pink in his arms. But it's still easy to tell that it's him.

I'd believed all along that he had a family, that he was a father. But seeing is different than believing. This image of him—happy, nurturing, loving, and supportive—is at odds with the psychotic, murdering narcissist I've come to loathe.

I'm so consumed by the image and my thoughts that I barely notice him close the door and lock it behind him. I'm in here alone now, with nothing to do but stare at this photo on the TV.

But then the image changes to a new photo. It's still him. Still the same baby. The first photo was taken inside a house or something. He was standing in front of a plain wall. But this photo was taken outside. He's taking her for a walk.

The photo changes again. This one is odd, though. There are other people in the picture, but their faces are scratched out. Only him and the baby are unmarked. Whoever the other people are, they have been intentionally obscured.

Intentionally and violently.

These images are scratched out with a blade of some sort. This wasn't done to protect their identities or even to protect his. It was done in anger. Blind rage.

Why? Who are these people? What happened to them? Did he kill them? Is this when he went mad? And if so, what sparked it?

Over and over, I see photos of him and the baby. Then after who knows how many photos, an image appears that makes my heart still and my lungs freeze. This photo is of a different man and woman with a little girl. I know this photo. I've seen it many times.

In our family photo album.

Only this time, Dad is crossed out.

Same with the next photo. And the one after that. These are *our* photos, covering years of my life.

If Dad is crossed out but Mom isn't, does that mean he only crosses out people who are dead? People he's killed?

I watch myself grow up in the photos, recognizing each one.

Then a few slip by that I don't remember. Then a few more. Suddenly I realize that not all the photos are from our family albums. They're candid. Shots of me cheering, shopping with friends, laughing. Some are closeups; others are from far away.

Did *he* take these? All of these? How did I not notice? How did I never see? They go back *years*.

Then my throat catches when I see a photo of me sledding with Dan. Even though I thought I was free, away from that man's prying eyes.

And then just like that, the very first photo reappears—that man and that baby. The slideshow is starting over again.

A tear slides down my cheek.

What is this?

Am *I* supposed to be that baby? Is he trying to say that I was once with him, but then I—

No. I don't want to think about it. I don't want to give him any more purchase into my life.

I *am* Bob and Sandy Smith's daughter. I *know* that. I've seen my birth certificate. And there are so many pictures of Mom pregnant with me and me as a baby with her and Dad. I was born exactly eight months after their wedding—four weeks early.

Or so the story goes.

But what about the pictures of that man with me?

How can I be their daughter and also his?

After the fifteenth time through the video, I can't stop the what-ifs.

What if I really am his child?

219

What if he had an affair with Mom, but then she decided to stay married to Dad?

What if Dad knew he wasn't my biological father?

What if he didn't know?

If it's true, it would explain why he was furious enough with Mom for lying and keeping me from him to almost kill her.

This is so messed up. No. No. No.

I can't deny, though, that Mom jumped into her role as this man's wife really quickly. And she never shied away from his touch. Maybe they *were* together before Mom and Dad got married.

The only thing I know is that *someone* is lying.

And I'm starting to think it's not him.

The logic flows now. He said he'd had problems. He said he'd been an alcoholic.

What if Mom was involved with this man, got pregnant, but then decided to marry Dad—Bob—because he could give her a better life?

For that matter, what if Mom isn't even my biological mother?

What if Sandy and Bob did some sort of illegal adoption arrangement? The pregnancy photos could be faked, right? A pillow or something under her clothes. Or what if they straight-up stole me? It wouldn't be the first time a wealthy family has been caught up in such a scandal.

The dark thoughts spiral, one after another, as my life scrolls by on the TV screen. Is this what it was like for him—watching me grow up behind the lens of a camera? Knowing I was his daughter, but never allowed to engage? Watching some other man raise me?

That had to hurt. That had to cut deep.

I can't even imagine.

I remember now what he said that first day he came into our home. He said he'd tried to reach out to me. Tried to get me back. But Bob wouldn't let him.

No wonder he went to all this time and effort to get me back.

What am I supposed to do with this knowledge? Am I supposed to understand him? Forgive him?

It's all so much.

I watch the slideshow over seventy times before he comes back. Wordlessly, he stands outside the door, staring at me in a way he's never done before. Actually, I've seen glimpses of this side of him. Moments here and there. But this time, it's on full display.

He's looking at me as a father. A father who has always loved his daughter yet somehow lost her for many, many years.

But he's also a murderer. An insane man who held us captive. Who tortured and beat me. Who gave me the wounds that pain me this very second.

His eyes point to the TV screen, where the slideshow is beginning once again. Then he looks back at me.

"You believe now, don't you?" he whispers.

My throat is too dry to voice it, so I settle for a nod.

The breath that leaves him is so full of relief that even I feel it.

"Good. That's really good, Jessy."

"How?" I barely manage to say. "How did they—"

Again, my throat goes dry before I can even finish. I hope he understands, though. I hope he understands that I want to know what happened. How he lost me.

What happened to us?

To my surprise, his face softens a bit. "I was sick, Jessy. I've told you that much before. I was an out-of-work alcoholic. Your mother and Bob could give you things I couldn't. Give you a good life while I straightened mine out."

Guilt, sadness, and anger race through me. He didn't have to give me away just because his life wasn't perfect. Plenty of people raise kids when they aren't fit to. Many of them find a way to beat the odds and make it work.

Then again, sometimes it doesn't work. Sometimes it's really, really bad. So maybe he did do the right thing for me—though it cost him everything.

His face hardens now. "But it was never meant to be permanent. Bob was never meant to keep you from me forever."

Questions flash in my head. What about the police? The courts? Couldn't someone step in?

But I suspect that's just naiveté. Who in their right mind would hand a kid over to a man like him when a man like Bob Smith was the alternative?

And so Bob raised me. I had a great life here. Picture perfect. Who knew it was built on lies?

"I'm sorry."

I've told him that before, but this time I mean it.

He half laughs. It's not a bitter laugh. More like his pent-up emotions getting the better of him.

"I appreciate that. But it's not your fault, Jessy. Not this part of it, anyway. But hopefully, now we can finally be the family I always wanted us to be."

He isn't a cruel, heartless monster. He's my father.

He reaches his hand out to me, palm up.

Instantly I take it.

His fingers curl around mine, tightening just a moment as if to check that it's real.

I pray to God it is. And I pray that finally the violence is behind us.

"Can we?" he asks, his voice full of longing. "Can we move forward?"

I smile. "I'd like that.

SEVENTEEN

ON WEDNESDAY, DAD ALLOWS DAN TO pick me up for school. It'll be my first day at school this week. I stayed home Monday and Tuesday to spend some time with Dad. Learn about him. About us. And heal.

The story I'll be telling people is that I've had a cold. Again. It'll allow me to take it easy now that I am returning to school.

Dan's waiting at the tree line for me, just as he said he would. He beats me to my door, holding it open. "Your chariot, my lady."

I can't help the snort that slips out as I ease into my seat. "Such a charmer."

"One of my best qualities," he says before shutting my door and dashing around the car. As soon as he's in, he cranks the heat. "For being sick for so long, you look great, Jess. How do you feel?"

"I feel good. Better than I have in a long time."

It's not a lie. These past few days have changed everything. We're finally on the right path at home, and things will only get better from now on. For a few nights now, I've even been allowed to sleep in my old room again.

My bedroom, that is.

"I'm glad to hear it," he says. "But if you start to feel sick at school, text me, and I'll take you home."

Even if he hadn't adjusted the heat, the warmth radiating inside me would keep me plenty warm. "Thanks. I should be OK. But if not, I'll let you know."

The rest of the drive is spent singing along to the radio. It's something Blake would never do with me. I love that Dan does it. He has a surprisingly great voice too. I could listen to it for hours.

When we arrive at school together, the happy buzz we built in the shelter of his car fades. It begins when he once again opens my car door. People milling around in the parking lot turn and stare. Whispers soar like vultures in the desert.

I'd almost forgotten how intense the pressure of their expectations can be. The weight of their judgments.

Something touches my hand. I glance down, finding Dan's hand in mine.

"Dang," he says. "If I'd have known we were gonna be in a parade, I would've brought candy to toss out to the crowd." He leans in closer. "Though I'd probably accidently hit everyone in the head. I have terrible aim."

"You do not! I've watched you play basketball in gym. You're amazing."

His smile shines so bright it rivals the sun. "I *knew* you've been checking me out!"

I shrug, not bothering to deny it.

Somehow, that only increases his good mood. He struts into school with his hand still in mine.

Rumors fly that we're dating. A few people are brave enough to comment about it to my face; the rest stick with loud whispers.

I spend every chance I get with him throughout the day. Part of it is him checking up on me, which is sweet. The rest is because I'm drawn to him in a way I've never felt before.

It's his energy. His positive outlook. It's addicting. Like nothing can get him down. I have a feeling that even if it were raining outside, he'd do something to make it fun.

I once had Blake, Cassie, and countless other friends, but now I see that there's truth to the whole "quality versus quantity" concept.

In order to maintain my place at the top, there was so much pressure to be in the know and have all the latest and greatest must-haves. Now that I'm on the outside looking in, it all seems so superficial. And by how quickly everyone has turned on me, it only solidifies that feeling.

Which makes Dan all the more contrary.

I've been around him enough to pick up that he was top dog at his school. Yet instead of acting like the king, like Blake does, Dan is different. He knows everyone from his school. Literally hundreds of kids, even the freshman. He knows their names. He knows their families and pets. If someone had an illness or injury, he asks how they're doing. He'd make a great politician.

The thought instantly makes me think of my old dad, which sours my mood for the rest of the morning.

At lunch today, Dan somehow picks up on it. But instead of coming right out and asking what's wrong, he tries to cheer me up by resuming our game of twenty questions. It's not that he doesn't care or is trying to distract me. Instead, I get the feeling that he's giving me time to sift through it.

"Which is better, Pepsi or Coke?"

The randomness of the question helps break up some of my thundercloud of emotions. I laugh, despite myself.

"Neither!" I reply. "Ginger ale wins, hands down. Or sometimes I'll mix things up with fruit-flavored sodas—maybe orange or grape."

He smirks and shakes his head. "You know, I've been asking people that Coke-or-Pepsi question for almost a decade, and you are the only person who's ever answered 'ginger ale.' You, Jess, are a one of a kind."

The last of the storm clouds burst at his praise. It's enough to carry me through the remainder of the day.

As the afternoon stretches on, I find my thoughts pulling toward Dan. Toward us.

Dan and I are not a couple. He wants to be, but he's waiting. For me.

I feel like officially dating Dan would be such a change. And I worry that changing something—anything—could jinx the goodness Dad and I just found at home. It would be like removing the wrong block in Jenga. All our stability would come crashing down.

That said, Dad seems OK with me hanging out with Dan. Dad and I talked about it a few times on Monday and Tuesday. He once again commented on how good it is to see me smile.

I guess that's his way of giving me his blessing to date Dan. Maybe. I don't know.

Still, I don't want to send us spiraling back into darkness. I want to play it safe.

So I'm going to test things out with Dan as a friend first. See how it all goes. I'll maybe only take the next step if everything goes well.

I hope it does.

‡

By Friday, most people have gotten used to the idea of *us*. Even the football team—with the exception of Blake—has stopped glaring at us.

The remaining holdout is Nick.

He's not sitting with us at lunch, when he and Dan used to always sit together. He's avoiding us in the halls. And he pretends I don't exist in the few classes he and I share.

Dan tries to brush it off, claiming that Nick's going through something of his own, but I can't help thinking it's us. More accurately, *me*. I can't stop thinking about how upset he was in the driveway, seeing me there. And as much as he denies it, I know this is eating Dan up too.

In gym, Nick surprises me by picking me as his partner in pickleball. Even Mr. Krause raises an eyebrow. Nick always partners with Dan. They're like the Dynamic Duo. Dan steps toward Nick, flashing his palms in an instinctively calming gesture. "Hey, man—I'll be your partner."

"No," I quickly reply, stepping forward too. "It's OK." Nick's eyes volley back and forth between us. Dan's trying not to frown—but failing. I give him a reassuring nod.

Even though whatever Nick is dealing with isn't my problem—Lord knows I have enough of my own—I can't help wanting to fix it. If I knew whatever was wrong, maybe I could help . . . ? And if his problem is truly with me, maybe smoothing things over would make Dan happy.

I follow Nick to the net that's farthest from the door. I suspect he chose it because it puts the most distance between us and Dan.

Nick serves first, sending a beeline straight for the far corner. I lunge but miss it. Instantly, my side flares with stabbing pains. I've been in my bed a few nights now, but my ribs and muscles are still sore from sleeping on concrete last week. And my body is still bruised from my mistakes over the weekend. For that matter, the bruises and wounds from my past transgressions will probably never fully heal.

Thankfully, that's all behind us. I promised Dad I won't disobey him anymore. Now that I know who he is and what he's done for us—for me—there's no reason to. We're healing now. As a family. The family we always should have been.

"Why Dan?" Nick asks as he serves again, smacking the ball toward the opposite corner.

I race for it and manage to hit it in the nick of time. "Why not Dan?"

"Because he's great, and you're a—" He smacks the ball

back to me.

Again, it's on the other side of the court. He's being an ass on purpose.

"I'm a what?" I grit my teeth and manage to hit the ball, barely. The ball just clears the net.

Caught off guard, Nick has to scurry to the net. He swings but misses. The ball bounces into another game. He runs after it.

"I'm a what?" I repeat when he comes back.

"I don't know anymore," he says. "And that's the problem!" He smashes the ball, sending it flying right at me. I squeal and duck.

Mr. Krause blows the whistle. "Smith!"

Both Nick and I turn at the sound of our name.

Mr. Krause points at Nick to clarify. "You, Smith— knock it off!" he warns.

I glance across the gym at Dan. He's watching us. And he's pissed.

I retrieve the ball and bounce it a few times, setting up my serve while giving myself a chance to breathe. I'm really overexerting myself. I know I'll pay for it for the rest of the day.

"Look," I say, "I get that you hate me and—"

"Would you stop saying that?" Nick snaps. "I don't hate you. I never have."

I suck in a breath, then wince from the pain it causes. He doesn't hate me . . . ? Is that true? Have I been wrong this whole time?

Questions amass in my head. If he doesn't hate me, then why has he stared at me all year? Why has he listened to my conversations at my locker yet refused to engage in conversation with me?

Then again, he's been decent since break ended. He was the first to ask if I was OK when Blake and I broke up. And then when Blake confronted me at my locker, Nick was right there, behind me. Nick and Dan.

The Dynamic Duo.

Our relationship bothers Nick so much. On Saturday, in Dan's driveway, Nick said something about how his feelings meant nothing to Dan. I accused Nick of hating me then too. Yet here Nick is, swearing that he doesn't hate me. So then what in the world is he so upset about? As much as I want to know, it's not like he'll tell me. I think he's made his thoughts on me quite clear now. It may not be hatred, but it sure isn't liking either.

"Whatever," I finally say with a sigh. "But whatever this is—between you and me—it's hurting Dan. Can we just pretend to get along for his sake?"

Nick frowns as he glances over at Dan, who's still watching us like a hawk. Even from here, I can see that Dan's usual, happy-go-lucky smile has been replaced with a scowl so fierce I have to stop myself from rushing over there and reassuring him.

"Fine. For him."

‡

At the end of the day, Dan's waiting for me at my locker to give me a ride home. Next to him, for the first time all week, is Nick. He's not looking at me or at Dan. Instead, he's silently gathering things from his locker. But it's a start.

"Hey, you," I say, smiling.

Dan smirks, the fluorescent lights twinkling in his eyes. "Hey."

I grab my stuff as he fidgets beside me.

"Um, there's something I wanted to ask you—but you don't have to say yes if you don't want to," he begins. The lights in his eyes fade and flicker with nervousness. "It's just . . . my sisters got busted for watching *Dexter*. Apparently, they didn't erase their viewing history or something. I don't know." He shakes his head to get himself back on track. "Anyway, they ratted me out for having you over."

I stiffen and suck in a breath, and the world seems to fall out from under my feet. He's in trouble. *I* got him in trouble.

"No, no," Dan quickly says, seeing my reaction. "It's all good. My folks are actually kinda happy about it. In fact, now they want to have you over for dinner tonight. I tried to tell them we're not, like, you know, dating or anything. But they still want me to ask you over. So like I said, you don't have to say yes or—"

"Dude—chill," Nick says. "Give her a chance to respond before you talk her out of it." Then he turns to me and adds, "But just so you know, Friday is spaghetti night, and Kate makes awesome spaghetti. You don't want to miss it."

Nick runs a hand through his shaggy brown hair, then tosses me a grin. I think it might be the first time he's ever smiled at me. Guess he's really trying to make this work for Dan. It's sweet.

Dan takes a moment to read Nick, unsure whether he can trust what he's seeing. Nick gives the slightest shrug as an acknowledgment.

"Yeah, it's true," Dan says, his eyes slowly lighting up again. "Spaghetti night is the best." Then he turns and blindsides me with the full force of his adorable lopsided grin and those bright hazel eyes. "What do you say?"

Immediately, I want to say yes just to keep this good vibe going between us. Between all three of us.

But meeting his parents is a big deal. Even though he explained that we're just friends, did they believe him? What did his sisters tell them? Do his parents know—like his sisters do—that he's been crushing on me for years?

Then, of course, there's the issue of my own parents. Eating dinner as a family is a big deal for Dad. He says it helps us bond. He goes as far to say that studies show that it helps kids eat healthier and reduces the effects of cyberbullying.

Would he be OK if I missed dinner with him and Mom? Just this once?

LAURIE WETZEL ‡ PICTURE PERFECT

The more I think about it, the more I think it'll be OK. I've earned a lot of Dad's trust back over the last few days.

Plus, we've talked a lot about how he wants us to have a normal life now. And for a teenager, a normal life means hanging out at my friends' houses every now and then. So maybe now that we're finally OK, we can find a new normal . . . ?

"I'll have to check with home," I finally tell Dan.

I expect him to be disappointed or, at the very least, to tease me. Instead, he grabs my backpack, tosses me his signature easy grin, and says, "Great! Text me and let me know what they say."

‡

When I get home, I rush into Dad's study, finding him watching the recording of my day. He doesn't watch it live throughout the day anymore. That's how much he trusts me.

Now he just double-checks the footage at the end of the day. He's watching for things I might not see. Like if someone is directing mean gestures behind my back or if Blake and his friends are giving Dan too hard of a time. It's nice that Dad's able to watch out for me in a way other parents can't.

"Hey, Dad," I say. "I was wondering if—"

I'm surprised when my words suddenly come to a halt. Nervousness flutters inside me.

Am I sure I want to ask this? What if Dad says no? That would suck. But it'd be worlds apart from what would have happened *before*. Back then, even just asking a question would result in strict discipline.

That was then. This is now. I can do this. I can ask.

"I was wondering," I begin again, "would it be OK if I ate dinner at Dan's house tonight?"

Dad spins around in his desk chair, giving me his undivided attention as he looks me up and down. "I thought you two were just friends . . . ?"

"We are," I say with sincere emphasis. "But his parents want to meet me."

A small smile appears. "Of course they do. You're a remarkable girl, Jessy. As long as missing family dinner doesn't become a frequent thing, I'm fine with you going tonight."

I can't help the squeal that comes out. I rush over and throw my arms around him.

"Thank you, Daddy!"

He tightens the hold. "Anything for you, baby girl."

I rush upstairs to get ready, then I head out to my car.

It's strange to be behind the wheel again. I haven't driven since my accident on the bridge.

But Dad and I both agreed that it just didn't make sense for Dan to drive all the way out here when he's already at home. Not to mention to then make him drive all the way out and back later.

I was worried my car wouldn't start, but I shouldn't have been. I guess Dad's been charging the battery and starting it every day while I'm at school. He even brought it into the barn and changed my oil. I didn't know people could do that themselves. Bob always made appointments with a mechanic for that stuff.

As the engine purrs to life, a warm feeling fills me. I'm so glad I have this chance to drive the car, after all the work Dad's done to take care of it.

To take care of me.

Plus, the drive over gives me a chance to settle my nerves for dinner. Dan and Nick played it off as a simple spaghetti dinner, but it feels like more. Meeting his parents . . . It sure feels like we're taking a step closer to something more than friends.

I pull up to his house, park, and draw a deep breath of courage before getting out. As I walk up to Dan's house, the front door opens. Leaning there against the doorframe, looking right at me, is Nick.

My eyes and my mouth open wide. I can't hide my surprise and confusion, though I do try to explain it.

"Sorry," I mumble with chagrin. "I just didn't realize you'd be here too."

Nick grimaces a little, then deliberately catches himself. He sighs. "I'm always here for dinner. Well, I was up until Saturday . . ." Now he's the one wearing the chagrin.

I get it now. That's why Nick was in the driveway that night—he was coming for dinner.

I nod, recalling Dan saying something to that effect about Nick practically being part of the family. I give Nick a small smile. I think he understands what it means. I'm glad we're all able to move forward.

"Jess!" Dan calls from behind Nick. "You made it!" He playfully shoves Nick out of the way as he reaches out for me, taking my hand. "Come on in. Everyone's out yet, so we're just watching TV."

I take off my coat and boots in the entryway and follow Dan to the living room.

Nick plops down, lying across the sofa. He grabs the remote and resumes whatever show they were watching. It looks like a cooking competition.

"Make yourself at home," Dan grumbles to him.

Nick crosses his ankles on the sofa's armrest. "Thanks."

Dan shakes his head, then grins as he looks at me. "What would you like to drink?"

"Whatever you have is fine," I reply.

"I'll take a pop," Nick says. "And some chips too!"

"Your legs aren't broken," Dan replies, still smiling.

I get the impression it would take a lot to upset him. And it's nice to see them in their element, joking around and having fun.

"Have a seat, Jess," Dan says. "I'll be back in a minute."

With Nick stretched out over the entire sofa, I survey what's left of the furniture. I decide on the love seat in hopes

LAURIE WETZEL ‡ PICTURE PERFECT

that Dan will sit beside me when he returns.

"How are you feeling?"

Nick's question sends me to that surprised and confused place again. "Fine," I quickly say. "Why?"

"You've been sick a lot lately. Two weekends in a row. But you didn't look 'sick' during pickleball."

I frown a bit. "If you're so worried about me being sick, then why did you play against me like we were in the Olympics?"

He shrugs. "It was a test."

That piques my interest. I scoot forward, leaning toward him. "For what? To see if I have what it takes to hang out with you guys?"

He shakes his head. "Nah." But then his gaze intensifies as if he has me under a microscope. "It was pretty clear from my test that you weren't sluggish or nauseous. Instead, it looked like you were in *pain*. Especially when you breathe too deep."

Stormy eyes pull me in, holding my gaze and daring me to look away.

I can't look away. I won't. Doing that would tell him he's right. The last thing I need is Nick butting in and ruining things.

I shift in my seat, trying not to flinch as I activate the sore spots—mainly my ribs. I remind myself that my sweaterdress and leggings cover all my bruises, including my stomach, which now looks like I rolled around in a field of grapes and blueberries.

A few more weeks, and I should be fine—provided I don't do anything to make Dad upset . . .

"I have been sick," I fib. "I get sick easily. It's a side effect of not having a spleen. And this time, I had a chest cold with a lot of coughing, so my lungs are still a little sore."

Nick's eyes narrow, and I fight to resist squirming under the weight of his suspicion. He seems ready to say something else.

But just then, Dan appears, holds a can of pop a few feet above Nick's stomach, then lets it plummet.

Nick grunts. "Jerk. Now it's all shook up."

Dan shrugs. "Don't like it? Get it yourself." Then he whips a bag of Doritos at him. "Let Jess pick what we watch."

Nick grumbles but hands me the remote.

I wave it away. "I'm good with whatever."

"See?" Nick says, resting back on the couch. "She doesn't want it."

"She's just being polite. Unlike *some people*." Dan hands me a glass of ginger ale.

I smile. He remembered. Do they have ginger ale in the house all the time, or did he ask his parents to get it specifically for me tonight?

"Thank you," I say.

"You're welcome."

My cheeks heat as he sits beside me. My body is flush up against his left side. I've misgauged how big this love seat is. Now that I think of it, it may not be a love seat for two but an oversized armchair for one.

I could squish into the pillow at my side, give him a little more room. But wouldn't that seem odd? Like I was trying to put space between us? Maybe he's OK sitting like this. I imagine he would have sat in the chair otherwise. Or made Nick get up.

"So where's everybody else?" I ask, fighting to keep my voice even. "Your parents and your sisters."

"Dad's still at work. Mom's with the girls at dance. They have practice every Friday. They'll be here soon."

"Oh," I say.

Then I frown.

I used to dance before cheerleading. I miss those days— the costumes, the choreography, the competitions. Most weekends, Mom and I would travel together from one event to the other. She would spend hours fussing over my outfits, hair, and makeup.

My heart clenches, missing her. I mean, I see her every day. But it's different. She's still different.

As wonderful as things are at home now, she's still a Stepford Wife. I don't know why. She's cold and distant. There's no spark. No emotion.

It's odd to be growing closer to Dad while drifting further apart from Mom. I can't even ask her why. Not unless I want to risk things going backward.

Dan yawns, pulling me from my thoughts. He stretches his arms up behind him in an overly dramatic way. When they come down, his left arm slides behind me, resting on my shoulders.

I gulp, side-eyeing his seemingly relaxed pose. He probably just needed the room, that's all.

But then his thumb brushes over my shoulder. Thousands of butterflies erupt inside me.

Nope. I don't think he did that for room. I think he did it to put his arm around me.

And I think I like it.

From the couch, I hear a hint of a snort.

"Is this OK?" Dan asks me quietly.

This. He means his arm around my shoulders. But to me, *this* means so much more.

This—especially this in front of Nick—feels like so much more than friendship. But at the same time, it doesn't feel bad or wrong. It feels good. Right. And maybe now that things are mostly normal at home, I really can have a normal relationship with Dan too.

Maybe I can even take him home and introduce him to my mom and dad. Maybe when Mom is better. Have him over for dinner and to watch football games with us.

A smile forms as hope floods me.

I lean into Dan. "Yeah. This is fine."

His arm tightens around me, pleased.

From the corner of my eyes, I see Nick staring, his brows

narrowed. I continued to look ahead and focus on the show. A few heartbeats later, Nick follows suit.

This is nice—hanging out.

With both of them.

EIGHTEEN

W E STAY LIKE THIS, TOGETHER IN A comfortable silence, until a car pulls into their driveway. Dan's mom and sisters are home.

The girls walk in first. Upon seeing us in the chair, Julie resumes her song from last weekend. Then they run up the stairs together, giggling.

As Dan's mom comes in, all three of us stand. With curly brown hair and kind blue eyes, she's prettier than the pictures I've seen on the walls.

Nick surprises me by rushing around the couch to help her with some grocery bags without her asking.

"Did you have a good day at school, Nick?" she asks, taking off her North Face jacket to reveal a red sweater and jeans.

He smiles, and it's more vibrant than any smile I've seen him make. "I did, Kate. Thanks."

Watching the two of them, it dawns on me: she's the closest thing he has to a mother now. Dan's family is Nick's family.

My stomach knots.

Dan clears his throat. "Uh, Mom, this is Jess. Jessy Smith. Jess, this is my mom, Kate."

I hold out my hand for her. "Hello, Mrs. McLeary. It's nice to meet you."

She stares at my outstretched hand. A moment later, she pulls me in for a hug.

My body clenches, caught off guard. I'm shielding myself from more pain . . . pain that, after a few seconds, I realize isn't coming.

I have to stop that reaction, that fear. Now that things are better, I need to relax. I'm sure it would upset Dad if he hugged me and I reacted this poorly.

But Kate's hug is warm. Soft. Safe. And she smells nice too. Like orchids. The whole experience reminds me of the way Mom used to hug me.

Kate pulls back and places her hand on my cheek as she looks me over. "It's so nice to meet you, Jess. And please, call me Kate."

I don't know what to do, so I just stand there. Other than Dan, no one has ever called me Jess. I don't even know why he does it. But I like it.

The door opens again, and in walks Dan's father, dressed in a charcoal suit. His badge hangs out of his front pocket, and a gun is holstered in his belt.

Suddenly, bloody images of Bob and Officer Adams pop into my head. I can't stop myself from taking a step back.

But then I focus on my breathing and shove those awful thoughts away, knowing those days are behind us. Thankfully, Dan's dad doesn't notice my freak-out. He's too preoccupied with taking off his gun and badge and securing them in a locked drawer in a cabinet near the door.

Now that I see him, I do remember him from Bob's time in office. I know I'd met Dan's dad on multiple occasions, but I don't recall our conversations. Just that he always had Jolly Ranchers in his pocket and would share some with me.

He spots me and smiles. "She's here!" Suddenly, I'm being hugged again, this time by him. "It's good to see you again, Jessy."

He's strong, tall, and stocky. Thin black hairs are matted to his head. And he smells just like Dan—that same woodsy cologne.

"I guess you know this already—but Jess, this is my dad, Tomas," Dan introduces even while we're already locked in an embrace.

Just like I did with Kate, I stand there, stiff as a board, unable to reciprocate. When it ends, I slowly release my breath, grateful it's over.

Dan's dad slams his son on the back, proud of him. Kate beams at them both.

I can't help but think it all has something to do with me.

I look away from the happy family and catch Nick's eye. He's watching them too. With a desperate need to belong.

I recognize it because I feel it too.

‡

We help Kate with dinner. Dan and I are on garlic bread, Nick has salads, and the girls help set the table. Tomas keeps swiping noodles and bread, getting his hand smacked by Kate each time, which makes us all laugh.

In all the many dinners I've had—with both versions of my family—none has ever been like this. With this many people in one room, it should be chaos, and it kind of is. But at the same time, it's perfection. Everyone is happy. Joking around. It's so lighthearted. No one is yelling or hitting.

But most of all, no one is afraid.

This is how our dinners at home should be. How they always should have been.

As wonderful as things are now, I realize they're not like this. Not yet. I'd like them to be. I'd love to see Mom and Dad joking around and having fun.

That same feeling is carried throughout dinner. Everyone talks openly about their day, the highs and lows—even Nick. The voices overlap and layer on top of one another, though no one is being interrupted or ignored. It's like a happy symphony.

Then Kate brings up the search for Officer Charlie Adams.

I choke on my ginger ale.

Everyone quietly watches on as Dan gently rubs my back.

"Are you OK?" Kate asks.

"I'm fine," I manage between coughs. "Wrong pipe."

After a few more coughs, I recover and join the others in waiting for Tomas to fill them in on the missing officer. I see the hope in their eyes. They're praying he has good news.

They must have known Officer Adams well. Did he join them for dinners too? Did he sit where I am now?

What would they think if they knew I'm the reason he'll never join them again . . . ?

"We found his cruiser today," Tomas says.

My heart stops.

"It was torched, but we haven't found any evidence to suggest that Charlie was inside it at the time."

"So he's still missing?" Kate asks.

Tomas nods. "That's what we're hoping for. We'll find out what happened to him, dear. I promise."

After that somber news, conversations continue, though with less enthusiasm. Their minds are all on their friend's disappearance, while mine is on his death.

Before I blacked out, the last thing I saw was Charlie's body still lying in the snow by the bridge and his cruiser still parked just yards away.

When did Dad set fire to the cruiser? Why? And what did he do to Officer Adams's body?

Oh God. If he didn't hide it well enough, if he didn't hide or destroy all the evidence, then Tomas will come for him. He'll take him away again.

Then they'll all know the truth.

I'll lose Dan.

But worse—I'll lose Dad all over again.

"So, Jessy," Tomas says, his tone upbeat again. "How's your dad? I haven't talked to him since before he left for Cameroon. He's back now, right? If so, I should see if he wants to play racquetball sometime next week. We used to play weekly back when he was governor. Matter of fact, I think he won the last game!"

Everyone stares at me. Smiling. Waiting for me to say something.

But I don't know what to say. Tomas is a cop. The chief of police. It's not like I can lie to him. But I can't tell him the truth either.

This—coming for dinner—was a bad idea.

Why did Dad let me come here? Why didn't he at least prepare me for this, for their questions about Officer Adams and Bob and everything else? Why didn't we rehearse something?

Without thinking, I stand. Actually, my first thought is to run, and the only reason I don't is because I know it'll be disastrously painful.

Instead I say, "Excuse me. I have to use the bathroom."

Before they can say anything else, I rush off down the hall. I shut the bathroom door and lean against it, trembling.

How can I stay here, in their home, staring them in the face, lying to them? Yet how can I explain the truth to them?

How do I say that the Bob they knew—the politician, the do-gooder, the devoted husband and father—stole me, kept me from my real father?

Tomas would know that that's illegal. He'd understand that Dad is the victim here. He's innocent. He *never* would have killed Bob or Officer Adams if I hadn't been kept from him like that.

Would Tomas see it that way? Would he understand?

How could he? It's a complicated situation that's hard to grasp. Look at how long it took me to understand, to believe. Dad had to go to great lengths with me—lengths he couldn't go with Tomas.

Tomas would go straight to the house and arrest Dad.

But Dad wouldn't go quietly.

How many more people would he hurt or kill? Would he kill other officers? Tomas?

And then Dad would come here for me. I know he would. Not to hurt me. To fight to the death for me. I cannot fathom what he'd do to Dan. To Nick. To Kate. Even to the—

No. That's enough.

I can't do this. I can't be here. But I don't know how to get out of this.

All I can do is pull out my phone and call Dad.

"Jessy, what's wrong?" he asks, answering before the first ring ends. The concern in his voice makes my stomach churn.

"Dan's father is asking about Bob. They're friends. I don't know what to say to him."

"Tell him the truth," he says, his voice now cold.

I gasp. He can't mean that. There is no way I can tell Tomas the truth.

"Tell him that bastard wasn't your father," Dad continues. "Tell him that the asshole left you and your mother right before Christmas. Tell him that Cameroon was just a lie to save face. You tell him that, Jessy. Then you tell him that you're OK. You're reunited with your real dad, and he loves you dearly."

A single tear runs down my cheek. It all sounds so simple, when it's anything but.

"Do it, Jessy—I'm trusting you." There's a pause. "Don't make me come over there."

I shudder. "But—but—what if he asks who you are? Your name?"

My body tightens. Even though I'm miles away from him, I still prepare for the pain that usually comes when I ask questions. Especially ones that start with *But*.

"Tell him my name is Jack. Jack Daniels."

Two thoughts collide in my brain at the same time: *Like the drink?* and *Am I really Jessica Daniels?*

"I-is that your real name?" I manage to ask.

"No. It's not. But it's memorable. And it's the only name he needs to know for now."

Another thought bursts into my brain, this time on its own: *What is his real name, then? Why don't I know it?*

I don't know what to say, so I say nothing.

"I hope you know I'm always here for you," Dad says.

"I do. I know."

Silence comes from his end, though I don't dare hang up. Not until he tells me to. He's waiting for something.

"Thanks." After a quick breath I add, "Dad."

"I love you, Jessy."

I close my eyes, leaning against the door again. He wants me to say it back to him.

While we've grown closer, he's never asked this of me before. Not that a father should have to ask. But the fact that I don't even know his name shows me that we still have a long way to go in our relationship.

I *should* love him. He's my father. He gave up so much for me. Sacrificed so much to get me back. So why do the words feel like acid in my throat?

I swallow back my emotions. "I love you too."

He hangs up.

My legs give out, and I slide to the floor with silent tears sliding right along with me.

I don't know what shakes me more: that I've forced myself to say those words when I don't mean them or that I don't love my own father.

I don't *love* Dad. Why don't I? I understand him and his choices now, yet my heart still won't budge.

And now that I've said it, he'll expect it all the time. Every day. Every time we're together. He'll keep forcing me to say it until the sentiment loses all meaning. I don't want that.

I want to love him. Maybe with time—

Soft knocks on the door ripple through me, interrupting. "You OK, Jess?" Dan asks.

Of course he—sweet, kind, caring Dan—would come check on me.

I stand. I don't bother to look in the mirror—I already know I'm a mess. Instead, I open the door, surprised to see both Dan and Nick there.

Dan takes one look at me, and instantly I'm in his arms. "Hey," he breathes into my hair. "What happened? What's wrong?"

I hold tightly to him for just a moment. I want to tell him what Dad told me to say. But those words are meant for his whole family—for Tomas, especially. If I tell my story now, I won't be able to repeat it.

I lean back, staring into his calming hazel eyes as his thumbs wipe away my tears.

"There's something I need to tell you and your family," I begin, slowly. "But before I do, I want you to know that I didn't hide it from you on purpose. It's just . . . it hurts. And I knew that if anyone found out, they'd pity me. I don't want that."

His face softens with concern. "What are you talking about?"

"Tell us, Jessy," Nick adds, leaning in. "Whatever it is, we'll fix it."

I turn away from them, both, knowing it has to be done. "I'll tell you, but"—I pause and grab Dan's hand—"I don't have the strength to say it more than once."

As we walk back into the dining room, all conversations stop. Eyes burn into me, peeling back the layers I've erected over the past few weeks. One meal, and they already care about me.

And that's exactly why they can't know the truth.

Yes, Dad wants me to tell them the truth—some version

of it, that is. I'll tell them that much. But no more.

I'm not sure who I'm protecting more: Dad or them.

I take a deep, shaky breath and meet Tomas's gaze. "You asked about my father. The truth is, he's gone. He left us right before Christmas."

"To Cameroon?" Kate says with a polite but tight smile. "Is he still there, dear?"

I shake my head. "He never went to Cameroon. It was a lie. He . . . he just left us."

My heart races in their silence. I watch as the confusion and sympathy set in.

"Why didn't you say something?" Dan asks, daring to speak first. "Why didn't you just tell us the truth?"

I shrug. "Initially, I guess I was in shock. I didn't want to believe it *was* the truth. So how could I say it out loud? Even now, some mornings it still takes a few minutes for me to remember."

"That's understandable dear," Kate says. "You're far too young to have to deal with something like this—especially on your own."

"How have you and your mom managed to keep up this charade for so long?" Tomas asks.

I wilt from his disappointment but try to answer. "Cameroon was a convenient lie. Bob—Dad—used to go there a lot, and people knew he was often unreachable over there. None of my parents' friends and coworkers have questioned it. And as for my peers"—I grimace against the painful memories—"well, Dan and Nick know how that's gone."

"Shit," Dan says, resting his forehead in his hand.

"Daniel!" Kate scolds.

"What?" he says, looking at her. "What he did is shitty."

She frowns, but then her sad, kind eyes fall on me again. "How is your mother doing with it all?"

I twist my napkin under the table. "She's . . . OK." My tone betrays the words. I know they can hear it.

"That's a big house for just you and your mom to care for," Kate says. "Do you two need any help? The boys would be happy to help with shoveling or whatever you need." Instantly Dan and Nick agree.

Oh no. They can't come to the house. Despite all the little dreams and fantasies I had just a few hours ago, no one can ever come to the house. Not Dan. Not Nick. No one. Not until I know for sure that Dad won't hurt them.

"It's OK. Actually, my mom's . . . friend is staying with us."

I look around the table and see the deep compassion in everyone's eyes. Even the girls—as young as they are and as little as they truly understand—gaze at me with warmth. For a split second, I consider telling them the rest of the story— that he's not "Mom's friend" but my biological father, that Bob stole me from him.

But just as I'm getting up the nerve, Tomas pounds his fist on the table, making us all jump.

"The Bob I know wouldn't do this. He's a family man to the core. You and your mother are his whole world. It's one of the reasons I supported him all those years and called him my friend." Then he leans back in his chair and shakes his head. "This doesn't make sense!"

My eyes widen. He doesn't believe me. I was right not to tell him the rest.

"Dear," Kate begins. Gently. "People change. You know that probably better than all of us."

He sighs. "What is the world coming to?"

He stands and disappears into the kitchen to clear his half-finished plate. A few moments later, the back door slams shut, making us all jump again.

"Daddy must be real mad," Julie whispers to Amanda. "He never smokes anymore." She then looks over to me and adds matter-of-factly, "That's what he's doing—he's out there smoking."

Kate clears her throat at her daughters before reaching

over to lay a light hand on my shoulder. "Well, you're welcome here any time you'd like, dear. You don't even need to ask. Our door is always open, and there's always plenty of food to go around."

On my other side, Dan takes my hand, squeezing it. I'm sure it's meant to be a gesture of support, but all it does is increase the guilt curling around in my gut.

Dan and his family are so nice. Happy. Compassionate. They've taken care of Nick, and now they're opening their door and hearts to me.

They shouldn't.

As much truth as I managed to share in veiled ways tonight, I'm still ultimately lying to them all. While I'd love nothing more than to deny it, the truth is, they're all still in danger.

Dad killed Charlie, their friend, just last week.

He killed Bob, Tomas's friend. And the only father I'd known my entire life . . .

"I can't do this," I say, standing. "I'm sorry."

I rush out of the room.

I can't put my shoes on fast enough. Before I can go out the door, Dan comes running up to me with Nick close behind.

"What is going on, Jess?" Dan asks.

I stop and stare, unsuccessfully ignoring the panic in his eyes. "I can't do this," I repeat. "This was a mistake."

"Dinner? It's OK. I mean, if I would have known what was going on in your life, I never would have pushed this on you. I know my family can be a bit overwhelming and—"

"No, they're prefect. Really. But that's the problem."

His brows narrow. Nick shifts closer, standing shoulder to shoulder with Dan while I stand on the outside. They look every bit like the Dynamic Duo. Like they're ready to take on the world together.

They're unsung heroes. The ones who quietly do good deeds for no other reason than it being the right thing to do.

If they knew what my world was really like, they'd try to fix it. And they'd wind up dead for it.

Before either of them can say anything, I keep going. "Dan, your family is wonderful and loving. But I'm a mess. I'm a walking disaster. And I'm not going to inflict my demons on you. I don't care what it costs. Goodbye, Dan. You were great."

I plant a swift kiss on his lips, then rush to my car.

NINETEEN

M Y CAR DOOR DOESN'T AUTOMATICALLY unlock when I reach it. It means my wallet or phone is blocking the signal on the key fob. Sometimes that happens. But why did it have to happen right now, when I'm trying to escape as quickly as I can?

"Jessy, stop!" Nick calls out behind me.

He followed. Of course. He's right up to the car before I can even dig into my purse to find the fob.

"Will you wait just a minute?" he says. "I have something I want to say to you."

I turn around, expecting to see Dan with him too. But it's just Nick. When I look over his shoulder, back at the house, I see Dan standing at the door, watching us. I get the sense that this was the plan—that Nick said he wanted to talk to me alone.

"Fine," I say, folding my arms across my chest. "What?"

Nick takes a breath. "Dan's family . . . they overwhelm me too sometimes. I mean, they're *great*. But they're so dang perfect that it's hard to handle."

I do a double take. That's what he wants to tell me? He didn't follow me out here to interrogate me? Call out my lies again?

Once that initial shock wears off, a new one emerges. I'm surprised by how much Nick's words resonate with me. He truly *understands* what I'm feeling. A small part of me wants to lean into it, but a larger part of me wants to run from it.

So I go into my purse, free the fob, and unlock my door. "You're just saying that to be nice," I say with my back to him, trying to end the conversation.

He shakes his head and steps closer to me. "I don't do 'nice,' Jessy. I do real, brutal, honest."

Something in me slows down. I turn around to face him.

"When my life went to hell," Nick began, "none of my other friends wanted anything to do with me. At most, they offered their condolences. Said their sorrys. But nothing beyond that. Only Dan and his family were right there, standing by me through the worst of it. They took me in. Looked after me. Gave me a reason to get out of bed each day, after everyone I loved left."

He looks at the ground for a moment, then looks up and locks eyes with me.

"I know it's hard to see that kind of life"—he points to the house—"when your own is a mess. I wanted to run away from it too. Many times. But they wouldn't let me push them away." He offers a small smile. "Even now, they're still helping me. Tomas helped me become emancipated so I could get a place of my own, be independent. And he helped me file appeals when John—that bastard who killed my sister—came up for parole."

My veins freeze as quickly as if I'd jumped into that dang river.

"Parole?" I have to choke the word out. "When did this happen?"

"This summer. Right before school started."

Images of that night—the accident, the pain, the hospital—spring forward. Every ounce of air rushes out of me. I have to lean back, using the car for support.

Nick's eyes cloud with worry as he watches me. "You

didn't know . . . ?"

I can only shake my head.

He frowns. "I'm sorry. I thought you knew. I assumed your parents told you. They were there too—they were part of the appeal."

I close my eyes and try to breathe.

"We lost," Nick says, a bitter clip to his voice. "He's out."

He's out. The drunk who killed Nick's sister and nearly killed me and my friends—he's out. My parents knew. But they didn't tell me.

Then I remember what else they kept from me: my real father.

When I open my eyes, I can see something on Nick's face. He has something more to tell me, but he's waiting until I'm ready to hear it. I lift my chin and prepare.

"No one knows where John is now. Tomas was keeping tabs on him for a while. But sometime around Thanksgiving, the bastard stopped showing up for his appointments with his parole officers. He slipped right off the radar."

I try to gasp, but there's nothing left in my lungs.

Nick kicks at the frozen clump of snow built up in my front wheel well. "Can you believe it? That murderer not only is out of jail but is God knows where right now." He scowls. "So yeah, between his release and then my dad getting out right before Halloween, I—"

"Your dad got out too?" It bursts right out of me. "I thought he got two years?"

Nick nods. "He did, but his time was up in October. Your parents didn't tell you that either?"

I give him a blank stare. Apparently, they withheld a lot from me.

Nick scoffs. "Yeah, your dad used his political connections to get that bastard transferred to a minimum-security prison and then get him set up with grief counselling and rehab therapy. I suppose it didn't look good that a 'grieving father' was rotting in state prison alongside the drunk that murdered his daughter." His words are now dripping with contempt.

My head is spinning with all the bombs Nick has dropped. This one about his father makes me dizzy in an especially unsettling way. I remember what Dan told me about Nick's father. I try to calm myself so I can focus on Nick and this moment with him.

"I take it you didn't agree with Bob's—my dad's— decision," I say.

"Far as I'm concerned, they should have kept him locked up and thrown away the key."

I can't imagine hating my parent so much that I'd wish to never see him again. But I was fortunate to have a wonderful life of privilege. Had. My real father *is* a murderer. What would I do if he went to jail?

The thought sours my stomach, so I refocus on Nick. "Where's your dad now?" I ask, my voice quiet.

Nick moves up beside me, leaning on the car too. "Last I heard, he went north to stay with his sister after he got out. He's called me a few times, but I keep ignoring him. I hope I never see him again."

My arms wrap around my torso as I move closer to Nick. "Why . . . ?"

I already know why. Or I can at least assume why, after what Dan told me. But I still ask because Nick's opening up to me. He's sharing with me. He's baring his soul wide open—and it's a kaleidoscope of pain, broken dreams, and nightmares. Just like my soul.

How many other people have souls like ours? How many other people can offer Nick not only sympathy and compassion but understanding and solidarity?

That's why I need to hear what he and Jessy went through—from his voice. I am one of the few who truly get it. Even if he doesn't fully realize it.

Nick taps his hands against the car, staring out into the

darkness. Then he lets out a long, drawn-out breath.

"My dad was a drunken asshole. He beat the shit out of us—me, Jessy, our mom. Tomas locked him up many times for it. But my mom was too afraid to press charges. So he always came right back home."

I look out into the same darkness that he's staring into, knowing he's seeing the past and not the little slice of suburbia. "I'm so sorry," I say.

"Wanna hear the ironic part? My dad had the balls to attack John for killing Jessy, even though he himself drove drunk all the time. Hundreds of nights. It's a miracle he never caused an accident like Jessy's—that he never murdered someone."

The word *murdered* makes me go numb.

"I told Jessy not to go . . ."

Nick says this so quietly that I can barely hear him. I lean in.

"I told her not to go to the game—the night of the accident. It's not like she cared about football or sports. But she said it was a 'historic moment in our lives.'" He almost smiles. "She said shit like that all the time. Drove me nuts. Anyway, she said it was historic and that she wanted to capture it. She loved photography. Dad had all these cool cameras, and she really got into it. That drove me nuts too."

He shakes his head in a slow, steady sweep.

"I should have gone with her," he says. "I should have been the one driving that night . . ."

"Don't." Without thinking, I place my hand on his arm. "Don't blame yourself. Even if you had been driving, you couldn't have changed a thing. It all happened so fast. There was nothing you could have done. Nothing any of us could have done," I add.

He's silent. I wait.

"You know what?" he finally says. "Sometimes I'm *glad* Jessy died. That means she got out. Then Mom got out. We all did, I guess." His desolate eyes turn to me. "Am I a horrible brother for thinking that? A horrible person?"

"No," I immediately say. "God, no. It makes you human."

He looks down at my hand, still on his arm. "I saw you that night—at the hospital."

The surprise makes my hand pull away, on reflex. "You did?"

"Yeah." He looks back out into the darkness, as if conjuring the memory. "Christ, I was so scared. When we got the call about Jessy, I had to drive us to the hospital. Dad was wasted, as usual. And Mom was a wreck, trying to keep Dad somewhat together. Even when we got to the hospital, Mom and Dad were still a mess, so I was the one who had to talk to the staff and figure out what the hell was happening. It was chaos. There were families everywhere. People panicking. Crying. Shouting. It took the staff forever to find Jessy's name. They finally told us she was in surgery."

My insides clench.

"So I left Mom with that drunken bastard, and I raced up to the waiting room. But no one would tell me any updates. I kept asking and asking, but all they'd say was that she was in surgery. For *hours* I waited, pacing in that damn waiting room, praying she'd be okay."

My heart stops. Just as it did that night, on the operating table.

"Finally, they said she'd made it," he says. "They said she was in serious condition, but still fighting. They said I could see her. Just me. Even the staff had figured out by that point what a shit show my parents were."

Nick snorts. Anger passes over him, like a cloud. Once it's clear, he takes a slow breath.

"I walked into Jessy's room and just stared at her. She was bandaged, head to toe. She looked so damn fragile and broken. But I didn't care. All I cared was that she was alive. That my sister was going to be OK."

I wipe away tears. I can hardly bear what he will say

next, but I don't want him stop.

"Then things went . . . crazy," he says. "Two strangers burst in, all panicked and hysterical. A nurse was right behind them. She grabbed me and tried to pull me away, get me out of the room. All she could say was 'There was a mistake—I'm sorry.' She said it over and over."

He slowly turns his head and looks right at me now.

"The girl in the bed—the one I'd spent hours praying for and losing my damn mind over—wasn't my twin." He swallows. "My twin was dead."

Tears pour down my face. All I knew about that night—about that mistake—was that my parents went into the morgue to identify a girl who wasn't their Jessy. I'd never once considered the other side of the story—that someone had been waiting outside a surgery room for a girl who wasn't *their* Jessy.

"I never blamed you or hated you, Jessy," Nick says. "But I understand why you might think that. I know I'm always staring at you." He scratches the back of his head in embarrassment. "It's hard to explain. I guess it's just—"

He stops and forces out a hard sigh, and his words seem to dislodge with it.

"I was older than Jessy—did you know that? Only by a minute, but it didn't matter. I took my role of 'big brother' seriously. I protected her from playground bullies and jerks. And I tried to protect her from the nightmare of our life. I didn't want it to diminish her light. My entire life was built around protecting my sister—and then she was suddenly gone."

He puts his hands in his pockets.

"But that feeling, that need to protect someone—it didn't go away," he says. "I didn't realize it at first, but it shifted to you. It's like, even though I *knew* you weren't my sister, I couldn't stop thinking about you and hoping you were all right."

My heart breaks just a tiny bit more for him.

He shifts, turning his body toward me. Our eyes meet, his wet with unshed tears. "I care about you, Jessy. More than I have any right to."

"I care about you too," I instantly reply.

He stares down at me, stunned by my words. Then he hugs me, clutching me to him.

I hold him right back. Just like Dan, Nick feels safe.

After a moment, he pulls back. "I'm sorry I've gotten in the way of you and Dan. I don't know—maybe that was some sort of protective thing too. I didn't want to believe it, but you two are good for each other. You really do make each other happy."

I can't help it. I smile—for a moment.

Then I stare off into the distance, recalling the drama I'd just put Dan through. I ran away from him and his family, right in the middle of dinner. I kissed him and left.

What did I say to him? *You were great?* Who says stuff like that?

"I don't know, Nick," I say. "Dan probably hates me right now."

"No, I don't."

I turn when I hear that familiar voice.

Dan is heading toward us, his hands in his pockets too. I'd totally forgotten about him standing in the doorway this entire time. He nods to Nick in a knowing way. Something about it makes me wonder if Nick had somehow signaled to him to come over.

Nick smirks at him. "Jessy has been listing all your faults. In alphabetical order. She's only on the *G*'s. This will take a while—you might as well head back inside."

Dan playfully shoves Nick's shoulder. "Shut up." Then he turns his cautious yet hopeful hazel eyes my way. "How are you feeling? Is everything OK?"

I want to keep looking into his eyes, but I can't. My head drops. "I'm so sorry I ran out like that. I'm sorry I never told you what was happening at home. I'm just sorry for it all." I pause, unsure of how to tell as much truth as I can. "I know you don't understand, but I was only trying to do the right thing."

Dan gently tilts my chin so I'm once again looking at him and his compassionate eyes.

"Look, I like you, Jess. I do. And I want us to be more than friends. More importantly, I want you to know that I'm here for you. I want you to know you can be honest with me. Real with me. You can let me in. Can you do that, Jess? Can you let me in?"

My insides twist in knots like the old corded phone Grandma has in her kitchen. Letting Dan in could cost him his life. And possibly his family's and Nick's.

Deep inside, a voice begins to whisper. It tells me I can't do this. I *can't*. It says that no matter how much I want a normal life, I can't have one. Not after everything that's happened. It tells me that I should just get in my car, drive away, and never look back.

My hand begins to reach for my car door.

But I stop myself.

Things are different now. Dad's changed so much. I don't have to be afraid anymore. Not for me. And not for my friends. We can finally have the perfect life he's created for us.

Over the last few weeks, I've become so accustomed to terror that normalcy now makes me uncomfortable. It's like I'm constantly waiting for someone to notice something's wrong.

I want to free myself of that feeling. I want to let Dan in—at least as much as I can without jeopardizing his life or sending Dad to jail. I don't want to push Dan away. I don't want to lie to him or Nick anymore.

"I'll try," I whisper to Dan. "I'll try to let you in."

He gives me a weak but sincere smile. "That'll do."

Then he hugs me.

I cling to him, holding back tears. I don't know why he

asked me out to the Grotto that fateful day, but I'm both sorry and grateful he did.

Dan places a kiss in my hair. Warm butterflies fill my stomach. I lean back, look up at him, and smile.

He stares down at me for a few seconds, then leans forward.

He's going to kiss me.

He leaves more than enough time for me to break away. For me to stop it. But I don't want to.

His lips seal over mine.

There is no urgency. No rush. No pressure. Just a sweet, perfect kiss.

Our lips move in sync, then his tongue tastes my lips. It's gentle, timid. He's once again giving me more than enough opportunity to pull away.

I don't want to. I like the way he makes me feel.

Here in his arms, I'm safe. He'll never hurt me. He'll never manipulate me or force me to do things I don't want to do. I don't have to pretend to be someone I'm not. I can just be a girl kissing a boy.

When Nick finally clears his throat, Dan and I gently part. Heat rushes to my cheeks, and I bite my sensitive lips.

Dan glances over at Nick and shrugs. "I'd say I'm sorry for doing that in front of you—but I'm not."

Nick laughs. "Dude, I wouldn't be sorry either. I just wasn't sure if I should give you some privacy or—"

"That," Dan interrupts. "Giving us some privacy. You should have done that."

I playfully smack Dan's chest and shake my head. "No, Nick. It's fine." I'm still blushing, but laughing together seems to help.

"Anyway," Nick begins, "if you two are all done, maybe we could head back inside? It's only seven. Want to watch a movie or something?"

Dan frowns a bit as he looks over at his house. I follow his gaze—and I think I see three heads gawking out the window at us.

"I'm up for a movie," Dan begins. "But I'm thinking maybe we'd like a little more privacy than what we'd get here." He runs a hand though his light-brown hair. "Maybe we could go to your place, Jess?"

"No!" I swallow and try to soften the tone. "I mean, I don't think it'd work at my place. My mom's not home. Neither is . . ."

What was that name again? John? Jack? That's it.

"Neither is Jack," I finish.

Dan looks confused. "Who's Jack?"

I suddenly feel cold. My lips have trouble moving. "My—my—my mom's friend. The one who's been staying with us."

They both stiffen.

"Like, *a man* Jack?" Dan clarifies.

I answer with silence.

"Well," Dan says, his voice clipped and wry. "*That* was unexpected." He looks up and to the side, as if picturing something. "When you said your mom's friend was staying with you, I just assumed a woman, you know?"

I need to reroute this conversation track. "It's just, well, Jack said not to have anyone over. And I wouldn't want to upset him."

As soon as the words come out, I regret them. That was a horrible reroute.

Sure enough, Nick pounces on it. "You don't want to 'upset' your mom's friend?" he asks, eyeing me suspiciously.

Visions of the box—and the beatings—dance in my mind. I rub my forehead, trying to push them away and replace them with the wonderful visions of the last few days.

"It's just . . . a strange situation," I finally say. "We're working through it. In the meantime, I don't want to do anything that could possibly create problems."

My gaze flickers between them, hoping they'll buy yet

another lie—mere minutes after I promised to be honest and let them into my life.

Actually, this is only a partial lie. It's true that Dad and I are working through things, and it's true that I don't want to create problems.

Nick stares at me a moment longer, searching for something. Then he shakes his head. "We could go to my place," he offers.

"Really?" Dan asks. "You hardly ever let me come over there."

Nick shrugs. "We going, or what?"

"I'm game," Dan says. "So I guess it's up to Jess." He places his palm on my cheek. "What say you?"

I once again realize that his soft, gentle touch is so foreign to me that a part of me wants to pull away. But another part—a bigger part—wants to lean in.

I smile. "A movie at Nick's place sounds perfect."

TWENTY

LESS THAN TEN MINUTES LATER, DAN AND I follow Nick to an old brick apartment building. "Just to warn you," he says as we stand outside the main door, "it's not great, but it's something."

Wordlessly, we head inside. An Out of Order sign is taped to the elevator, so we climb three flights of stairs before turning down a narrow corridor. Lights hum and flicker, flowered wallpaper hangs off the wall, and many stains mark the carpet. I don't even want to know what they are. Given the darkness I've recently seen in my life, my guess immediately jumps to blood. But maybe it's just spilled pop. Or maybe a pet got loose. A lot.

Nick stops at door 318, then unlocks and opens it. A mattress sits on the floor with blankets unmade. On the wall across from the bed is a small TV with a cracked screen. To the right is a tiny kitchen.

A narrow hallway leads to two more rooms. All the doors are open.

This is it? This is where he lives?

Just then, the click of the deadbolt sliding into place echoes through me. I shiver.

Behind me, I hear Dan whisper to Nick, "She doesn't like

closed doors. She's claustrophobic."

Nick gives me a look. He seems a little confused yet also a little understanding. "I'm not a huge fan of closed doors myself," he says, confirming my earlier observation. "But it's good to keep this one locked. Everything is valuable to somebody, especially when they have nothing." He shoots me yet another look as he walks past me. "And since when are you claustrophobic? I don't remember ever hearing you say that."

"It's a recent change," I say, then bite my lip.

After our talk out in Dan's yard, I now understand why Nick has watched me and listened to most of my conversations—yet I'm still surprised by how much he retained. He knows me better than any of my former so-called friends did.

Nick heads to the fridge and opens it. "What would you like to drink? I have"—he pauses as he gazes inside—"water."

From my angle, I can see inside the fridge. It's empty, aside from a package of bologna and a loaf of bread.

"I'm fine," I say.

"Me too," Dan adds.

We're quiet for a moment as we stand there, looking about the sparse apartment.

"I think your place is great," I say. "It's a space all your own."

Nick smiles.

The more I stand here, the truer my words are. This place is great. The old me would have been shocked and appalled. But now I'm jealous. This is bigger than my room. My new room, that is. And it has lighting and a bed and a TV—all things I once took for granted.

More importantly, this place lets Nick be completely independent. There's no one here, watching his every move, setting high standards and severe punishments. Here, he's free.

And I understand the value of that now.

"Want the tour?" Nick offers, grinning.

"Sure," I say.

Nick begins pointing. "Kitchen. Living room slash bedroom."

Then he takes a few steps down the hallway and flicks on a dim light to show a small room with a shower, toilet, and sink.

"Bathroom," he says.

As I follow Nick down the hall, I suddenly realize that the doors aren't open. The doors aren't there at all. Not even on the bathroom. I know this apartment complex isn't in the greatest of neighborhoods, but don't they even provide doors to the bathrooms?

Nick's eyes follow mine to the open doorway. He looks a bit sheepish. "Ah, yeah, about that—it's only ever just me here. Dan is the only visitor I've had, and even that's been only a few times." He cringes, then shrugs. "Like I said, I'm not a fan of closed doors."

Wait—does that mean he did this himself? He removed the doors? Why?

I hate to admit it, but the lack of doors does feel more comforting than it should feel. I guess once you've been trapped inside a room for days on end, doors and locks take on a new meaning.

Then I finally put two and two together. Based on what Nick said about his dad, it's likely that he experienced some form of this too.

"And this . . ." he says with great buildup as he stands in front of the doorway to the left, "is where the magic happens." He waggles his brows, reaches for the light switch, then steps aside.

In the center of the room sits his drum set. I crack a huge smile. This is supposed to be a bedroom, but of course Nick would give his drums the prime spot in his home. I love it.

"When's your next gig, by the way?" I ask.

"Next weekend," Nick replies.

"Wanna come?" Dan instantly asks, his face brightening.

"Yes!" I don't hesitate.

It's one of the first times I've been able to give a response without fretting and fearing about what Dad would say. It feels so good to know that Dad would be fine with me going.

We move back into the living room slash bedroom, and Nick gestures to the mattress. "Wanna watch TV? Sorry— it's not the greatest."

"It beats lying on cement," I say before I can stop myself.

They both eye me, then Nick chuckles. "Like you've ever slept on the floor a day in your life!"

I smile, trying to pass off my comment as a joke too.

If only they knew the truth.

The three of us sit on Nick's mattress and prop our backs against the wall. I'm in between them, sitting so close that there's barely enough room for air to flow between us. The funny thing is, we didn't have to sit this way. The mattress is wide enough for us to space out a bit. But I don't mind it. It feels nice. Safe. Like nothing bad can get to me when the three of us are together.

As Nick surfs through the channels to find something good, I find my mind swimming with thoughts about these two guys flanking me.

First, Dan. It's getting harder and harder to resist his charms and not make this official. He's just so carefree and fun to be around—which is amazing, considering all the crap he's putting up with at school for associating with me. A lesser man would have shunned me too. Especially after the bomb I dropped tonight at dinner. Yet he's still here, wanting to be my light in the darkness, to guide me out of it.

Nick too. He wants to be my light as well. Knowing what I now know about our history, it makes sense. My connection with him is different from my connection with Dan, of course. Nick truly is like a brother. Protective. I'm glad I have him in my corner.

I'm grateful for both of them.

Nick finds us a sci-fi show, and we settle in. Slowly, as the show plays on, I find I can relax. Breathing becomes easier. Any lingering anxiety from earlier fades. I even laugh at a few of the show's jokes.

This—right here—is the best I've felt in over a month. If I'm truly being honest with myself, it's the best I've felt in a very long time. I mean even before Dad came into our lives. Back when I was with Blake and my old friends, there were all these expectations about who I was and how I had to be. But with Dan and Nick, there's none of that. I can just be.

"So, Jessy," Nick begins, "is it really true you beat Dan in pool?"

I blush. While that night at the Grotto ended tragically, I do cherish my memories of playing pool with Dan, chatting, laughing.

"No," I say. "We didn't finish the game, so I technically didn't win."

"You totally would have, though," Dan says, bragging me up. "You should have seen her," he says to Nick. "I'm glad I bet questions and not money. She would have cleaned me out."

I play with my bottom lip to hide my smile.

"So how do you know how to play pool like that?" Nick asks.

"Because of my . . . dad," I say, stumbling on the words. I should probably leave it at that, but I continue. "We got a pool table when I was four, and we played together all the time."

"Shit," Nick curses. "I didn't mean to make you think of him. I'm sorry."

"It's . . . fine. I like keeping the good memories close."

It's true. Mostly. Those memories are happy. Yet they seem wrong now. Tainted with lies.

I don't want every memory of Bob to be like that. It

LAURIE WETZEL ‡ PICTURE PERFECT

would be a disservice. He raised me for a reason. He wasn't my real father. He didn't have to be wonderful, devoted, and loving, but he was. I was his whole world. And in that respect, I can understand why he kept lying to me. Why he didn't want the illusion to end.

"Maybe we can go over to your house sometime and play on your turf," Dan adds, trying to lighten the mood.

Nick glances at his watch. "The night is still young. How about now? Beats sitting on a mattress, watching a cracked TV."

I freeze, my body instantly clenching. *Now? Tonight?* No.

I do want my friends to come to my house someday. I do. But when I know they'll be safe and when that box of a room no longer exists. The day is coming. I think. I hope.

"It's too soon . . . ?" Dan questions.

I nod.

Nick shrugs. "We get it. Change is hard."

I lean my head on Dan's shoulder, partly for comfort and partly to hide my emotions. Yes, change is impossibly hard. And Nick, more than anyone, understands that.

"So," Nick says. It's just one word, but it's loaded. "Tell us about Jack—your mom's friend."

My heart stops.

"You said some guy named Jack is staying with you, right?" he continues.

Dan is quiet, but now he's staring at me too. This is not good. So not good. Knots tighten inside me, clamping down so strong that it's as if I can't breathe.

"C-can we not talk about Jack, please?" I stutter.

"Who is he?" Nick presses, his voice like hardened steel. "How long has he been at your house? Why did you wait so long to tell us there's some man living with you guys?"

Intense emotions roll off him and onto me. The sensation literally makes me itchy. I jump off the mattress.

"I'm thirsty. Anyone else need water?"

I feel two sets of eyes on me as I move to the kitchen and begin filling a glass from the sink.

Coming up alongside me, Dan leans on the counter. He idly runs his finger over the outdated Formica pattern. "I mean—it's just strange that your dad suddenly leaves, and some guy is already in your home." He pauses. "Is that why your dad left . . . ? Because of, well, this guy and your mom . . . ?"

I turn off the water and glare at him. "Are you asking for yourself, or for your dad?"

Dan grimaces and straightens, his jaw clenching. "That's not fair."

I look away.

"I care about you, OK?" he continues. "You clearly have a lot happening in your life right now, and you're keeping it all secret. I—we—just want to make sure you're all right. And that means we want to know more about this Jack guy."

Every time someone says that name, my body tenses even more. I know it's not even Dad's real name, but it feels as if he'll walk through the door at any moment. As if we're invoking the devil or something. I can't help but glance around the room and ceiling, half expecting to see cameras that of course aren't there.

Instantly, guilt vibrates through me. This is my dad. Not the devil. He's been through so much for me.

I shouldn't be terrified of talking about him or bringing my friends home to meet him. I shouldn't feel the need to hide him away like some shameful secret.

But until I know he won't harm Dan and Nick, I have to. I have to keep that part of my life separate.

Now Nick appears beside me, all hard edges. There's a desperate look in his eyes that has me wilting.

"You're afraid of him."

I try to deny it, but my mouth has gone dry.

"What has he done to you, Jess?" Nick demands.

Dan's head quickly darts from me to Nick and back

again. "*Has* he done something to you?" he repeats.

"You're both being ridiculous."

I grip the glass and try to dodge past them. I want to go back to watching the show—back to when things were good and safe. But my still-bruised hip catches on the countertop. Pain radiates through me, and I drop my glass.

It shatters into dozens of tiny pieces.

My heart pounds in my chest, as I recall another broken glass and the pain that night brought.

Broken.

Pieces.

So many broken pieces.

Something inside me shatters too. Dad has *murdered* people. Dad has *beaten* me and my mother.

Before I realize what I'm doing, I'm picking up the pieces, trying to fix it. Fix everything. Before someone else gets hurt. Because of me.

Frantic, I grasp at the shards and drop them into what's left of the glass.

"Jess," Dan says, pulling on my arm. "Jess, stop!"

I can't. Not until I find every piece.

"Jessy, stop!" Nick says this time, reaching down at me. "It's OK."

"No, it's not!" I shout.

Heat rises, and my heart pounds in my chest. I know there are no cameras here, yet my gaze still flies all over the place, double-checking that Dad didn't see this—see me fail again. I'm kneeling, rocking.

"It's not OK," I repeat. "Nothing is OK. I have to fix my mistake."

"Shit, your hands," Dan says, pointing.

I look down at my hands—and I see right through them, as if they're transparent. All I can see are the remaining pieces of glass on the floor, glinting, covered in blood. I tried to fix it, but I only made a bigger mess.

"Dammit, Jessy," Nick says. He lifts me by my elbow

and pulls me up.

"Stop!" I shout as he gently yet firmly moves me away from the glass. "I have to fix it!"

But he doesn't stop. Not until we're in the bathroom. He sets me on the toilet lid, standing over me. Dan is right behind him. The three of us in this small space makes my already-labored breaths quicken.

"What the hell was that, Jessy?" Nick shouts.

I flinch, my body preparing itself for impact.

After several seconds pass, I open my eyes, cautiously glancing at both Nick and Dan.

They're silent, eyes wide and mouths agape. Neither is going to hit me. Even though I made them mad, even though I messed up, and they yelled, they're not going to hurt me.

They would never hurt me.

I am safe with them.

The muscles in my body loosen, and my breaths slow.

Dan squeezes forward so he can kneel down in front of me. He gently reaches for my hands, though stops short of touching me. He seems to sense that I need a moment.

"Are you all right?" he asks quietly. "What happened?"

I can't answer him. The glass broke and then . . . I don't know. I had to fix it—fix something—even though I knew it was pointless. I just had to. I don't know why.

Suddenly, my fingers burn. I hold them up under the glow of the light. Blood drips out of dozens of little cuts that line my fingers, cuts that will eventually blend in with the others that mar my skin. I didn't even feel it—or see it—until now.

"Oh God," I whimper.

"Let me see," Nick says. Nudging Dan out of the way, Nick now kneels in front me.

I ball my hands, wincing from the pain. "It's fine."

Nick sighs. "No, it's not."

Slowly, wordlessly, he holds his hands out to me. Like Dan, he doesn't touch me. He waits for me to be ready to give him my hands.

So I do. I put my hands in his.

Behind him, Dan lets out an exhale.

The two of them go to work, needing few words between them. Nick instructs Dan to grab the first aid kit from under the kitchen sink. As Nick brings the tweezers to my skin to remove the glass, I tense, awaiting the sting. But it doesn't hurt. He's tender. He's taking the utmost care to ensure he doesn't hurt me as, one by one, he plucks the tiny pieces from my skin. Next, he helps me stand and run my hands under the faucet, washing away blood.

My stomach sinks like a rock in the ocean as I realize this isn't his first time tending to someone with wounds. Was it his mom? Sister? Himself?

Once the blood is cleaned away, Nick gently twists my fingers under the light, inspecting them before drying them with a towel. "Well, I don't see any more glass, so that's good."

He then sets me back down on the toilet seat, kneels in front of me, and begins the painstaking process of bandaging my hands. He uses nearly his entire box of Band-Aids.

"Want some ice for your hip?" Dan chimes in.

"My hip?"

"You hit it on the counter, remember?" he says. "It's probably going to bruise." He looks at Nick. "You got an ice pack, right?"

Nick bobs his head, thinking. "Yeah. Sort of. Your mom bought me a bag of veggies once—they're still in the freezer."

"It's fine," I say, yanking my hands away from Nick. I tug my shirt down to make sure no skin is showing. My hip and my torso are still littered with bruises that haven't completely faded.

Bruises that my dad caused.

Bruises from beatings that nearly murdered me—like Bob and Officer Adams.

How is this my life?

My hands begin to tremble again.

Nick glances down at them, then slowly glances up at me. His eyes are full of so many emotions I can't even name.

"Why did you say 'I have to fix it'?" he asks.

No one speaks. The silence sucks the oxygen right out of this small, cramped bathroom. The walls move in.

"I have to go."

Dan and Nick exchange a look that's too quick for me to decipher.

"But you're shaking," Dan says. "Let me drive your car, and Nick could follow in his truck."

With crystal clarity, I envision what would happen to them if they were to come out to my place tonight—and it's not the fantasy I'd previously envisioned.

"Nope."

I stand, taking extra effort to calm my racing heart. It doesn't work. The room seems even smaller, even more cramped now.

Dad has *murdered* people. He's *beaten* me and my mother.

How is this my life?

I have to fix this.

"No, I'm fine," I say as I push myself out of the bathroom. "Really. I just have to go."

I stop long enough to press a kiss to Dan's cheek. Just as I did a few hours before.

When I step outside, the chilly air burns my throat. As I begin racing to my car, I stumble and slip in the newly falling snow. But then I find my footsteps. They are quick, sure, steady.

By the time I'm pulling out of the parking lot, I understand what shattered inside me.

Delusion.

The delusion that Dad has been trying to plant inside me, like some kind of malignant tumor, every moment of every day since he burst through our front door. The delusion that he can brainwash me into being the perfect daughter for his perfect family.

The delusion that Dad had some right to reenter my life in this way. The delusion that Dad had some right to manipulate and brainwash my mother. The delusion that Dad had some right to abuse me, emotionally and physically. The delusion that Dad had some right to murder Bob and Officer Adams. The delusion that he can get away with it.

The delusion that Dad can be trusted. The delusion that we could ever be a picture-perfect family. The delusion that this is—in any way, shape, or form—what love looks and feels like.

The delusion that I've done something wrong. The delusion that I *deserve* any of this abuse. The delusion that I have to be who he wants me to be. The delusion that I have to live my life in fear. The delusion that I have to fear for the lives of my loved ones. The delusion that any of this is my fault.

Most importantly, the delusion that I am not strong enough to stop him.

TWENTYONE

A S I PULL UP TO THE HOUSE, I PUT THE CAR in park and shut off the engine. I don't get out. Instead, I grip the steering wheel tightly and stare through the windshield at the dark house.

Dad no doubt saw me pull up. He knows I'm home. He'll be waiting for me inside. He'll likely be happy to see me. His daughter. His Jessy.

Snowflakes dart and race in the wind, blowing away from the house. The way they swirl, it's as if they're begging me to not go inside. They know what will happen when I do. All it will take is for him to see my hands, and he'll hurt me. Maybe even go after Dan and Nick, even though it's not their fault.

But I will go inside.

I'm going to fix this.

I don't know how, but I don't care. I also don't care that I've failed on all my other attempts to stand up to him in the past. That was then. This is now. Or better yet, that was me then. This is me now.

And what I understand now is that Dad isn't my only obstacle. As much as I hate to admit it, Mom is too.

I tried repeatedly to get her to see his darkness. To get

her to leave. But she refused. She was and is still his perfect little housewife.

But I broke through his delusions, so I'm confident she will as well. Someday. I just need to get her away from him and his influence.

Maybe that should be my goal tonight. Just take Mom and finally run.

I reach for the door handle, my pulse pounding in my ears.

Just then, I hear a noise. Something faint. It's the sound of tires crunching on snow.

I whirl around and see headlights coming up the driveway, toward the house. They get bigger and brighter, and the crunching sound gets louder and louder. In seconds, the unknown vehicle is right behind me. I raise a hand to cover my eyes from the blinding light now filling my car.

I hear car doors opening and slamming shut. Footsteps rushing toward me.

Every muscle inside me tenses and prepares for battle.

A face appears in my driver's side window. Then another.

It's Nick and Dan.

Knowing it's them and not Dad, I don't know what I feel more—relieved or terrified.

I scramble out of the car, keeping my eyes on the front door. Dad has to appear any second now. There's no doubt he knows Dan and Nick are here.

He's going to kill them.

"Get out of here!" I frantically hiss, trying to keep my voice down.

I don't know why. The fact that Dan and Nick are here is no secret to a man who has cameras on every inch of this property and beyond.

"Please!" I say, my voice rising now. "You have to leave!"

Both guys move to stand in front of me. Between me and

the house.

Dan's face is tight with worry. But Nick isn't even looking at me. He's staring at the house, and there's a stormy glint in his eyes.

"It's Jack, right?" he asks, spitting out each word. "That asshole is hurting you!"

I don't deny it. There's no point.

"You have to leave—now!" I repeat. I point to the road. "*Now!* You're not safe here!"

"I can take a hit," Nick says, fists clenched.

He wheels around and heads straight for the front door. I try to cut him off, but he moves around me. We sidestep each other until I'm finally the one blocking him.

"Jess, stop!" Dan calls out, rushing up behind Nick. "What's going on? What do you mean we're not safe? Doesn't that mean you're not safe either? Is Jack really hurting you?"

The questions swirl around me like the snow. The wind picks up even more. My head whips between Nick, Dan, and the door. The danger they're in is like a drum beating inside me. Each step they take makes the drum beat faster and faster toward the crescendo—their death. God, I can't lose them too.

"You don't understand—" I begin.

"Don't give me that bullshit!" Nick snaps, cutting me short. "I had to listen to my mom make excuse after excuse for my father for years. So don't tell me I don't understand. Just get out of my way and let me at that bastard!"

Nick bursts past me in rage. But to my surprise, Dan leaps forward and grabs his arm.

"Wait!" he says, holding his best friend tightly and pulling him back. "Just give her a moment!" Dan then turns to me, his blue eyes so soft, pleading. "Jess, tell us what's going on. Please. Let us in, remember? Whatever is happening right now, we're here to help you. *We're here.*"

Once again, I look at the door. Where *is* Dad? What is he

doing? Is he not home? Or does he just want me to believe he's not home? Is this some sort of game or trap? Is it— No. Stop.

I'm feeling it again. The fear, the terror, that has gripped me since Dad arrived. The delusion.

And that delusion has shattered.

I draw a deep breath, then turn away from the door so I can face my friends. "There's no time to explain it all," I begin.

I barely recognize the voice coming from me. It's so steady, determined.

"Jack is my dad—my real, biological father. My whole life has been a lie, a coverup. But the time he spent away from me . . . it messed with his head, and . . ."

My determination falters. The words I need to say are beyond understanding and belief. It's as if my mouth refuses to form them.

"And what?" Nick presses.

I wring my hands. "Well, and he's done some truly awful, terrible things . . ."

"Like what?" Nick demands. "Abuse you? Lock you up? Tell me I'm wrong."

I don't. I can't.

Nick steps closer, his focus still on our front door. "I saw a lot of shit growing up, Jessy. Tell me what he's doing. There's nothing you can say that will stop me from confronting him."

"No!" I shout. "He'll hurt you! *He kills people!*"

I immediately cover my mouth in shock.

Dan goes white.

Nick turns his eyes on me. Instead of fear, I see a determined fire burning so bright that I can almost feel the heat. He's not going to let this go.

"How many?"

I wince. "Two. That I know of. Bob and—"

"Charlie." A painful gasp escapes Dan.

Just hearing it makes a sob catch deep in my throat. I wish I could have broken it to him more delicately. And given him the time and space to grieve his friend. But the danger is still high. I have to push past it in order to speak and get them to understand what's truly at stake here.

"I thought that in time, Dad would get better. But he won't. It won't. He's always watching me, demanding I do everything he says, punishing me if I don't do it right or if I fight back. And my mom—I don't even know her anymore. He's brainwashed her. Beaten her." I rake in a breath, then lift my chin. "And now I'm afraid he'll kill you. Both of you. And my mom. Maybe even your family, Dan." Tears flood my eyes. "Everyone but me. So that's why I have to get away from him. I can't do this anymore. I just need to grab Mom and go."

"*God*, Jessy," Nick says.

He hugs me, holding me tight. Less than a second later, Dan joins in, both of them holding and supporting me. It's such an intense embrace that it hurts and feels good at the same time. Safe.

"You can't run," one of them whispers through the folds of my hair. "The only way to ensure you're safe—that you're both safe—is to stop him. We'll help. You're not alone anymore."

I don't know who said it. I know it doesn't matter. They're both here for me. And with that, the final delusion shatters.

The delusion that I have to do this alone.

Nick is the first to break from the embrace. "Let's go, then," he says, his stormy eyes darkening. "Let's get your mom and do this."

Before I know it, he's moving toward the house—but Dan yanks him back again.

"Are you out of your mind!" Dan exclaims.

"I thought we said we're ending this," Nick says through gritted teeth. "Nothing ends while we stand out here. She's suffered long enough. And who knows what he's doing to Sandy right now!"

Nick's right. It's time to face Dad. Even I give Dan a confused look.

As if answering us both, Dan removes his phone from his pants pocket and makes a call.

I hold my breath, suspecting who it is.

"We *will* end it—but not on our own," Dan says as he waits for a pickup. "Don't you get it? That man has murdered people. If we step inside that house, we're dead. *Dead.*"

Picturing Nick and Dan succumbing to the same bloody fate as Bob and Officer Adams did makes red spots fill my eyes and my head hum with tension.

"Look," Dan continues, staring hard at Nick. "Dad and the force are trained for this. But what the hell can *we* do against a murderer? We're not even armed. And if her mom is hurt, the sooner help is here, the better."

Nick looks back at the house, grimacing. I know that if it were up to him, he'd still charge inside, this instant. Truth be told, I'd follow him. After all, marching right into the house had been my plan, too, before Nick and Dan arrived.

But this time, Dan is right. This fight is more than we can face on our own.

My heart soars and drops at the same time. This is it, then. The police will be coming. But Dad won't go quietly. He'll try to kill them all.

Though Dan has his phone plastered to his ear, I still hear the sound of a mailbox greeting.

"Voicemail—shit!" he curses before the beep sounds. "Dad!" he almost shouts. "I need you to get to the Smith farm right away. Jessy's place. Bring backup. The guy staying at Jessy's house killed Charlie and her dad! Call me back— right now!"

Dan ends the call, then glances at the house, nervous in a way he hadn't been before.

"I'll call the station too, but we have to get the hell out

of here. Now."

"But my mom—" I begin.

Dan shakes his head and holds out his hand. "No. It's too risky for us to go inside, even for her. But don't worry—my dad and the response team can get her. It'll be OK."

My chest hollows at the thought of leaving her behind, but Dan's right. She'd fight us and bring attention to us. And that would lead to the guys getting hurt. Or worse.

Nick stares at the house for several long moments, then his gaze turns to me.

I'm not prepared for what I see. The storm in his eyes is suddenly a hurricane. It's not fear but an intense, grim acceptance of the danger we're in. I feel myself quaking in the force of its winds.

He nods. "Get in my truck."

We take a step forward.

"You didn't tell me you were bringing friends over, Jessy."

All three of us whirl around, hearing the voice suddenly behind us, in the darkness beyond the reach of the yard light. We hear the click of a gun cocking.

My eyes widen. My heart stills. My breathing stops.

Instantly, I step in front of my friends and hold my arms out, shielding them. Well, if he's going to shoot them, he'll have to shoot me first.

"Drop the phone," Dad says from the darkness. "All of you—lose the phones."

The gun barrel emerges into the light, and it's all I can focus on. At any moment a bullet could come flying out of that darkened tunnel, ending it all before I can even realize what is happening.

I've seen death many times now. Came close to my own a few times too. But none of those moments were as terrifying as this one. And that's because I know, without a shadow of a doubt, that he won't just stop with my death. He'll take Dan and Nick out too.

Dan drops his phone, and Nick and I follow.

Only then does Dad move into the light.

"*You*!?" Dan gasps.

"*No!*" Nick shouts at the exact same time.

I glance back at Nick and Dan. Their faces are twisted in shock and horror.

And recognition.

"You know my dad?" I ask, the words nothing but chokes of air.

"Don't call him that," Nick seethes. "He isn't your dad. He's mine."

TWENTYTWO

N O.
That one word is all my brain can manage. I don't
know whether I'm thinking it or saying it out loud.
No.

The wind whips around us, driving the snow into an intense frenzy. Then my thoughts begin to race and swirl as well. It's as if they, too, must obey the wind. They twist and turn so much that I can barely follow.

Nick's dad is up north, living with Nick's aunt. That's what Nick said just a few hours ago. How could this be—

I *knew* I'd seen this man with shaggy brown-and-gray hair and muddy eyes before. I must have recognized—

What is Nick's dad's name? Eric—

Nick's dad was in prison. Just like Dad said he—

Nick's dad lost his daughter. His Jessy.

Dad said he'd lost me before and doesn't want to lose me again, so he'll—

Nick's Jessy had dark hair. The color Dad made me dye—

The beatings. The box. Mom. The cameras and pictures—

The slideshow. The photos of Dad and a little girl. The

crossed-out faces of the other people. I think one was a little boy—

Nick—

As my mind spirals, Dad rushes forward. He keeps the gun pointed at us, but his face is tight with panic. "Don't listen to him, Jessy!" he exclaims. "I'm *your* father! Don't let him come between us again!"

"Stop!" Nick yells. "Stop lying to her, you piece of shit!"

Fury flashes in Dad's eyes as he glares at Nick. It's a fury I've never seen. Not even when he was beating me within an inch of my life. This is pure hate.

"Why would you do this?" Nick shouts, his voice now breaking. "Our Jessy is *dead*!" He points to me. "She is not *our* Jessy!"

Just like that, my thoughts stop whirling. They're still. Silent. Free-floating in midair before crashing down around me.

This whole time, I've been trying to reconcile his truth with my own, but it never felt right. It was like trying to force a puzzle piece into the wrong slot. Only now do I see that the piece—him—belonged to a whole different puzzle.

So it's true.

This man is not my biological father.

Bob. Oh God. *Dad.*

The world tilts. I grab Nick and Dan to keep from collapsing.

I stare at Eric. At this man. At this monster.

At *him.*

My stomach churns, and I cover my mouth. "You murdered my father," I gasp from behind my hand. "You tortured me for over a month. You forced me to believe you were truly my dad. You forced me to play into . . . whatever the hell this is."

"I just want to be a family again!" Eric pleads, his eyes flooded with pain. "I just want you back."

He reaches for me, but Nick blocks him. And so does

Dan.

"Stay the hell away from her!" Dan bellows. "My dad and the others are on their way," he adds. "It's over!" His voice is bold, maybe even triumphant.

I want to feel that same triumph inside me too. But we're fifteen miles from the police station. And the roads are quickly being covered in snow.

Eric smirks. "Yeah, I heard you make that call. Too bad they're already a little busy on another call, on the other side of the county. Someone gave them a tip about Officer Adams's body. By the time they realize the tip is false, it'll be too late."

Even though we've been standing outside in a snowstorm for many minutes now, my blood suddenly goes cold. Too late? For what?

Eric then turns his eyes to me. His mouth is twisted up in a joyous grin. He's not scared at all. He's enjoying this. Enjoying toying with us.

"Do you want to see your mother?"

Mom.

"What have you done to her? Where is she?" As strong as I want to sound, my voice trembles with terror.

"Come see," Eric says, waving the gun toward the woods. "This way. Go."

Dan and Nick don't move an inch. They stare at me, their faces gripped with anger and fear.

All I can do is nod and start walking. The guys follow. Their eyes flicker from me, to Eric, to the gun.

I don't know what he's done to Mom. I think of the beatings she's taken. I think of her eyes, which were once filled with fire but have become more and more vapid with every passing day. Has he beaten her again? Has he finally just killed her this time? Have I lost her? Lost the only parent I had left?

A numbness settles over me. I can't feel my own legs trudging through the snow. Frozen branches crunch under our feet as we cross the tree line behind the house. Then Eric stops in a small clearing. Beyond it is the old machine shed. Light streams out from many missing boards in the walls and roof. It shines on the falling snowflakes, making them seem like diamonds. Dad kept meaning to fix this place up. Guess he'll never get the chance now.

Eric motions with the gun for us to head inside. A shop light is hooked up to a generator in the corner. Beside it is a shovel. Which means this isn't the first time Eric's been out here.

The thick groves of trees help block us from most of the harsh wind—but it also cuts us off from Tomas and the police. It will take them forever to find us back here.

I stop, unable to command my legs to move another step. In front of me are three long, rectangular mounds of dirt. I stare at them for a long moment. Then it hits me.

Graves. They're all graves.

Dad.

Officer Adams.

But who's in the third? Mom? Is this what he meant . . . ?

Eric follows my eyes to the third mound. "Did you know that they let that drunken son of a bitch out early? For 'good behavior.' He stole the most precious thing in the world from me, but he didn't even serve his full sentence." He sneers and shakes his head. "I'd tried—and failed—to take him out before. But I made sure he got what was coming to him this time."

So it isn't Mom. It's John, the drunk driver from the accident. The man who killed their Jessy. Nick said he's been missing since Thanksgiving.

Knowing that Mom isn't in that grave brings no comfort. My stomach still plummets.

"My mom," I say, trying to keep the words steady. "Where is she?"

Wordlessly, he motions ahead.

That's when I see it.

Behind the three mounds is a large pile of fresh dirt and a deep hole. The hole is about the same size as the mounds.

It's another grave.

An open grave.

Eric motions again with his free hand, though he keeps the gun trained on us. "Go on. Take a look."

After a second to gather my courage, I step up to the hole. Nick and Dan are right beside me. Together, we peer down, seeing a large plywood box. A coffin.

My hand covers my mouth, but my cry still escapes. "*Mom! No!*"

"You bastard!" Nick shouts.

Both he and Dan jerk forward.

"Hey!" Eric yells, now waving the gun madly.

I grab Nick and Dan tightly, pulling them back to me. If it's true—if my mom is in that coffin—then Nick and Dan are my entire world now.

As I cling to them, I strain my ears as hard as I can, hoping I can miraculously hear sirens approaching. But I don't. I hear nothing but the groans of the old shed as it battles against the wind and my own galloping heart.

Please let Tomas have checked his voicemail. Please let him get here in time.

Or maybe it's better this way. Once again, I picture Eric starting a shoot-out. There's only one door to the shed. Eric will pick them off like flies as they enter. He'll kill Tomas. He'll kill them all.

Eric stares at us—at me. His eyes are so crazed that they practically glow. "This was meant to be your mother's grave, Jessy."

I suck in a breath, and I feel Dan and Nick stiffen beside me. Is she not in that coffin, then? Is she alive? I'm too terrified to even guess.

"You're *sick*!" Nick spits at his father. "You've killed people. You've destroyed a family. Why? Because you can't accept that our Jessy is really gone. But she's *dead*! And I'm glad. She's free of this hell!"

At this, Eric lets out a long, gutted cry. When he finally quiets, he runs a hand through his hair, then looks back up at me. There's something different in his eyes now. Pain. And . . . clarity.

"Deep down, I knew you weren't her," he says softly. "I knew you weren't my Jessy. But I guess I kept lying to myself. I thought maybe if you became my Jessy, then it'd all go away. The pain. The emptiness." He rubs the sleeve of his free arm on his eyes, my eyes glued to the gun he so carelessly dangles in the air. "God, I miss her so badly!"

My bottom lip quivers, and I blink back tears. For a moment, I feel pity. Not pity for Eric the murderer. But pity for Eric the father. Eric the father, who lost his daughter to a horrific accident, a tragedy so unthinkable that it twisted his mind into violent, murderous delusion.

"I'm sorry about your Jessica," I whisper. I swallow a lump in my throat, then meet Eric's gaze. I lock eyes. *"But I'm not her.* I'm not your daughter. She's dead."

"They buried her while I was in jail," he says. "I wasn't even there. I didn't even get to say goodbye to her. My own baby girl."

"Don't give me that 'baby girl' shit," Nick snarls. Spit flies from his mouth. "You *beat* her! You beat us all."

Eric glares in rage at his son, pointing the gun at him.

My body braces for the impact, while Dan and Nick are silent statues beside me. We're clinging so tightly together that I cannot imagine how Eric could shoot Nick without also shooting Dan and me. I never wanted any of this—for this to end in blood and violence. But if it has to go this way, at least we're together.

But then Eric grimaces in agony and thankfully lowers the gun. The relief is minimal, though, as the danger is far from over.

He lets out a long, defeated exhale. He nods. "You're right. I wasn't a good father."

Nick staggers, his jaw popping open. Even Dan lets out a shocked breath. All I can do is cling to Nick a little tighter, knowing I was seconds away from almost losing him. Losing both of them. Losing my life as well.

Silently, Eric stares down inside the hole. At the coffin. For a long time, he doesn't move.

"All this time, I haven't been ready to let her go. But I think I am now."

My brows narrow as I stare at him. The clarity that filled his eyes moments ago is gone, replaced again by crazed delusion.

"I'm ready to say goodbye to you, Jessy," he says.

Everything inside me stills.

"Get in the coffin."

Nick and Dan scream and shove me behind them. Protecting me—putting their lives in greater danger—just as I have protected them.

Eric lifts the gun and sweeps it between the two of them. "Who should I shoot first, Jessy? The boyfriend? Or the brother? Doesn't matter to me."

"Stop! No!" I shout—but not at Eric. At Nick and Dan.

If Eric hurts them—if they die—I'll never be able to live with myself. In this life or the next.

Using a strength I didn't know I possess, I yank them back, twisting their bodies back toward me.

"Stop!" I repeat, more softly now. "Stop, or you're gonna get yourselves killed."

I know Eric is still pointing that gun at them, at all of us. Once again, I know he could shoot, and it would be over in an instant.

Knowing all this, I still reach up and place my hands on Nick's and Dan's cheeks. I need to hold them and their attention. I need them to hear me. I need them to listen. I need them to cut out the rest of the world for just a moment and focus on us.

Dan instantly leans into my touch. Tears stream from his

eyes.

Nick hesitates and tries to recoil. He won't rip his furious, stormy gaze away from his father. He won't leave us unprotected.

"It's OK," I tell them. "Whatever happens next, it's going to be OK."

Dan's jaw tightens. "My dad *is* coming," he whispers. But I don't think he believes it anymore.

I nod and force a smile through my heartache and tears, though I don't believe it anymore either.

Suddenly, Nick pulls me into him and shocks me by kissing my forehead. "We'll get you out of this," he whispers, then slowly releases me.

Dan is quick to follow suit, wrapping me in a hug that on any other day would erase all my problems. "You're part of us now, Jess. We're a team. A family. We're not letting you go. I care about you so much."

"Jessy," Eric says. His voice is sharp. "Now. In the coffin. It's time."

Dan and I break away. Nick and Dan step forward, once again shielding me.

"You two," Eric snaps at the guys, "get back. Way back."

Their bodies shake with barely contained rage, but they obey, backing up toward the far wall, where even the light struggles to reach. They're ten feet away now, but it feels like miles.

Once again, I peer down. The hole is deep, dark, and cold. *Six feet under* isn't just a saying.

I let out a shuddering breath, then bend down and sit on the edge on the hole. My feet dangle over the coffin; my heart hammers in my chest.

I cast one last look at Eric, hating him, then I drop down.

Instantly, I'm in a new world. I can't see anything but the rough black edges of the grave, gnarled tree roots, and the cold, harsh reality of my rapidly approaching demise.

This won't be the quick plummet into death I'd once

envisioned for myself on the bridge. I'll be cut off from air a different way. A much slower way. I'll have plenty of time to panic. To be gripped in terror and agony as Death wraps me in its cloth.

Above me, a shadow appears. It's Eric, peering down. Beyond him, dozens of snowflakes fall in through the gaps in the roof, uncaring and unaffected by the predicament we're all in.

"Open it," he orders. "Quit stalling."

There's only enough room for me to straddle the coffin. I reach for the lid, my ears pounding with each furious heartbeat. My fingers curl around the top-left corner.

Wait—what if Mom *is* in here?

The sudden thought sends me scooting back. I fall on my ass.

"Jess!" Dan shouts, hearing the scuffle.

"I'm OK!" I call out. It might be more for my own reassurance than for his.

I wrap my fingers around the lid again. I count to three before lifting it.

It's empty. I'm not sure if that's better or worse.

"Get in," Eric says flatly. "It's time to say goodbye. Time to say goodbye to my little girl. But first, I'm gonna say goodbye to that worthless excuse of a son."

With that, Eric disappears from my sight.

What happens next happens fast.

I hear footsteps. A gasped "Sandy?"

Mom?

"Do it," Eric says.

A flash of light tears through the air above me, and a loud bang echoes with so much pressure that I cover my ears.

A gunshot.

"*Nick!*" Dan howls.

There's an awful moan of pain.

Oh God. Nick's been shot.

"*No!*" I scream.

With a flood of adrenaline and fury, I scramble and claw at the dirt walls, trying to climb out of the hole. Dirt slips through my fingers like sand, sending me back to the bottom. I fight, I scream, but I still can't find a good purchase.

If he's dead . . .

No. I will *not* lose Nick too. He's suffered too much to die at that monster's hands.

My clawing is getting me nowhere. Every second feels like ages.

Without fully realizing what I'm doing, I shove the lid back on the coffin, then stand on top. I leap off the lid, bridge myself with both hands and both feet on the dirt walls, and climb out in a matter of seconds.

The electrified muscles that pulled me from the grave are ready now to sprint to Nick's side. But standing right before me, blocking my view of him and Dan, are two people. Eric and Mom.

He's beaming with pride. Something silver glints in his hand. A knife. I recognize it. Flashes of that first night return. The night he turned my world upside down.

When I look back at Mom, I see the gun in her hand. The barrel still smokes in the bitter-cold air.

She shot Nick. Mom. My mother shot Nick. And from the empty glaze across her face, this act was no different than doing the dishes.

I lean over, trying to see around them, looking now for the two people who mean the world to me. Dan's kneeling over Nick, who's writhing on his side. He's pale and shaking. Blood gushes from his shoulder. All around him, the dirt is turning a muddy red.

Nick looks up at me. With wide eyes full of agony, he gapes at his dad and my mom—then looks back at me. In that look he conveys my worst fear. None of us are getting out of here alive.

I can't just stand here and let my mom kill him. Kill both of them. Eric has done so much to her, but I won't let him warp her into the same vile monster that he is. I won't let him win.

I charge at Mom, tackling her from behind. We drop to the ground, wrestling for the gun.

"Jessy, stop!" Eric cries. "You're ruining everything! You never listen!"

I see flashes of his arms and hands trying to stab me, but I twist and roll out of his way.

Finally, I throw an elbow, popping Mom in the nose. She cries out in agony.

Ignoring the guilt, I scurry back to my feet. The gun is in my hands.

Eric inches toward me, one hand extended with the knife while the other is held open. "Jessy, sweetheart—give me the gun."

I raise the gun, pointing it at his head.

"You were right," I say, my whole body shaking from the adrenaline. "You were a shitty father."

He lunges. My body spasms in fear.

I squeeze the trigger.

A shot rings out, momentarily overriding all sounds.

My arm flails from the force of the recoil.

Eric slowly looks down at his chest. Blood is spreading out beneath his shirt, right where his heart would be. If he had one.

He falls to his knees, then slumps facedown in the dirt.

I shot him.

Killed him.

I'm a murderer.

Oh God. I'm just like him.

"Drop your weapon!" multiple people shout.

Suddenly, a blur of tan-and-brown uniforms and unfamiliar faces fill the space, all with guns pointed at me.

"Stand down!" one of the blurry faces shouts. The man then holsters his weapon, lifts his hands up, then takes several steps toward me. "Jessy, hun—it's all over. You can put the gun down now."

I blink, fighting back the pooling moisture in my eyes. That's when this man's face finally registers.

Tomas. He made it.

A sob breaks. I blink again, shifting my focus to the wall of officers behind him—who thankfully have all put their guns away too. They all made it.

"Jessy," Tomas repeats, inching closer. "Give me the gun, sweetie. You're safe. You're OK. It's over."

"I killed him," I whisper.

Tomas will have to arrest me now. I'll go to jail. Have a trial. Be sent away for a very long time. Will anyone understand why I did it? Why I had no choice?

"I shot him," I repeat. "But he—"

Tomas holds out a hand, quieting me. His kind eyes fill with sympathy as he shakes his head. "No, sweetie. I shot him. I'm the one who killed him."

My mind whirls, trying to determine if he's telling the truth. Lies have destroyed my life. I want to believe him. It would be easier than facing the consequences of what I did.

I study him closely. One hand is still reaching out to me. The other is by his side, next to the gun he put back into its holster.

"But—but—my gun went off," I say. "I know it."

Tomas's kind eyes never waver. "Yes, it did. But I promise you, Jessy—you didn't kill him. The kickback sent your hand flying. I saw it with my own eyes. Give my team one minute, and they'll find your bullet over there, in the wall somewhere. But they're gonna find *my* bullet right in his chest. Center mass."

He takes a deep breath.

"Eric was a deeply troubled man—more so than I knew. I wish this could have ended with him in handcuffs, but when I came through that door and saw Nick bloody on the ground and Eric lunging at you with that knife, well, I did what I had to do to protect you kids. Taking a life is hard, Jessy. Even

293

in a situation like this. So please believe me when I tell you that you're free from that burden. *You did not kill him.*"

With that, the gun in my hand instantly weighs a hundred pounds. My arm drops. My knees give out. A rattled sob leaves my throat.

Suddenly, I'm in Tomas's arms—my body boneless under the crushing weight of what I almost did. One of his hands rubs my back as the other hand gently removes the gun from me. He tells me over and over that I'm safe. Behind him, the other officers and paramedics rush to tend to Nick and Mom.

"Jess!" Dan yells.

Tomas releases me, and I instantly run to them. My guys. I fall to my knees beside Nick as the paramedics work to pack his wound. Even still, he throws his good arm over me.

"Thank God you're OK," he breathes into my hair.

A second later I feel another set of arms embracing me. Dan.

I cling to them both.

Many voices sound around us, shouting commands at each other. Dozens of officers and paramedics now comb through the crime scene that is the shed. The paramedics ask for some room, so they can tend to Nick.

I stand, and Dan moves beside me, taking my hand.

"I'm going to be fine, Jessy," Nick says as we step away.

"Thankfully, you all will be," Tomas says.

He tosses his arm around Dan, holding him close. Dan leans into his dad's embrace, though he doesn't let go of my hand.

"I've never been more scared in my entire life than when I got your message," Tomas confesses. "We were clear on the other side of the county—following a 'tip' about Charlie . . ." He grimaces with realization. "We arrived as fast as we could. We were about to search the house when we heard a gun go off out here."

Dan looks Tomas in the eye. "I'm pretty sure Charlie is

in one of these graves, Dad."

Both father and son turn their attention to the three unmarked graves.

I squeeze Dan's hand, then step aside, giving them a moment to themselves. Fighting off more tears, I blink up at the snowflakes falling through a missing board in the roof. I think of Officer Adams and what he did for me that night on the bridge.

We're all jarred, though, when a hysterical scream fills the shed. It's Mom, fighting the paramedics trying to restrain her.

"Murderer!" she shrieks at Tomas. "You murderer! You killed my husband! You killed him!"

I watch numbly as paramedics finally manage to place her on a stretcher. She continues to rage as they wheel her away. The curses—the delusions—echo through the woods.

I blink back a tear. "Wh-where are they taking her?" I turn to Tomas, my eyes pleading. "She didn't know what she was doing. She—"

"She's on the way to the hospital," Tomas says. "Don't worry—they'll take good care of her. Get her the help she needs."

Several paramedics step up behind us, pushing another stretcher.

Dan looks at Nick and nods. "Dude, your ride's here."

Nick nods. They lift him up, and I give him one last hug. "I'm so sorry."

"Never apologize to me for what that monster did. I'm fine. Besides, chicks dig scars."

I laugh and let go of him. As I step back, I accidently bump into Dan. Silently, we watch as they maneuver Nick through the trees, trying not to jostle him too much.

When he's out of sight, I turn to Dan. Blood—Nick's blood—covers his clothes.

I grimace as my heart constricts. More tears race to the surface.

"I'm so sorry—"

"Jess," he says, grabbing my hand and quieting me. "It's OK. Remember? That's what you said before you went into that grave. You said that whatever happens, we'll be OK. And we *will* be. All three of us. I'm not going anywhere. Nick isn't either. You didn't ask for any of this to happen to you, and we're not gonna let you deal with it alone."

My lips tremble as a tear spills over. Instantly I'm in his arms.

I'm safe.

TWENTYTHREE

"**S**AY CHEESE!" KATE CALLS OUT.

Dan, Nick, and I humor her, smiling for several more pictures. We're in front of the school, surrounded by all the other graduates, clad in caps and gowns, posing for pictures for their families.

I'm standing between my guys. Their arms rest around my shoulders, while my arms rest behind their backs. Kate didn't tell us to pose this way, with me in the middle. It's just what naturally happens whenever we're together.

Behind Kate, Dan's sisters make funny faces at us, trying to get us to crack up. Tomas clears his throat, and they stop—for a second. As they resume their antics, he lets out such a heavy sigh that it makes us all burst out laughing.

After a few snapshots, I push the guys forward. "How about a few of just you two?"

Before I can even step away, my guys are already hamming it up. I laugh as they josh and joke while Kate snaps away.

"Jess, honey, now it's your turn," Kate says. "Let's get a few of just you—for your mom."

She says this with such positivity that my heart aches.

It's a different ache, though, than the one that comes

from Mom's absence on this special day. As much as I wish she could be here, I'm grateful for the care she's getting at the local psychiatric hospital.

And then there's the ache I feel for Dad—Bob, my real and only father.

Unconcerned about the tears building, I stand tall and smile big for Kate's snapshots. This is me. This is who I am. Sadness and joy. Struggle and triumph.

It's picture perfect.

"That was lovely, dear," Kate says, her own tears pooling. "Thank you."

As soon as she lowers her phone, Nick and Dan wrap me up, sharing in the bittersweet moment.

This is how it's been since that awful night when the nightmare ended and the long, hard road of healing began.

That night, Kate and Tomas opened their home to me. Their home is so warm and full of love. It reminds me of how my own home used to be, before my world imploded. The McLeary dinner table is chaotic, as is the rest of the house, but it's a wonderful chaos. This family has provided me the safe, stable foundation I need to move my life forward, one day, one moment, at a time.

Nick and Dan have been the core of that foundation. They were there for me during the nightmare, and they're there for me now.

As I see it, Nick truly is my brother. My twin. He feels the same. Nick said that if Jessica were alive, we'd be triplets. It's hard to believe he's the same broody, silent guy who used to stare at me and listen in on my conversations. What I didn't understand back then was that he *saw* me, he *knew* me. And that's what ultimately saved my life.

As for Dan . . . the special bond between us continues to grow and deepen. It's friendship, yet it's more. I can feel it. But we're giving ourselves the freedom to not label it, not rush it—especially not now, during these first months of recovery.

There's so much time ahead of us. All I know is that I'm thankful that he has been, and always will be, by my side. I draw a deep breath as emotion courses through me. In response, Nick and Dan hold me even tighter.

"Hey, guys," I hear a familiar voice say behind us.

Dan and Nick release me, and I look up to see Blake in front of us. He smiles at the guys, and they exchange fist bumps and shoulder pats.

"Jessy, can I borrow you for a moment?" Blake asks. "My parents would love some pictures of the whole group."

"I'd love that too," I say, beaming.

I follow Blake to where Cassie, Nevaeh, and several of my other friends are gathered. We huddle around and smile, and all the parents start clicking away. No one knows which phone or camera to look at, which makes us crack up. This, too, is wonderful chaos.

It feels good to capture this moment together.

Once the nightmare ended and the truth was slowly revealed, these friends rallied around me. I know nothing will ever be the same between us—how could it? But we're standing here now as friends of a deeper kind.

Once the pictures are done, I reach over to hug Blake. We don't need words. We both know we'll always have a history and a connection, even if our paths are now diverting.

After hugging the others and vowing to keep in touch, I make my way across the parking lot, back to Nick and Dan. With every step I take, I think about the steps I'll soon take on the life path ahead of me. It includes a few detours.

I've been accepted to a four-year university on a cheerleading scholarship, but I've decided to put that plan on hold. Ms. Shueller, my counselor, reached out to the university to explain my situation. They assured us that the scholarship will always be there, whenever I'm ready for that next step.

I'm confident there will be time, later, to focus on my education and my future career. But right now, I need to focus on healing from my past and living in the present moment. I've decided to attend the local community college for my general classes.

Dan and Nick enrolled there too. I know they've been accepted into four-year universities as well, but they feel the same way I do—we have so much time ahead of us for school, but we just want and need to be together right now.

In fact, the three of us will soon move into an apartment near campus. We're excited to have our own space and to start this adventure together. We're grateful, too, that Kate still insists we eat dinner every night at the McLeary house.

"Who's ready for pizza?" Tomas asks, as if sensing that someone is thinking about food.

Of course, Dan's sisters jump up and down, shouting and cheering. They race off, heading for the minivan.

"I take that as a yes," Dan quips.

"We'll meet you kids there," Tomas says before hurrying with Kate after the girls.

Nick, Dan, and I watch them pile into the minivan, then we turn to take in the scene around us. Photos are winding down, and groups are parting. A few classmates rush for last photos, hugs, laughter, and tears.

This is an ending but also a beginning.

As we head for Nick's truck, I grab each of their hands, lacing my fingers with theirs.

Nick smiles.

Dan does too, and he brings my hand to his lips for a kiss. "You ready for this?" he asks.

"Absolutely," I say.

I'm not sure if he meant being ready for dinner, the three of us moving in, college, the future—or maybe all of the above. It doesn't matter. No matter what the situation, I'm absolutely ready to face it head-on.

The nightmare I endured was more than anyone should ever have to endure in their lifetime. My age made it even more tragic. I could have let it break me. Destroy me.

But instead, I choose to fight. I choose to battle the darkness and the nightmares, to lean on my support system, and to heal and grow. To rise up in spite of the awful things *he* did to me. To us.

It is not an easy path. But missing out on my future would let him win, and that is something I will never allow.

Neither will they—Dan and Nick. My Dynamic Duo. As long as I have them by my side, I'll never be fighting alone. As long as I have them by my side, I'm ready for anything.

NOTE FROM THE AUTHOR
‡

Thank you very much for reading *Picture Perfect*. It was definitely an emotional roller coaster, but I'm glad to see you made it to the end. And what an ending it was! While the story didn't end in a "picture perfect" way, the ending felt true to the characters. And who knows—maybe Jessica, Dan, and Nick will make an appearance in future books. I'd love for Nick to find that special someone who heals his broken, rock-god heart.

If you enjoyed the book, I'd greatly appreciate it if you could help in the following ways:

Leave a review on your favorite book site! Reviews, even just star ratings, are a huge help! They increase the book's visibility and help readers decide to take a chance on it.

Recommend it! Share this book with your social media groups, friends, family—anyone you think would enjoy it as much as you did. There's nothing better than word-of-mouth to spread awareness for a book.

Connect with me! I'd love to hear from you! Visit my website at lauriewetzel.com. Or follow me on your preferred social media platform:

/LaurieRWetzel.   authorlauriewetzel

laurie_wetzel   Laurie_Wetzel

Always,
Laurie

ABOUT THE AUTHOR
‡

L AURIE WETZEL lives in Minnesota with her husband, two sons, and lab Knight (who is a total Momma's boy). Given that Minnesota is a frozen wasteland two-thirds of the year, Laurie is quite content to gaze at the beautiful snowfall from inside her home, most likely near the fireplace, under a blanket, with her laptop or a book. She's an avid sports fan, especially when her sons are playing. (Since the Vikings will probably never win a Super Bowl, at least she can watch her kids win.) In addition to writing novels, she also writes for Aequitas Comics.

Her works include:

Unclaimed Series:
Unclaimed
Ignited
Revealed
Series finale in progress

Anthologies:
Quillandria: A Quill of Hope

Made in the USA
Columbia, SC
31 October 2022

70230182R00170